TAKE *only* PICTURES

Laina Villeneuve

Bella
BOOKS
2014

Bella Books, Inc.
P.O. Box 10543
Tallahassee, FL 32302

Printed in the United States of America on acid-free paper.

First Bella Books Edition 2014

Editor: Cath Walker
Cover Designer: L. Callaghan

ISBN: 978-1-59493-414-8

About the Author

Laina Villeneuve admits that her real-life courtship would read like a blatant plot manipulation. In the last ten years, she and her wife have been married, had a baby, been legally married and had twins. An English professor and voracious reader, she also has a lifelong love for horses.

Dedication

For my wife
The trail is sweeter with you

Acknowledgments

Time is precious, so I must first thank my family for weekend date nights that allowed my wife and me to get out and see where the story wanted to take us. Thanks especially to my mom, Aunt Diane and my niece Emily who gave us a few weekend getaways that became writing retreats.

Nat and D, thank you for looking at early chapters and encouraging me to keep going. Wes, thanks for the pep talks about wrangling words to paper. Jennifer, you were so kind to listen to all the progress reports, especially during the editing process. Roberta, thanks for being my emotional buttress.

Many many thanks to Carsten for the first major revision suggestions. I thought your character suggestion was crazy but am very glad I listened. The plot and action are so much better because of your help—a true testament to the benefits of peer editing!

Thanks to the generous Mammoth Lakes rangers who helped me with so many of my backcountry facts. If I've gotten it wrong, it's my fault, not theirs.

I am so thankful for my editor, Cath Walker, who asked such good questions, pushed me for more detail and saved me from embarrassing grammatical errors. I appreciate your patience and guidance in the process.

My lovely wife, I still remember introducing you to Kristine and Gloria across the street from the old house on our way to drop the kids at school. I hope you don't regret saying it would be good to have something other than parenting and work to talk about.

CHAPTER ONE

Kristine felt her father stop in the doorway, but she kept her back to him and continued piling clothes into her duffels. She counted out her underwear, hoping to make him uncomfortable enough to leave. Her subtle gesture did nothing to throw him off.

"You planning on staying there the whole summer, or do you even have a plan?" Cliff Owens demanded, no amusement in his deep voice.

She faced him squarely. Even in socked feet, his frame filled her doorway, a technique which once cowed her into seeing things his way. Though she'd physically grown to almost match his six-foot stature, he still treated her like a teenager.

"There are two ways off a horse, you know."

"When it's their idea, and when it's yours," she recited, knowing that in his eyes, she was letting her little brother control her life. He hadn't approved of or understood why she returned from her summer job years before. She had failed his expectation to get back on the horse when the next season rolled around and she refused to go back. Trying to acknowledge his concern, she said, "This is my idea."

"Gabe'll get over his heartbreak like he always does. Put your things away."

Kristine recalled how free she had felt at seventeen when she'd first accepted the job offered by her father's top buyer. She spent that whole summer, as well as the following three, out from underneath her father's thumb. She clenched her jaw and added more underwear to her bag. His attitude cemented her resolve to get away. "I promised Gabe I'd be there for the summer."

"And I told Leo to hire another packer," Cliff said, running his hand through his coarse, near-black hair in agitation.

"You're the one who needs to hire a hand here on the ranch."

"You said that six months ago when you finished your internship."

"That was a job…temporary, but still a job," Kristine argued.

"You live here, you work for me."

"I help out here. Leo's offered me a job."

Cliff scoffed. "Till it gets too tough like it did last time? You have no idea how long it took to live down that embarrassment."

Kristine bristled, knowing that he and the entire staff still believed she'd left because she'd been injured by a horse in the backcountry. "I expected you to be happy that I'm getting back on the horse."

"It's time you committed yourself here to the ranch."

"I'll find something in photography. I still have applications out."

"When are you going to give up that childish dream?"

"I've been called back for a second interview several times. I'm close."

"You're ignoring the fact that you belong here." He punctuated his sentence with a sharp thwack of his palm to the doorjamb before disappearing down the hallway, giving her no opportunity to engage further in their recurring dispute about why she, and not Gabe, had to be the one to take over the ranch. She kept telling her father that it was his dream not hers, but he always countered with a horse analogy about how a horse is only capable of being a horse—you don't try to make him something he isn't. According to her father she had a gift with horses. It was in her blood, thus she belonged on the ranch not goofing off with a camera.

Arguing with him was pointless. Her father understood livestock, not art. Art was foreign and held no weight with him. To suggest otherwise just got a tired dismissal and his usual disappointment. She was used to seeing it in his eyes. However, this morning, she'd seen his anger, and anger, Kristine decided, was good. Anger might help him see that she was serious about walking her own path, not the one he'd put her on.

Being passed over after what she considered successful interviews with the message that she had talent but just wasn't the right person had made her angry, too. She embraced the feeling, pushing out the self-doubt her father had been fanning since she'd come home. More importantly, she felt this anger replace the worry and dread she felt whenever she pictured returning to The Lodgepole Pine Pack Outfit. She reminded herself that she was different now, not the tagalong girl who felt like she needed to prove herself. At least that's what she wanted to believe.

Arms wide, she bowed her head and took deep breaths, bracing herself against the bed. She felt as sick as she had when she'd taken off from the Lodge, run home from the last trip she'd done. She hadn't thought she'd ever go back, but here she was answering Gabe's call, not just for him but for herself.

A warm hand settled between her shoulders. "Are you sure about this?" Roberta Owens's calm voice washed over her.

She turned and sat on the edge of the bed. Her mother followed suit and stroked her hair. She had her father to thank for her height and thick hair, but in coloring and features, she and her mother matched. When she'd worn her light brown hair long like her mother, people often mistook them as sisters, noting the same pixie shape of their faces. "I'll be okay," Kristine said.

"Your father's right. I know Gabe's been looking forward to running the Aspens, but he'll be fine at Leo's main outfit."

"I know he'd be. It's just that…" Kristine couldn't explain how she was motivated by more than the fact that Leo was giving the autonomous position at the smaller outpost to an established team if Gabe was returning to the outfit by himself. She owed it to Gabe to go back. She studied her mother's strong hands hoping she took some of that strength with her because her future depended on being able to confront the past. Once she put things right, she knew she'd gain the confidence she needed to land the job that would take her away from her father's ranch forever.

* * *

Kristine's journey to the Lodge was a study in contrasts. Previously, she would have been blazing the road with an eye out for cops, blaring the radio and singing at the top of her lungs to the songs she adored. When the season started early enough, she could drive to Mammoth straight from her college campus, first at the local community college in Quincy and later when she was studying agriculture at Cal Poly San Luis Obispo.

The school year drained her, juggling the demands of her coursework and what social life she could piece together. The Lodgepole Pine Pack Outfit offered the complete opposite. She thrived at the outfit that offered an array of day rides led on horseback as well as all kinds of guided trips out into the backcountry. At school, she learned equine training techniques and some of the basics for packing. The Lodge offered total immersion to the art of taking a pile of camp gear and loading it into two balanced packs onto a mule to carry into the backcountry. She learned some hitches from the old-timers that her professors back at school had never even heard of.

Each summer she gorged herself on the social opportunities first denied by her small-town origins and later by her heavy course load. Her gregarious nature was an asset in interacting with the tourists who chose to experience the backcountry on horseback instead of by foot.

Since she'd left the Lodge so abruptly six years ago, her summers had been completely different. She'd done photography internships that were often so rigorous she was relieved to get back to school. The last one was a position at a museum. Unfortunately, it ended when the funding to keep her permanently had fallen through, and she'd reluctantly returned to the ranch. For a few weeks, she'd enjoyed its quiet, but while her days were peaceful, her mind was not. She sensed her father watching her. If she could have simply accepted her place on the ranch and settled happily into the work, she would have been fine, but they both knew she was biding her time, wanting to be anywhere but rural Quincy, California.

She eyed the speedometer and applied the gas, climbing back up to the speed limit. Clearly, her feet were not anxious to make good time on the five-hour drive. She could have explained it as her maturing in the years since she'd been gone if only the increased speed didn't make her break out in a sweat. She should have felt relieved to be back on these once-familiar roads, snaking her way through the mountains. But she was not the innocent girl who had last driven there, and, she hoped, not the terrified one who had hightailed it back home.

That was the only time she'd driven the route in the dark, and when she'd arrived as the sun broke over the familiar valley of home, she'd hoped it was a symbol for leaving it all behind. The truth was, she'd never been able to put it fully to rest. It still ran inside her like a dark and cold undercurrent, one she constantly tried to avoid, fearing if she stepped back into it, it would suck her in completely.

Now that she was finally returning, she dreaded the questions she knew would come. They'd be on her like a bear who remembers scoring at a Dumpster. Every summer since, the staff had peppered her brother with questions even though he had never had anything to offer them. It didn't matter. She'd been the one to feed them something in the first place, making her an easy target. Now that she was there in person, would the questions come immediately, or would they wait? In her worst possible scenario, their anger washed over her from the moment she arrived. Her former friends might bombard her with accusations and insults. She braced herself, knowing she would not be able to defend any of their charges.

Steeling herself, she pulled off at the Devils Postpile parking lot about a mile from the Lodge and a good fifteen miles from the outpost she would share with Gabe. Stock wasn't allowed near the national monument, a stand of symmetrical columns created by lava flow, so she had only ever viewed the natural wonder on horseback from the trail way over on the other side of the San Joaquin River.

She rolled down her window, filling her lungs with the crisp pine-scented air before flipping open her phone, pleased to find she had service. She dialed the outfit's number and asked for Gabe, waiting as the employee with an unfamiliar voice went to track him down. "Gabe here," he said.

"Give it to me straight. Who's back, and what are they saying?"

"Where are you, sis?" he asked.

"Almost there," Kristine answered honestly.

"Dozer's still chewing on why you left, but the others are just curious about you being back. It won't take long for them to come around. And hell, we'll be up at Aspens most of the time, so fuck 'em if they're pissy."

She tipped her head back against the headrest, grateful for his unquestioning support, but he'd only answered the second question, the one she considered less important. What she really wanted to know was who was back, banking on a passing comment her dad had made about the possibility of Nard buying a tourist shop up in Mammoth with his stepsister instead of spending the summer at the Lodge. It would be so much easier to make peace with the way she left without having to confront him, but she feared that if she asked about him specifically, her brother would suspect the truth about why she had bailed and make it his responsibility to protect her.

"Thanks, Gabe. I'll see you soon."

"Drive safe, hear?"

"I will."

"Can't wait to see you." She could hear his beaming smile in his words. "We're going to kick some serious ass this summer!"

That made her laugh out loud. "I sure hope so," she said, soaking in his enthusiasm.

She grabbed her camera and walked the short trail to the Postpile to grab some shots before she finished the drive and faced the past head-on.

CHAPTER TWO

Gloria woke with hard nipples and the mouth that had brought them to attention kissing its way down her abdomen. She parted her legs, groaning as her sometimes lover rolled between them and pushed against her center with her breasts. "What time is it?"

Meg crawled up her front, pulling again at Gloria's nipples with her lips and a little nip of her teeth. "You seriously want to know what time it is?"

"I'm due in Mammoth tonight. I have to get on the road." Though she protested verbally, she raised her hips, grinding into Meg.

"I don't think it'll take long to get you there."

Gloria gasped as Meg entered her with two fingers. She rode the hard thrusting, climaxing quickly as Meg had predicted. "God, you're good at that." She scooted her hips and rocked Meg onto her back, stretching her out in the morning light. Meg's confidence in her body and what she wanted made it easy for Gloria to fall into bed with her whenever she was home from her research projects. She traced one finger from clavicle to navel before wrapping her hands around Meg's bountiful hips.

"Inside. Now," Meg growled as Gloria teased her, tracing a finger through her folds. "I'm so ready for you."

Gloria gave Meg what she wanted. They had explored each other's bodies enough times to know exactly what the other liked and needed, and the familiarity was part of being home. She was aware of the curve of Meg's hip, the arch of her back as she got close, how she held the sheets, tilted her head back, enjoying Gloria's touch. When Meg tipped into her own climax, Gloria held her palm tight against Meg's curls, waiting for the shudders to stop before she stretched out next to her.

"How long are you going to be gone this time?" Meg asked, turning to face Gloria.

"Couple of weeks, maybe a month."

"Depending on what the pickings are in Mammoth?"

Gloria swung her feet over the edge of the bed and began collecting her clothes, not wanting to deal with the undercurrent of insecurities that resurfaced for Meg when she traveled away for work. She threw on some sweats and a tee and folded her work clothes over her arm.

"I'm due at work," Meg said, backpedaling. "Want to grab a bagel?"

"I need to check in with my folks and get on the road. I'm heading in for a shower."

"My cue to leave." Meg flopped back across Gloria's bed, brown curls splayed across the pillow. She was short enough that she looked comfortable stretched out in the cramped bed. Gloria could only almost achieve that if she lay diagonally.

Gloria tried to tamp down her frustration. She pulled her shoulder-length blond hair into a messy ponytail. Meg knew that she had already kept her longer than she should have this morning. As much as she enjoyed the alive hum in her body from the morning sex, she hated the guilt that came with it. She should feel a pang in leaving instead of relief to be away again, but she'd never made any promises to Meg. She tried redirecting to the positive. "Thank you for a lovely wake-up."

Meg frowned. "I miss you when you're away. I only feel complete when you're home. When are you going to get something permanent here? There's probably something at the local field office."

"You sound like my mother," Gloria sighed. She rested her hip against the bed but didn't sit down.

"Good," Meg said, stroking Gloria's thigh.

She couldn't help but laugh. "Good?"

"I have this theory," Meg said, lounging back against the pillows. "If a straight girl supposedly marries her father, wouldn't it stand to reason that a gay girl marries her mother?"

"First you need the marrying kind," Gloria said as gently as she could. She leaned in for a quick kiss, escaping before Meg could wrap her arms around her and pull her back into bed. "I'll call you when I'm back in town," she said at the doorway.

Stepping out into the heavy mist, she let the door to her camper slam shut, hoping it would jar Meg from her bed and to work. It would be hard enough to say goodbye to her mother. She didn't need another Meg extraction to worry about before she made the ten-hour drive from Eureka to Mammoth.

The camper was already packed, so once Meg was gone, she was ready to take off on her latest field project. In between projects, it stayed in the shed that she and her father had built together when being a helper had meant handing him nails. The shed protected the camper they had bought for their summer family vacations. Walking to the house, she noticed that Richard Fisher's car wasn't there, so she knew he'd already gone to work.

Still, she held her breath as she eased shut the back door of her parents' house behind her, not wanting to disturb her mother if she was still sleeping. Before the tongue had even engaged the jamb, her mother's voice carried from the kitchen, startling out the breath she'd been holding.

"Eggs for Meg or just for you?" Kate Fisher called.

"Just me."

"That's too bad," her mother continued. "I'll have to stop by the bagel bakery later to tell her not to be a stranger when you're away."

Gloria rolled her eyes. "I'm grabbing a shower."

"My bet is you need it. Hurry up, I'm cracking the eggs."

She paused, considering whether to complain about her mother's observation but continued without saying anything, knowing how lucky she was to have parents relaxed enough about who she was to joke with her about it.

Freshly scrubbed, she scooted onto a stool opposite her mother, and dug into breakfast. Gloria found a note on the counter from her father wishing her well on her journey and felt only mildly guilty about the reason she wasn't in the house earlier to say goodbye in person.

"Ready to take on a new set of bears?" her mother asked, sweeping from her forehead her wispy bangs that were surprisingly more gray than blond. She, too, was dressed for the day in her gardening jeans and one of Richard's old sweatshirts that she more than swam in now.

Gloria smiled, grateful that she didn't pick back up on the Meg topic.

"I have to get acquainted with the staff there first."

"And that's what's got you nervous?"

Quizzically Gloria looked at her mother, who motioned to Gloria's plate with her fork.

Gloria answered the motion with a smirk and tried to eat as if her stomach wasn't full of butterflies. She concentrated on her toast, hoping it would settle her belly.

"You don't have to worry about me, you know. I'm a tough old hag who didn't even need you to fly halfway across the country, and now you're just across the state." Though her face was lined, much thinner since before her fight with cancer began, her jaw was strong and firmly set.

Gloria's mouth was so dry she couldn't even swallow. She sipped some coffee, trying to force the solids into her stomach. "There's still the issue of my being out of cell range a good amount of the time." She'd inherited her mother's stubbornness along with her slim nose, high cheekbones and dark blue eyes. Her father often joked that he wasn't sure he'd contributed anything, but since her mother had become sick, Gloria had begun to see more of her father in herself, the way they both worried.

"I'm sure the Forest Service in Mammoth is every bit as good at tracking you down as they were in Tennessee. If you'd been up early enough, you could have heard all of this when I covered it with your father…" Her knowing eyes pinned Gloria's and forced a blush from her. Gloria couldn't help but glance out back, wondering if Meg was still in the camper. "She's already gone," her mother said, rising to clear her dishes. "She cleared out while you were in the shower. You know you could have let her shower here."

"I wanted to talk to you, just you, before I go," Gloria said, tackling a small bite of egg.

Her mother's eyes brightened. "Why? Are you finally thinking of settling down with her when you get back?"

"Mother."

She frowned. "I keep telling both you and your father to quit worrying about me. You, especially, need to worry about yourself. How long do you think Meg's going to let you treat her like a plaything you can pick up and discard whenever you feel like it?"

"I know you don't understand our arrangement," Gloria began.

Her mother waved her off. "And I don't need to. But pretty soon, she's going to find the person who can give her everything."

"And I wish her the best when she does," Gloria interrupted.

"I just don't understand why you distract yourself when you know she's not your forever."

"So now you want the details." Gloria wiggled her eyebrows, and her mother threw a dishtowel at her. When she busied herself with the breakfast dishes, Gloria felt chagrined. She carried the towel and her plate to the counter, leaning her back against the surface to try to catch her mother's eye. "I'm sorry," she said.

Her mother shrugged, refusing to look at her. "You avoid forever just because it doesn't come with a guarantee."

"I'm not avoiding. I'm open to the idea, but you know that my work…"

"Don't. If your work was your real priority, you wouldn't have quit Tennessee. Your idea of family is this circle, this tiny circle. It scares me to think of you and your dad…"

Gloria wrapped her arms around her mother, resting her chin on top of her head. "I don't think I should marry someone so you think I have someone to take care of me."

"I know you can take care of yourself," her mother said, swiping away a tear. "So you quit worrying about me, and I'll try to quit worrying about you."

"Deal," Gloria said. She glanced at the clock.

"Get going. I taught you better than to be late your first day."

"My first day is tomorrow."

"Then get out of here so I can get on with my morning."

Gloria gathered her toiletries and paused at the back door, her eyes resting on a photo album that sat by the couch.

"I can't wait to see where you're going," her mother said.

Gloria nodded because she was sure if she answered, her voice would crack. She readied her camper for travel and opened up the gates. Her mother remained inside, never one to make a big deal of her departures. Gloria pursed her lips as she eased out onto the road, plenty of time ahead of her on the long drive to work through all her mother had given her to think about.

CHAPTER THREE

It's funny how quickly it all comes back, Kristine thought, bent down on one knee next to the sorrel mare. Like riding a horse...or is it supposed to be a bike? Having been on a horse since the time she could sit up, years before attempting to ride a bicycle, had forever ruined the phrase for her. She smiled to herself and turned to the task of getting her tiny rider into the saddle.

"Trust me," she said to the adorable pigtailed young girl whose head tilted all the way back to get a look up at the saddle. She had her father's jet-black hair and almond eyes and her mother's dimpled chin, Kristine noted, patting her chap-covered thigh. "Put your right foot here. Left foot in the stirrup, and swing aboard."

The girl's feet followed orders, and the seven-year-old sat proudly in the saddle.

"A natural," Kristine said, making sure the girl's feet were secure in the stirrups. She handed her the reins. "You remember her name?"

"Goldie!" she shouted.

She could feel both the approval of the little girl's mother and the scrutiny of Brian, the young cowboy learning the ropes who would be making this same trip at least two hundred times over the course of the summer. He at least had the costume down with his Western brushpopper shirt, Wrangler jeans and black felt hat. When they got back to the corrals, she'd let him in on some of her secrets to securing better tips from the dudes who did the shortest of their rides down to Rainbow Falls and back. So many of the kids Leo hired cared only about spending the summer in the saddle. They treated the guests, who very often had never been on a horse, disdainfully simply because of their lack of experience, their being "dudes." But he surprised her, dropping to his knee in front of the beautiful twenty-some-year-old woman whose horse he had pulled around.

Kristine dipped her hat to hide her embarrassment for him. Though the young woman was short, she was clearly experienced. He might have noticed that if his eyes had gotten past the vest zipped tight over her long-sleeved polo shirt and her form-fitting riding pants tucked into her paddock boots. She proved Kristine's intuition true when she took the reins, captured the stirrup and launched herself into the saddle.

They finished loading the rest of the riders, Brian leading the three other dude horses to the stump that served as a mounting block. He and Kristine rode the as yet untried horses from the employee corral. The willowy redhead who had refused Brian's leg up angled her horse behind Kristine for the loop down to lower falls.

"How long have you been riding?" Kristine asked, turning in her saddle to make sure the whole group fell in behind her.

"Since fourth grade," she answered, "but all English, hunter/jumper."

"Clearly, the skills translate to Western," Kristine said with a quirk of her eyebrow, smiling at the blush the woman didn't try to hide.

They fell into easy discussion about the different riding styles, horses they'd owned, how great it must be to get to ride all summer and get paid for it. Engaging her in discussion had been easy, and, as usual, it made the ride go so much faster. Kristine had always had a knack for being able to find something to talk about with anyone. She pointed out wildlife and flowers and hollered the story of the fire that raged through the forest in 1992 and what the outfit had done with the stock. It was a talent that had been rewarded with rave reviews from the guests and extra cash to help with her college expenses.

They returned to the Lodge via the wagon trail and riding between the mule corral on their left and the horse corral on the right. The horses automatically lined up at the tie rail by the horse corral. Kristine wasn't surprised when she circled around to tie them up and Miss hunter/jumper handed her some bills. She also wasn't very surprised when she whispered that she was in campsite seventeen and would really like to get to know her better. The guest winked and sauntered away as the little squirt ran over with her own fistful of bills.

"Don't go asking mom for a pony," Kristine said to the youngster, tucking the money into the breast pocket of her plaid shirt. As mom smiled on, she bent down to whisper just to the little girl, "tell her to start you on a horse." The little girl beamed and galloped off toward the café.

"How do you DO that," Brian grumbled.

"Get tips or get campsite invites?" she asked.

Brian's head snapped in the direction of the young woman he had attempted to help. "She invited you over? YOU?" The scrawny teen tipped his hat back and scratched his red hair.

Feeling like she had shared too much with the newcomer, Kristine slipped off Rip's bridle before tying it to the saddle, steering the conversation away from the personal. The tack shed behind them held four-by-four beams, two high, to house the saddles. Kristine heaved the first saddle onto a top rung. Brian followed her lead, grunting to push the saddle into place.

"Watch your guests," Kristine said, as they worked on the next two horses. "You pick up on little things. Bigger kids like to try on their own. They're independent—as are most women." He hung his head. "You'll get the hang of it, and fast with three rides down to the falls every day."

"You make it look so easy."

Kristine shrugged but remembered very well feeling awe-struck by the day-ride crew years ago when she herself had been the newbie, learning the trails, the horses, the soap-opera dynamics of the people she worked with.

"Teeny!" a deep voice barked.

She groaned at the annoying nickname of her youth. "Where the hell you been, girl?" The voice came from a cowboy so old and bent by time that he had to peer up at her. She saw the smile behind his eyes, his brown skin darkened and wrinkled from years in the sun and couldn't deny him a hug. She snapped his red suspenders as they pulled apart.

"How'r you, Sol?"

"Still dodging the question, I see. I knew your daddy made a mistake listening to Leo about going to school. Can't see what they have to teach you that you haven't already learned from us…"

"How are my mules?"

"Yeah, I figgered that's why you were back. Not for us geezers. C'mon." He tugged at his battered baseball cap and limped across the yard.

Kristine gave Brian instructions for putting up the stock and joined Sol down at the mule corral. She scampered onto one of the felled trees that served as the corral and gazed out over the stock.

"Suuuuuuuzy-Q! Scooter!" Out of the thirty head in the corral, four long, dark ears swung her way. The pair broke from the herd and strolled over to put their faces in Kristine's lap, snuffing for treats in her chap pockets. Most of the mules in the corral were bred and trained by Kristine's father, but Kristine considered Suzy-Q and Scooter her babies since they were the first her father had let her train on her own. Amazingly, they had not forgotten her.

"You been spoiling this year's foals, too?" Sol grumbled.

She shoved him with her shoulder. "I don't have the time to live down at the corral like I did when I got these guys. I grew up with them. I learned a hell of a lot having free rein with their training. They taught me about boundaries, so no. No more spoiling. Don't go telling my dad he was right."

Sol worked the chew in his lip a minute his eyes still on the mules in the corral. "How's the old man?" he finally asked.

"Same pisshead he's always been."

"You watch your mouth, girl," he growled.

But Kristine laughed at his attempt to scold her. "And who taught me about pissheads?"

He hmphed and joined Kristine in scratching the ears of the mule in front of him. "Clifford might be an asshole, but he sure breeds a fine mule."

"You're the only person in the world I know who calls him that."

"You talk him into doing a draft horse cross, get something a more respectable size?" he asked. "Get a Belgian mare and one of those Mammoth jacks. He's got more than those bitty donkeys now, right?"

"We picked up a Mammoth jack stud."

Sol rubbed his hands together. "A cross like that would make a fine mule."

"Only problem is how attached we are to our Morgan mares on the ranch. They're always going to throw a smaller mule, and there are plenty of people who agree that it's a great cross. Not everyone thinks bigger is better," Kristine said even though Sol was one of the few packers who agreed with her. She straightened Suzy-Q's forelock. "They all need haircuts."

"Unlike you."

Kristine hid her smile by tilting her hat, shading her face from Sol.

"You got any hair under that hat, or'd someone scalp you?"

"Not scalped, Sol. Just grown up."

"You sure about that?"

"Hell, I'm not even sure you're grown up, old man."

He laughed then, his eyes disappearing into his weathered face and chins multiplying. "C'mon, young 'un. You can call me anything you like…"

Kristine smiled and couldn't resist completing the sentence. "But don't call me late for supper." She swung her arm around

Sol, always thankful for his support. She'd missed the gruff cowboy and felt guilty for the years she'd let pass without at least contacting him. Her mules a close second, he'd been the hardest part to leave, especially since she'd lied about why she had to go. She knew he'd suspected but hadn't pushed, for which she was grateful. His questioning eyes resurfaced time and time again in her mind. When it came to flight or fight, she'd chosen to run, and she'd always wondered what would have happened if she'd stayed instead.

CHAPTER FOUR

Gloria swung the postcard rack a third time staring at the beautiful vistas, sunrises, sunsets, scenic panoramas of the Red Cones, Rainbow Falls, Devils Postpile and more. As a wildlife biologist who had worked for the Forest Service and was now conducting research for the Department of Fish and Wildlife, she had worked in some beautiful places, but she rarely took photos. She'd been disappointed too many times by her images which failed to compare to those done by the professionals. They were somehow able to portray the awe she felt when she was out in the wilderness.

"Against the wall, we have cards done by local artists," the clerk offered from the counter across from the doorway. She had a classic outdoorsy look and had probably taken the job here so that she could hike every second she wasn't working.

Gloria smiled her thanks and walked across the store. No doubt the Lodgepole Pine Pack Outfit's store charged more than the larger places up on Mammoth Mountain, but it was a lot closer. It looked like they had a little bit of everything as far as staples went as well as some tempting treats. She again looked at the young woman, probably still in college, absorbed in a supermarket thriller.

Far too young, she chastised herself, remembering what Meg had said to her just that morning. She thumbed through the rack of tees and sweatshirts. When she was new to the area and on yet another temporary assignment, she forced herself to orient to the community instead of tucking herself away like a hermit, which came much more naturally to her. Having arrived in Mammoth the evening before, she had spent the morning at the Forest Service office. Scott, the Wilderness and Trail Supervisor, was welcoming enough but clearly distracted by dozens of pressing tasks, all of which would have been effortless for a fully-staffed department. They were a clear challenge for his small staff of three, all of whom she'd been able to meet since the camping season had not yet officially begun. Lean times everywhere, she mused.

She wondered what it was about any ranger station that drew together a standard cast of characters. The supervisor was always a fatherly type, stern and distracted but also concerned with the welfare of his employees. She'd met Mitchell, their touchy-feely guy, laid-back and relaxed about everything including casual sex. This type was always the first to hit on Gloria, and he was no exception, standing close and offering to walk her through their past season ranger reports personally.

Rick held the high-strung wilderness ranger role. She'd seen both female and male rangers fall into this category. People came second to him. He barely had any energy left over to communicate with people because so much of his attention keyed in on the current state of the entire ecosystem. He would be extremely knowledgeable and informative, but any information would feel like it was distributed. He kept professional distance from everyone.

Some stations had the backcountry hostess ranger—the soft-spoken gentle soul who took personal responsibility for every guest's camping experience. Gloria's job was to reduce the interaction between humans and bears. That more often meant managing people, not the bears, so she was used to causing conflict by demanding that people respect the rules of the backcountry. Thus, she usually butted heads with the hostess ranger type.

But not as much as she butted heads with the straight competent ranger. Juanita fell into this, her least favorite of the female ranger types. Her first priority was for people to know that just because she wore comfortable shoes and enjoyed the out-of-doors did not mean that she slept with women.

Occasionally, she ran into the gruff one-of-the-guys dyke rangers. Friendly enough, but never a romantic interest for Gloria.

Professionally, they'd all be helpful, but socially, she'd be on her own. Mitchell would be sure to offer his assistance with her acclimation to the area. She frowned. Why wasn't it ever a charismatic and friendly woman making the offer?

Gloria moved to the display of mounted enlargements on the wall of the store. The individually crafted and packaged cards had a different feel from the postcards she had selected. The commercial version of the Devils Postpile picture, for example, was obviously taken directly at the site and captured the fascinating detail of the geographic formation. The local photographer had taken the picture from across the San Joaquin from atop a mule whose ears framed the tiny, but clear, national monument. She liked the sense of familiarity that the artist had captured. This photo wasn't for the hit-and-run tourist. It was for the nature enthusiast who cherished the wilderness like she did, who saw, she laughed at herself for thinking the cliché, the whole picture. She scanned more of the cards by the same artist.

A smile touched her lips as she selected another from the rack. Two border collies lay on a bedroll. One's muzzle was snugly tucked under its tail; the other had its head tipped lazily back. It stared familiarly at the photographer. She wondered if the dogs belonged to the photographer or if the photographer had been on one of the outfit's many overnight trips and had caught the image of the employee's pets. Her mother would love it.

She added the card to her stack, already seeing it in the photo album back in Eureka. Whenever she began a new job, she made sure to find a store that had postcards of the local scenery. She'd buy several and send them home. Her father had recently told her the tradition meant more and more these days. It used to be that she'd send images to help her mother picture their next vacation destination, plan out the hot spots she'd like to visit. As her mother's leukemia had worsened, the postcards began to take the place of those trips. She surveyed the cards in her hands. Would her mother be up to the hike down to Rainbow Falls? Maybe. But Pond Lily was out. Having surveyed the map of the valley, she knew her mother would never see it firsthand. It'll still bolster her spirits, though, Gloria thought, and she'd send off this one of the pups as soon as possible. She turned the card over and read the stamp. The artist's logo was a sketch portrait of a mule and read Suzy-Q Cards. Gloria heard "cue-card" and wondered if the artist intended the wordplay. She added the card to her stack and went to the register.

"These always fly off the shelf," she said, ringing up the purchase. "She's one of our own."

"Suzy?" Gloria guessed.

"No, Teeny. Used to work out at the corral and always had her camera with her."

"She's good."

"That's what I've heard," the clerk said with a wink.

Gloria blinked in surprise at the double entendre. She wasn't surprised by the clerk's message—she'd definitely pinged Gloria's gaydar—it was more that they'd only exchanged a few sentences.

The clerk, not seeming to have noticed Gloria's surprise, continued. "And she's back this summer."

"Tell her I love her work."

"Oh, she'll be at the meeting. You're the bear expert, right?"

"Guess the uniform gives me away," Gloria answered. Thanks to her mother, her Fish and Wildlife uniform was crisply pressed. Since she anticipated a tough sell to a room of seasoned cowboys, she'd worn the optional tie with her tan shirt. The forest green jacket, DFW logo on the shoulders, matched her slacks.

"I'm glad you're here," the young woman continued, "because last year, the bear here was just out of control. He was going through the Dumpster all the time. You should come by my cabin. I'm right behind the store here. I've got a picture of this little cub that was with the mama last year. He's got a pack of smokes in one hand and a candy bar wrapper in the other. It is just too funny." She beamed.

Gloria studied the woman. Every utterance made her reconsider the conclusion she'd drawn from the last. She couldn't tell if the invitation to her cabin was just part of the verbal explosion she was familiar with as the "bear expert." It was typical of people to react to her job by pouring out their bear encounter stories, but they didn't usually invite her to take a look at photos. The woman in front of her was certainly charismatic and cute. Perhaps she would seek her out. She glanced at her watch. "Guess it's close enough to dinner to head over."

"Close enough?" The clerk laughed. "You better hustle on in. Nobody's late for dinner."

"It's just now going on six," she said, double checking her watch.

"Oh, they say dinner's at six, but I'd be surprised if there's a seat left. I'd be there already if I wasn't on duty."

"Thanks for the warning." Gloria smiled, tucking her stack of cards into her day pack. She took a step toward the door, but the clerk stopped her.

"Tourists have to go around, but you're official. Go on through the double doors. You can go through the kitchen to the dining room."

Gloria thanked her and pushed through the swinging door.

CHAPTER FIVE

A few days after Kristine arrived, Gabe announced that Leo had called them back down to the Lodge for dinner. They entered the building together, but while Gabe headed straight for the cluster of cowboys by the diner-style counter, Kristine snuck into the kitchen angling to steal a candy bar from the lunch station before Jorge noticed. The wiry Ecuadorian had been with the Lodge years before Kristine had joined the crew, and she remembered how fiercely he protected the snack shelf. Her eyes on him instead of the direction she traveled, she did not notice a figure pushing through the double doors that led to the store. The quick "excuse me" meant to avoid the collision scared a yelp from her lips.

"Hands off the candy," Jorge said without turning from the grill.

Kristine's face radiated a wide grin, thinking of how accurately the cook's words could be attached to the woman standing in front of her. She couldn't help but let her eyes roam down the newcomer's body, appreciating how well she wore her uniform. "He knows me too well," Kristine said, meeting the attractive woman's eye. She nearly got lost in their deep blue, that color the sky turns just before nightfall. "Can't get over the sweet tooth," she said, motioning with her chin to the shelf behind the woman. "You look lost. Where are you headed? I'm Kristine Owens, by the way." She offered her hand.

"Gloria Fisher. I'm here to talk about bears. The store clerk said it was okay to go through the kitchen."

Kristine took a moment to enjoy the feel of Gloria's firm, warm handshake. The woman radiated a relaxed confidence. The pressed uniform said professional, but the way she'd swept the top portion of her blond hair back from her face leaving the rest down around her shoulders and carried the goofy Fish and Wildlife hat said "not uptight."

The slight advantage in height that Kristine had might have been from the thick-heeled White's she wore. She held Gloria's hand three beats longer than considered polite simply because it felt so right nestled with hers. She found herself thinking how easy it would be to pull the woman in for a kiss, her lips ever so much more enticing than the original sweet she was after. She frowned, admonishing herself for slipping into the persona she'd been the last time she was here. "Ah, you're the reason boss-man called us all the way down from Aspens for supper. All the staff is this way, in the dining room. Have you met Leo yet?"

"No," Gloria said, pushing through another set of swinging doors after Kristine.

Kristine spotted Leo at the old-timers' table. "He's the most scraggly cowboy over in that corner." Then she considered Sol, sitting next to Leo. "Or second scraggliest. Maybe tied for the most scraggly cowboy here. Shouldn't you be following my finger instead of staring at me?"

"Would it help?" Gloria asked, amusement in her voice.

Kristine tipped her chin to the side, truly considering her answer. "Fair enough. He's the one in plaid."

Gloria continued to stare.

"Fine. I'll introduce you myself. Right this way." She smiled impishly.

After the introductions, she wove through the tables where the cabin, store and café staff sat. They looked comfortable in the café, surrounded by all of the junk on the walls that made the place look "authentic." Whenever something was too broken for the corral staff to use, it got tossed up onto the wall. Rusted out bits, an old cowbell probably missing its ringer, cracked harnesses and horseshoes all gave the café a rustic feel. The first year, she'd studied all of the pictures, her favorites the staff pictures taken at the beginning of each season. She passed all of them without a glance, settling onto a stool at the counter with the other packers next to her brother, Gabe.

He flicked the brim of her cowboy hat, adding, "Hiding a rooster?"

She narrowed her eyes at him as she removed her hat, tucking it beneath the counter. The brim caught on the bar she rested her feet on. She scritched her fingers through her short brown hair, unplastering the fine waves from her crown and pulling a few bangs over her forehead.

"Damn, Teeny," a bear of a cowboy quipped. "Did Gabe get you by accident when he was shaving all of his mules for the season?"

Kristine gritted her teeth, annoyed. They'd worked a few seasons before she'd left, and according to her brother, he'd become one of the Leo Armstrong's main packers. "No more Teeny."

Without acknowledging the comment, he looked to the front of the room. "Tell me she's the entertainment tonight," he drawled.

"She's a stripper?" Brian gasped, turning on his stool and straining his neck.

Leo's son, Nard, glared at the youngster. "Dad's just kissing political ass letting some bear specialist come down and tell us what we already know. Bears are a problem. Bears are dangerous. Don't play with the bears. Should be very educational."

He'd slowed down on the last two sentences, directing them right at Kristine. She flicked her eyes to him, considering the challenge only she heard. "Give her a chance," Kristine said, keeping her voice even.

Nard snorted. "Seems like your type, you mean?" he sneered.

Kristine didn't respond to the barb though her pulse thrummed in her ears. His eyes stayed on her, that stare that she'd been happy to leave behind, but she held his gaze. She would not engage him. She would not let him win. Thankfully, the kitchen staff brought out heaping plates of pork chops, potatoes and corn. Everyone dug in.

Kristine would have said Nard had always been an ass, but that would be disrespecting the burro, the donkeys which were an integral part of her father's breeding program. She tried to be fair. Who could blame a guy for having an attitude problem when the world called him Nard because his father, Leo, had already taken the logical shortened version of Leonard? Why not go by Leonard? Leo Jr.? But here he was, thirty-six and still at his dad's pack station. She wondered if he'd improved in the job in the six years she'd been gone. He wasn't sitting with the old-timers, but Gloria was. By the way the visitor studied her food, it looked like she was also thankful for the diversion a meal provided.

"You know she could be, if she wanted," Gabe whispered, interrupting Kristine's thoughts. "A stripper," he clarified, wiggling his eyebrows and sharing the target of Kristine's gaze. "Maybe I should ask after the presentation."

"Save it, Gabe. You're not the one she'd be taking it off for."

"Oh, really," he said, turning to look at the woman in question again. He pushed his plate away from him. "You sound pretty sure, there. What exactly happened in the thirty seconds it took for you to walk her over to Leo's table?"

"She shook my hand back in the kitchen," Kristine said, tossing her napkin onto her plate. "And hers is definitely a hand that has graced the glorious body of a woman." She glanced back in Gloria's direction as she said the words, and though it wasn't possible for the woman to have heard what she said, her eyes locked with Kristine's sending a rush of heat through her body.

He brother glanced between the two women. "Guess Nard was right," he said, chuckling.

Kristine broke eye contact, meeting her brother's eyes with no hint of humor. "Don't."

Gabe's brow furrowed in confusion, but before he could respond, Leo stood, ringing one of their bell mare bells. "Please turn your attention to Ms. Fisher. She's a specialist on bear aversion training. She's got some reminders for us and, ahh…" he looked down at her, at a loss for what to say, and she rose.

"And to enlist some of you in helping us take care of what has become a real danger. As Leo said, I'm Gloria Fisher. I'm a wildlife biologist with the Department of Fish and Wildlife. I work out of the Ontario office in southern California and have been studying interaction between bears and humans for a little more than a year. In reviewing reports from your local Forest Service rangers, a trend has emerged, revealing that encounters are on the rise. Yosemite has successfully reduced their bear encounters. I applied for a grant to try implementing some of their techniques in this region to see if balance can be restored before bears have to be relocated or destroyed." She pulled out a stack of notecards and started giving statistics from the incidents recorded from campgrounds and the strategies needed to prevent them.

Nard sighed loudly and rolled his eyes. Kristine turned completely around on her stool trying to concentrate on Gloria, but she couldn't ignore the comments of her fellow packers. Every item on Gloria's list elicited a smartass response.

"Bears are attracted to FOOD?" Gabe whispered.

"But they never disturb a family pic-a-nic," Dozer said, not as quietly in a pretty decent Yogi Bear impression.

"They're smart?" Gabe gasped.

"Smarter than the average bear," Dozer continued.

"You grow much more hair on that face, and people will start to believe you're a bear," Gabe said.

"Let's see the expert lady try to scare me off."

"Wouldn't work. You hear banging pans and come running for supper."

"If she were supper, you bet I'd come running," Dozer purred.

Kristine reached beyond her brother to smack the large cowboy, unable to take more of their banter. Less than a minute later, though, her brother gasped again. "Bears get into TRASH CANS? Even if the LID is on?"

Even Kristine had a hard time suppressing a giggle. Surely, this woman had to know that people who worked in the backcountry had the sense to do what they could to keep bears out of the outfit or their camps. No one wanted to be in the backcountry with hungry guests and have to explain that they'd lost all of their food to a domesticated bear.

She took advantage of the opportunity to evaluate Gloria unimpeded. Again, she appreciated her confidence. Clearly, Gloria was used to addressing large groups of people and commanding their respect. She was professional, ticking through her points, but Kristine had to agree with the cowboys at the table about the usefulness of her information.

Not that she minded, Kristine smiled. The ranger could be reciting the elevation of all of the peaks in the Minarets and giving rainfall data for the last hundred years, and Kristine would have listened. Gloria had no trouble projecting her low but powerful voice through the room. Kristine remembered what it was like in normal conversation and took a moment to wonder what it would be like brought down to an intimate whisper. She imagined that voice raising the hair just behind her ear, but before she could anticipate what she'd be saying, the words Gloria had uttered snapped her out of her reverie.

"Did she say something about shooting the bears?" she whispered to Gabe.

"Yeah," he said, sitting up straighter. "With rubber bullets."

Kristine quickly shifted away from Gloria's physical attributes to what her intellect had to offer about dealing with the animals in the backcountry.

"It's important to establish that the area you inhabit is your den and that they are not welcome. Bears are extremely territorial, and if you claim the territory effectively, with noisemakers and some zings to their hide, they'll get the message that they need to forage elsewhere."

The entire café was silent.

"At the end of the week Leo will help me set up a practice area in the meadow where we'll have the opportunity to practice some of the techniques I went over tonight."

"The Forest Service is going to sign off on our carrying in the backcountry?" a skeptical Dozer shouted out.

Kristine admired the way the ranger deftly shepherded the conversation back to how she hoped Leo's employees could participate in improving the balance between human and nature. After a half hour or so, the questions ceased, the crew cleared their plates and drifted to their evening chores.

Kristine sat tipped back in a chair on the porch that ran along the main building, her boots resting on the railing. Waiting for the rest of the corral staff to emerge from the store, she enjoyed an after-supper ice cream. Who was she kidding, she thought, letting the chair's feet thump back to the porch. She was sitting there hoping to get another glimpse of the presenter. She toyed with the idea of inviting her to join the group which had decided to get a campfire going after the evening feed.

Again, she remembered her promise to herself. By facing her past instead of continuing to run, she could use that strength to finally stand up to the force of her father. She could leave the ranch and find her own path as a professional photographer. A summer fling sounded enticing, especially after being in the small, socially dry town of Quincy for six months, but she knew that it would only distract her from getting on her own feet.

Having gone through the kitchen to the store, the corral crew emerged from the door on her left just as Gloria exited the diner's door on her right. Did Gloria look pleased to see her sitting there? Meeting her eyes, Kristine felt a pull between them, the instinct that had her fantasizing about kissing her when they'd first met instead of offering to point out her boss.

"Teeny!" Dozer shouted, making her whip her head in the opposition direction. "There's a hay hook with your name on it up at the corrals if you've still got something to prove."

Kristine ground her teeth. He hadn't changed at all, and she found that she still had a difficult time not letting him get under her skin. True, she had felt the need to keep up with the guys back then, but she'd had to when they always treated her like a helpless girl. Risking another glance in Gloria's direction, she met those blue eyes once again. She seemed to be observing the scene with interest. Best to walk away now, Kristine told herself. Their paths weren't likely to cross, and it would be easier to resist the very real temptation she presented if Kristine didn't spend any more time talking to her.

She sighed, bowing her head before she pushed to stand and join the crew stepping off the porch to the hard-packed dirt yard between the building and the corrals, not to prove anything to Dozer but to prove to herself that she had returned a different person, that she was in control.

CHAPTER SIX

Gloria enjoyed her walk back to the campground, taking in the details of the mountains she would call home for the summer. A gentle breeze played on the Jeffrey pines, the air carrying their faint vanilla sweetness. Far down in the valley as she was, direct sunlight disappeared early, leaving the rest of the day to fade to darkness.

She found the campground as deserted as she'd left it. Besides her ancient camper there were only two other vehicles backed into campsites, which didn't surprise her. Mid-June was too early for any but the most serious of campers and backpackers. Most families traveled later in the summer when the temperatures were friendlier, though they would pay in mosquito bites. Gloria enjoyed the colder months with minimal pests, both insect and humans, to disrupt her solitude. During the summer, she'd talk to hundreds of people a day and feel completely sapped. These quiet times recharged her batteries.

Wasn't that why she'd turned down Sol's invitation to join the cowboys at their campfire pit? Part of her current project did involve the crew, but beyond a few meetings, she wasn't likely to work with them. Usually, the local Forest Service crew were the only ones she saw regularly, and she accepted invitations to hang out primarily out of professional courtesy. Tonight, though, she was tempted by the group of cowboys. She recalled how unruly they'd been in the meeting, the classic back-row students poking fun the whole time, not taking her seriously at all.

She could pretend it was their behavior that kept her gaze returning to the back, but she knew that it was the tall cowgirl who had captured her interest and held it. Thinking about Kristine brought a smile to her lips. She had a youthful playfulness about her but a cleverness in her banter that suggested she was older than her fair skin and tousled brown hair suggested. She wondered how much she was likely to see her during the summer. Surely she'd be at the welcome-back campfire Sol had mentioned to her during dinner. The few minutes she'd been in Kristine's presence had piqued her curiosity. She'd felt a spark when their hands met and the way Kristine's eyes had traveled down her body made her feel like she was charting a course for her hands. Just the thought sent a warm rush through her.

Her campfire pit sat cold and empty. She could skip a fire altogether and bundle up in her camper with her book…she shivered involuntarily…or she could take a chance and test the warmth of the company Sol offered. Turning on her heel, she headed back in the direction of the Lodge.

"Ms. Fisher," a deep voice boomed. "I thought campground duties had claimed you."

Gloria paused to let one of the back-row cowboys catch up to her.

"No campground duty for me. I'm a biologist, not a host," she explained. "My specialty is actually scaring off unwanted guests."

"That mean I should be feeling scared right now?" A familiar smile played on his lips.

Gloria tilted her head, trying to discern why she felt like she recognized his smile. "I'm off duty."

"Gabe Owens," the cowboy said, offering his hand.

Recognizing the last name Kristine had given her, Gloria decided charm must run in their genes. At five foot seven, she was used to men being taller than she was, but this man towered over her. He was the classic tall, dark and handsome cowboy from the westerns, with a thick mustache and close-cropped hair. She took his hand and held it long enough that he began to look worried. She gave a final hard squeeze before saying, "You were one of the peanut gallery. Were you Yogi or Boo-Boo Bear?"

Gabe tucked his chin and removed his hat, looking appropriately chastised. "Just a cowboy, ma'am, and you know cowboys are very near to rascals who are practically heathens. I do apologize. Let me make it up to you? We've got a campfire going to warm your outsides and some drinks that are sure to warm your insides."

Gloria studied the cowboy, wondering if flirting was a staff requirement at the Lodge. "Lead the way," she said. "I'm sorry you had to sit through my lecture. I imagine you and the other Boo-Boos must have a lot of experience with bears."

Gabe shot a broad smile and looked relieved. "Yeah, we do our best to keep them at bay. Haven't had too many run-ins the years I've been here. Mostly the Dumpster down by the café and the campgrounds that get hit the hardest if I remember correctly."

"How long have you been working for Lodgepole Pines?"

He laughed. "Everyone just calls it The Lodge."

"Thanks for cluing me in to that," Gloria said.

Gabe scratched the back of his head as he calculated. "This makes my seventh year here. Not that Leo gives out any fancy pens or anything."

Gloria felt scrutinized by the corral staff as she approached with Gabe. Eyes moved from him to her. A few of the cowboys gave Gabe a facial thumbs-up with the purse of their lips and slight nod. She didn't see the one person she had hoped to see, the only one she wouldn't want thinking she was here for Gabe's company.

"You're welcome to sit anywhere," Gabe said. "I've gotta grab my guitar from my truck, but I'll be right back."

Gloria sat upwind of the firepit and watched the group work together to stoke the fire, sparks flying as they dropped on large sticks of wood. A short, broad cowboy with more facial hair than she'd ever seen on a human approached her.

"Dozer," he drawled, offering his hand. "Like a drink?"

"I'm fine, thanks," she said.

"Let me know if you change your mind. I've got just about anything you'd want in my cabin there." His chin jutted in the direction of the cabin behind them, and his voice dripped innuendo, confirming her suspicion about the flirting requirement.

A woman slid a possessive arm around the man's waist. "As long as it's Jim Beam." She held out her hand. "I'm Sandy. I'm cooking for Dozer's trips this year."

And you're welcome to that fine specimen of a man, Gloria thought as she shook the woman's hand, not sure how to relate to her that she was in no way offering competition. "You weren't at dinner," Gloria said. She had a skill for remembering faces and names.

"No time," Sandy said. "I have to get my kitchen together. We're off on the Horseshoe Meadows trip at the end of the week."

"Everyone is required to attend the rifle training with rubber bullets at ten on Friday," Gloria said. "It's my understanding that you typically sleep near the food to prevent nighttime raids?"

"I'm there to do the protecting," Dozer said, his chest puffed out. "I haven't ever lost any food out in the backcountry." He glanced around the campfire, missing Sandy's eye roll. "Where's Teeny? We lose her to the campground girls already?"

Gloria's ears perked at the question, remembering what the store clerk had said about this Teeny being good. The cowboys must be her source of information. The youngest cowboy at the fire looked surprised. "I thought she was joking about being invited down to the campground by one of our guests in Campsite Seventeen today," he said.

Dozer slapped his thigh. "Oh, ho! She got one already? Can't say I'm surprised. Teeny always did take the girls seriously."

"Too bad you don't take women as seriously," Kristine said as she strode up to the fire, shrugging into a thick tan coat. Distracted by the banter, Gloria had missed Kristine's approach, and seeing her again produced a tickle of excitement. Kristine pinned Dozer with a furious glare. "And it's Kristine."

Kristine. Teeny. Gloria's mind got busy matching the woman who had some sort of reputation that the cowboys and store clerk had been talking about with her own initial response, when she felt the cowgirl's eyes on her. Kristine's expression shifted again, but Gloria didn't know her well enough to interpret it. It was not delight, but it wasn't dread either. Gloria felt herself warm as Kristine held on to her gaze. Gabe's voice broke the contact, allowing Gloria to release the breath she'd been holding.

"Quit picking on my sister before she decides to hightail it out of here again," he said, returning with a guitar. "I trusted you'd be giving her a better welcome back than this."

She couldn't help notice how appealing Kristine was in her tight Wrangler jeans. The coat she had added concealed her tailored plaid shirt that, tucked in, highlighted her narrow hips. It added to her rugged appeal that Gloria was sure went over well with vacationers. It was easy to imagine women getting swept off their feet.

"It's you she's doing the favor for," Dozer said. "Us she quit out on, no goodbye, no nothing."

A tense silence followed his statement, and it was clear in the way everyone looked at Kristine that they wanted an answer from her. Gloria saw a blush rise on her cheeks and wondered what could throw off the woman who had seemed so sure of herself in earlier conversation.

"I needed a change of scenery," Kristine said.

"Didn't the scenery down at the campground change enough to suit you?" Dozer goaded.

"Drop it," Gabe said.

"What? It's no secret how she chased tail. Always wanted to have what we've got." Dozer reached down and rearranged his package.

Kristine's color deepened. She'd opened her mouth to reply but bit back whatever it was when Sol walked up behind Dozer and roughly patted his back.

"You're the only one who's ever been in love with that thing," Sol growled. "Where the hell's the Jim Beam, and why aren't you playing that goddamned thing?" he barked at Gabe. The entire demeanor of the campfire changed as the old man pushed through the group and sat next to Gloria.

"Don't let these pissheads scare you off, girl," he said, pouring two cups of bourbon and handing one to her. She blinked and accepted the cup, wondering where the conversation would have gone if Sol had not interrupted. She watched Kristine as she assessed the seating options, caught her eye and motioned to the chair beside her, inviting her to sit.

Again, she couldn't read Kristine's expression. After a moment's hesitation, she took a few steps and dropped into the camp chair to Gloria's left. She raised her lips in a courteous smile that didn't reach her eyes. Her shoulders still held tension as she opened a microbrew and tilted it back.

They sat in silence as the rest of the group settled in, and again Gloria wondered about the group's history, why Kristine had left and why she was back now. Kristine rolled the bottle in her hands, seemingly uncomfortable in the circle, and Gloria struggled to think of something appropriate to say. Gabe tuned his guitar. She didn't recognize the song, but a few voices joined Gabe's. Kristine finally breathed out, appearing to relax a little. She glanced at Gloria and offered the smile that had captivated her in the café.

Gloria took Kristine's smile as an all clear. "So…Teeny? How does a woman of your stature get a nickname like that?"

"Ugh. I was a late bloomer," she responded, swigging from her bottle. "I was a regular beanpole when I was seventeen. But later, even when my size didn't match the name, it was their way of reminding me of my place. You heard Dozer, I'm sure.

They've always seen me as the tagalong for wanting to learn what they were doing…well packing the mules anyway. I never wanted to cook for the overnight trips or lead the day rides. I've always wanted to be with the stock, and some didn't take to that too well." Her eyes stayed on her bottle instead of targeting anyone in the circle.

"You look a lot like your brother. Who's older?"

"He lords his seven inches over me, but I've got two years on him, and I don't ever let him forget that."

Gabe wrapped up a song, and Dozer shouted across the campfire. "Teach me that one you say works wonders on the ladies."

Sandy smacked Dozer's arm.

"It's good for tips," he defended himself.

"I'm sure that's Kristine's excuse, too," said a cowboy so lanky his chest seemed concave. He wore a mean expression with a hawkish nose and dirty blond mustache. She recognized the speaker as Leo's son and read the animosity in the eyes that blazed in Kristine's direction.

"Nothing wrong with being a flirt," Kristine said, lightheartedly, eyes not meeting Nard's.

Dozer guffawed. "Your reputation goes way beyond flirting!"

"C'mon. I was a teenager away from my parents trying to set a good example for my little brother. Sing that George Strait song for us. The chords are easy enough for Dozer, and it's always a crowd-pleaser."

Gloria noticed Kristine's hands tight on the bottle she held and realized that she was uncomfortable with the ribbing from her friends. She could easily read the dynamics between Dozer and Kristine, his crassness something she, too, experienced from colleagues who argued that their pushing the line with their jokes was their way of accepting her as "one of the guys." His taunts, though, didn't rattle Kristine in the same way Nard's did. He'd fixed his hard stare on Kristine, and she studiously kept her eyes from him.

From the stories they told of their past summers, their triumphs as well as their disasters, Gloria gathered that most of the group had worked many seasons together. Since she had become a specialist, traveling around to work with different crews on bear/human cohabitation, she often found herself the outsider observing tightknit groups.

Most of the time, she enjoyed her solitude, but the banter at the campfire made her realize how much she missed the camaraderie that came along with the chaos. The warmth of the campfire extended beyond the flickering glow of the flames. Their shared memories made Gloria miss her family back in Eureka. Her earliest memories were of singing rounds at the campfire with her mom and dad in the summers, back when they used to pick a different camping destination every summer. Back when her mom had the stamina to hike the most difficult terrain.

"You have siblings?" Kristine's voice interrupted her memories.

"Nope. Just me."

"All the attention lavished on you, huh?"

"You could say that." Gloria admired Kristine's natural beauty. Flecks of gold in her brown eyes reflected the dancing flames of the fire.

"I imagine it would be even more fun to be the one lavishing attention," Kristine said.

A wave of warmth shot through Gloria's body, and she openly stared at Kristine, who was leaning back into her chair, propping her feet on the stones of the firepit. Nothing in her posture suggested she'd uttered the come-on, yet Gloria's body hummed with the prospect of Kristine's scrutiny fixed upon her. Wood popped and shifted in the pit, sending another shower of sparks beyond the ring which Kristine quickly stamped out. Smoke rose into the canopy, and owls hooted as the night deepened.

Kristine spoke, a smile playing at the corner of her mouth. "Don't they miss you? I imagine you're out in the forest quite a bit." The fire popped sending a spray of sparks into the night.

Gloria frowned. She thought they'd been flirting, but there was certainly no innuendo in Kristine's question. "They do. But I'm their vicarious link to all this," she said, gazing up at the treetops. A stronger wind moved in the canopy, a distant roar like the ocean in a seashell. She shuddered as much at her memory of the ocean and home as how cool the evening grew as the sky deepened to the blue-black before dark.

Kristine shrugged out of the heavy cowboy coat she wore and held it out to Gloria.

"I'm about to head out anyway," Gloria said, shaking her head.

"Not quite," Kristine said, quirking an eyebrow.

Gloria raised her eyebrows in question, waiting for Kristine's explanation.

"You've hardly touched your drink. And besides, what if we have a bear visitor?" she winked.

Gloria accepted Kristine's offer. She thought about the heat of Kristine's body as she settled into the warmth of the coat that already smelled of woodsmoke. She couldn't help thinking of Kristine's arms wrapped around her body. Kristine was right. She did want to stay. All that waited for her back at the campground was a very cold sleeping bag.

"You're not uncomfortable?" she asked, feeling guilty for accepting the coat.

"Just the opposite."

Gloria tipped her chin, listening.

Kristine leaned in close and whispered, "It's nice to have an intelligent woman who plays on the same team to talk to. This crowd…" She frowned, leaning away from Gloria and letting the thought drift away as she finished off her beer.

"And you'll work with them all season?"

"No. My brother and I are up the road at the Aspen Outpost."

"So you don't work for the Lodge?" Gloria asked, puzzled.

"Oh, we all work for Leo. He's got another station about fifteen miles down the road."

"By the Aspen Grove Campground."

"Yep."

"He owns both?"

Kristine nodded. "The outpost is smaller. Gabe and I don't do the long travel trips that stay out in the backcountry overnight. Teams like Sandy and Dozer take trips out anywhere from five to seven days. We do what are called spot trips, dropping stuff off in the backcountry. Sometimes they ride with us, but others they hike in on their own to where we've left their gear, and we coordinate with them to pick up everything on the day they hike out. Travel trips leave out of the outpost, too. Leaving out of there shaves a day off trips out to Yosemite or gives a good starting point to trips that return to the Lodge. So we'll see this crew a bit, but only when they ship their stock up and then pack up their trips that leave from our trailheads. Most of the time, though, it'll just be me 'n Gabe."

Gloria felt disappointed. She realized she'd been anticipating chance run-ins with Kristine since the campground where she'd parked her camper was so close to the employee cabins at the Lodge. "Sounds quiet."

Kristine laughed. "I've got Gabe. I'm sure my life's a whole lot less quiet than yours down at the campground."

Sol, who must have had an ear on their conversation, said, "We'll be trying to get the two of you down here to play. Isn't anyone else who picks a tune like your brother. Play me one more song, that one about God being a cowboy, before I take these old bones to bed."

Gabe extended the guitar to his sister. "That one's Kristine's specialty."

"You do a great job with that one. Keep it up."

"Your turn to play, my turn to drink," he winked.

Kristine took the guitar and looked a bit sheepish. Gloria was grateful for the dark as she wondered if the song Sol had requested was one of Kristine's conquest specialties. She knew the group thought she'd come with Gabe but was pretty certain her expression would betray her interest in his sister. She didn't know them well enough yet to feel comfortable revealing that.

Kristine kept her head bent as she found her way through the chords. She sang more quietly than Gabe, but her voice was beautiful and true. As she neared the end of the chorus, her voice gained strength, captivating all at the campfire.

Longer silence filled the night when Kristine handed the guitar back to Gabe. "Thanks, Sol. It is good to be back, but I'm beat, and if I remember, morning comes early around here."

Gloria stood as the others tipped their hats to acknowledge her departure. She, too, thanked everyone for the evening.

"Want a lift to the campground? It's on my way over to the outpost," Kristine said to Gloria as they stepped away from the fire.

"That'd be nice. Thanks."

They climbed into the cab of Kristine's truck and sat in silence as Kristine rubbed her hands together in her lap while she waited a few minutes for the engine to warm.

"I should give you back your coat," Gloria said, though she made no move to take it off.

"It's mostly habit," Kristine said, stopping the motion.

Gloria searched for something else to say. Kristine put the old truck in gear and eased out onto the road. After spending the evening enjoying her company, she should be able to think of something during the short ride, but she was at a loss. "This small camper here in Slot One is home," she said. She started to shrug out of Kristine's coat.

"You're fine," Kristine said. "Keep it. The cab's warm, much warmer than where you're headed."

Gloria pulled the collar around her again, smelling saddle oil and horse and Kristine. There was no reason for her to continue to sit in the cab, but still, she could not motivate to open the door. Nothing in Kristine's body language conveyed that she was anxious to get going. Nothing encouraged pursuit, either. That her job entailed teaching a local team to manage bear problems meant that after a few weeks, at the most a few months, Gloria would move on. Because of this nomadic existence, she never worried about being forward when the opportunity arose, not having the luxury of time to draw out a courtship. Short and uncomplicated worked for her, and the places she worked were usually filled with other seasonal employees who felt the same way. Something about Kristine intrigued her, but she was having a very difficult time reading whether the feelings were reciprocal.

"I'm not keeping you from your campground exploit?" she asked, unable to resist her curiosity.

"I'm liking the company here just fine." A slow smile crept across Kristine's face.

"Better than the company at the campfire?"

Kristine smirked. "That company is exactly why I'm headed back to the Aspens."

Gloria laughed, enjoying Kristine's candor. "With friends like that, I wouldn't blame you for wanting to help someone warm up her sleeping bag."

"That an invitation?"

The question flooded her with desire. "Like you said, it is cold where I'm headed…"

Since her previous question had come so quickly, Gloria was thrown when Kristine sat quietly. She seemed to weigh her decision. For a moment, her eyes held desire, but then it was like Kristine shut the door on them. "Six years ago, I'd have jumped at the chance to help you out with that, but that's not what brought me back to Mammoth."

"You have to know that your reputation in no way bothers me," Gloria said, hoping Kristine would change her mind. Instead, her words seemed to make Kristine bristle more. Hoping to clarify, she added, "I'm a seasonal employee and get the 'Take only pictures' philosophy."

"What does that mean?"

"You know the motto: Take only pictures; Leave only footprints. Dating can be like that. You don't disrupt the habitat. You take your memories and leave as little trace as possible."

"I'm sure Campsite Seventeen would be willing to play that game if that's what you're looking for." Kristine tipped her hat to hide her profile. Gloria tried to think of something that would bring the flirty, fun atmosphere back, but Kristine added, "It is late," effectively dismissing her.

Reluctantly, she let herself out of the truck, stepping out into the cold. She watched as Kristine pulled away, the taillights quickly disappearing around the bend, plunging her into utter darkness. The level of disappointment she felt from Kristine's departure surprised her. Reviewing the day, it was clear that the store clerk welcomed her presence more than the cowgirl. Too bad the evening had served to pique her interest in Kristine. She wondered what Kristine had meant about the reason she'd returned to the Lodge. A smile crept to her lips. She had at least a few weeks to work her charm on Kristine and felt pretty confident that it wouldn't take long to bring her around.

CHAPTER SEVEN

"I knew it was a brilliant plan to have you run the Aspens with me." Gabe sighed, helping himself to coffee, eggs and toast.

The last thing that Kristine wanted was to be Gabe's caretaker. She wouldn't have been surprised if Gabe's sloth and desire to be looked after had scared off Bridget, the girlfriend he'd been set to run the outpost with before she'd dumped him, prompting his plea for Kristine to come back.

"Because Bridget got tired of cooking you breakfast?" Kristine asked pointedly.

Gabe covered his tracks quickly. "Thanks for breakfast, sis. We could, uh, take turns?"

Kristine smiled. "That's better."

"Surprised your truck was already here when I rolled in last night. Sure seemed like the bear lady was into you."

"C'mon, Gabe. If that's what I was after, I would have been at Campsite Seventeen."

"I can't believe you passed up on that. You think she plays for both teams?"

She threw a towel at him.

"No, seriously, sis. You're on fire from day one, hitting it off with all of these hot ladies. How about a little help here?"

Kristine sat down opposite her brother and tried to console him. "You're assuming the day rider was hot."

"No. Brian told me just how hot she was. He's got a little crush of his own going, if you ask me."

"You want me to ask Brian if he thinks you're hot?"

Gabe scowled. "You're dead if you do. But the new day-ride girl, Takeisha. There's someone you could ask."

"You're on your own there, buddy. I am not getting mixed up in your disastrous love life. Though it would be fun to see what dad thinks of interracial dating."

"Some help you are."

"I only agreed to help you with the Aspens. Ready to get the stock?"

"Not even close. We show up at the Lodge this early and they'll start expecting us to work hard." He put his feet up on the table. Kristine swatted them away.

He smiled his Cheshire cat grin. "Plus, you're changing the subject." A surprised look crossed his face. "Or is that your plan? We're leaving early to swing by the campground next to the Lodge on our way in for you to 'pick up your *coat.*' Is that what you girls call it?"

"I lent her my coat because she was cold, not because I was angling to get in her pants." Kristine cleared her dishes.

Gabe looked stumped. "But she's hot."

"Yes, and so was Campsite Seventeen."

"I thought I knew you," Gabe said, shaking his head.

"It's called growing up, baby brother." She patted him on the cheek and slyly grabbed his coat off the antlers hanging by the door.

They went their separate ways at the Lodge, Gabe off to find Nard and Kristine down to the mule corral with five halters slung over her shoulder and her camera hanging from the other. With Suzy-Q and Scooter trailing, she grabbed a few shots of the mules loose in the corral, noticing as she framed the latter that Dozer had joined her at the fence. She zoomed in on his cowboy scowl before slinging the camera around to her back.

"Never knew what you saw in those bitties," Dozer said, resting against the corral observing her progress.

"They do the same work your giants do just fine," Kristine retorted.

"No one likes that string but you. Any packer stuck with 'em is the sissy packer of the summer."

Though tempted to bite at the childish remark, Kristine knew that it would only egg him on. Instead, she concentrated on catching her five mules, smiling to see them make their way immediately to the gate as soon as she'd swung their lead ropes over their withers. They walked obediently without her having to grab them because they knew grain waited for them at the tie rails. Dozer didn't move to help her open or shut the gate.

She glared at him as she fastened the gate after the last mule. "What?"

"Nothing. Nothing at all," she said, pointedly latching the gate behind her.

"See anyone out there who needs shoeing?"

"Not my job to look," Kristine said crisply. He didn't offer to help her but routinely expected her to lend a hand when he was doing anything.

"What'll it be, Smoke?" she rubbed the mule's ears as he munched his corn, oats and barley treat, soothing him to a sleep-like daze. "The standard mane buzz and cropped tail? Whiskers?" His lower lip hung low, telling her that he could care less what she did as long as she continued rubbing his ears.

She asked him questions about the years she'd been gone, noting the white patches around his girth area and armpits that betrayed careless handling by other packers. She apologized and got to work, hoping Dozer was just yanking her chain and that they'd had some decent packers in the years she'd been gone. When she was done with his cut, he was the handsome mule she remembered, the sleek well-balanced animal her family specialized in.

"You think I'm crazy for going home last night?" she asked Scooter. In all honesty, her twenty-year-old self wouldn't have headed back to the Aspens to sleep in her own bunk. Objectively, Gloria tempted her in multiple ways. She was unassumingly beautiful. Her appeal radiated from her self-confidence. Plus, Kristine enjoyed her company a great deal. But this summer, she had bigger things than satisfying a sexual urge to worry about.

In her experience, a seasonal thing never had a chance to become something permanent. Even when she'd dated someone for a while at school, it never got serious. At every milestone, the term ending, finishing a degree, the path she envisioned had never included someone by her side, and the partings had always been mutual, the next step in each woman's personal life taking precedence over a relationship.

Those musings brought her to Suzy-Q. "When is it going to stop mattering?" she asked, scratching the mule's ears for a moment. "I'm twenty-seven at the end of the summer. You'd think it wouldn't matter what Dad says. But he's totally right about my not being able to support myself. Forget about dreams, how am I going to pay off my student loans?"

Suzy-Q sneezed brown goo all over the front of Kristine's sweatshirt.

"That's all you've got?" Kristine laughed, wiping away the mess. "You may be beautiful, but you're not very helpful."

As she worked on clipping the mules, she relished in the atmosphere of the yard as it came to life. She watched the day-ride girls catching and saddling stock, bantering about which horse was which. Kristine felt a pang of regret. She'd been gone so long that few of the dude horses were familiar to her. There'd been a time when she was queen of the yard, aware of which horses could be trusted with kids, which traveled out and which ones poked along the trail.

She smiled remembering how she could make the packers' lives hell if she wanted by sending stock with them that she knew would bolt for home the minute they were turned loose in the backcountry. Some of the cowboys made an effort to stay on her good side. For them, she'd set aside her favorites. Peacock, Lumpy, Chief. They'd been old-timers when she was here, and she wasn't surprised that they'd moved on, died or been traded in during her absence, but they'd always been the choice horses to have in the backcountry.

Then there were the tough-to-bridle horses, the ones who nipped when cinched. She had always sent those with Nard. Because he never remembered to untie Gulliver when he bridled the gelding, he'd ended up with more than one broken lashrope. Kristine drew immense satisfaction from his seething about his broken gear and how much trouble she caused him when he went to tie a load onto a mule with a shorter lashrope. All that had changed when she joined him in the backcountry.

Kristine rolled her shoulders and stretched her neck, remembering how she'd told herself that it was those childish pranks that had prompted Nard to request her as the helper on his travel trips. She tried her best to stay out of his way on the trips and knew she could have avoided a lot of conflict with him if she'd just done her work, but his incompetence bothered her so much that she couldn't help herself. She couldn't hold her tongue and continued to needle him.

The jingle of the harness on the team her brother and Nard had taken down the wagon trail signaled their return. Kristine snapped the clippers back on, vowing to ignore the guys as she finished her task. Peripherally, she watched the day-ride crew join them. Once her stock was presentable for the season, she drifted to the shoeing shed to watch Dozer work, noticing his grimace as she pulled her camera out again. Just to mess with him, she kept taking shots from behind him, framing the mule's foot with his rear.

"Any of these kids need sneakers?" Gabe asked, making her jump. She tried to hide how much he'd startled her.

"All of them," she responded. "But I'll tackle that tomorrow. Leo hasn't said anything about having any spots for me yet."

"Nard's got a big trip leaving in a few days. He was talking about how you could be second packer on it."

Kristine tensed at the suggestion and more so as she watched Nard approach her mules. She gathered her strength and marched across the yard. "I didn't pack for any overnight trip," she said pointedly.

Nard ran his hand along Suzy-Q's freshly-shorn mane. "I've got an extra bedroll you can use. It's the Horse Heaven trip, too."

"I came back to work the Aspens with Gabe."

Nard moved with her, dropping his voice low enough that Gabe wouldn't be able to hear. "You sure you didn't come back for something else?" He openly leered at her. "Seems like a big coincidence your coming back right when I'm heading out there. I always thought it a shame...all those years you worked here and never once saw Horse Heaven."

"I never lost sleep over it," Kristine said, knowing what he was insinuating.

"I have." He ran his hand down the mule's rump, giving it a smack that made both the mule and Kristine jump. That made him smile. "I'll tell my dad we're all set with you as second packer."

She suppressed a shudder, trying to find a way out of the trip. She knew she'd have to face him this summer, but it was going to be on her own terms, not his. She glanced at Gabe, took in his puzzled expression, and knew she couldn't say anything to Nard as he walked away.

She untied Scooter and Suzy-Q from the rail and led them toward the stock truck they used for hauling horses and mules between the two pack outfits, leading them up the wooden platform. Her brother loaded Joker and Pepper.

"Still spooked?" he asked.

"No," she lied, hating that now she also had to figure out how to divert her brother. When it first happened, it had been easier to tell him she'd been hurt tying one of the horses to the picket line in the backcountry. Being back, though, she could feel how closely he watched her, and his tone was serious and protective, something she hadn't heard before, emotions she'd hoped to see in her father. Although he'd hesitated when she'd gone through her carefully crafted details, he accepted her story without question. She knew he'd be disappointed that she hadn't followed the cowboy code of getting right back in the saddle, but even he couldn't ignore that she wasn't up to it physically for quite a few weeks. He couldn't argue with her logic when she insisted that she wasn't useful to Leo if she hurt too much to get in the saddle. Usefulness, that was the answer.

"It's that he's still such an idiot. It makes no sense at all to have me out on that trip. Obviously, he needs to be training one of the new guys. I'm not going to be riding any of the trails on this side of the valley. I'm sure Leo will shut his idea down and send someone who actually needs to know the stopovers."

Her brother smiled.

"What?"

"You know it's that common sense that makes Dad think you're destined to run the ranch. You have a business sense of the big picture that I'll never have."

"Don't you dare tell him," Kristine said, punching him.

"No. It's our secret," he said, holding her eyes. He hesitated, but then continued, "You sure that…"

She waved him off with an excuse of wanting to get the stock over to the Aspens.

As she drove back, a wave of guilt crashed on her. She understood how angry and hurt Gabe would be if he found out what she'd been hiding all these years. At first, she'd been too scared to tell him. Then too embarrassed. She felt guilty for keeping him in the dark but saw no easy way to tell him now. It was so long ago.

Do you even have a plan? Her father's words mocked her. She had no plan at all. Had she come back specifically to confront Nard? The tangled knot in her stomach betrayed that she'd rather not. She'd returned for Gabe, she reminded herself. In helping him, she hoped to remove some of the sting from when she'd left. If she was able to work the summer through to the end, she hoped to redeem herself, at least in her own eyes. She wondered whether that was possible without having to dig up the past.

Kristine reflected on how things were when she'd run home to Quincy so unexpectedly six years ago. It was clear that her dad hadn't fully believed her explanation. She'd worried so much that he'd push for more details, more answers about why she didn't finish out the trip. At first, she was relieved that he'd let it go, but then the fact that he did so actually hurt. He'd always taught her to tough it out, but when she'd bailed, he hadn't pushed the issue. The way he'd dropped it confirmed for her that he saw his daughter as a weakling. She'd been battling that perception ever since and needed to prove to herself that she wasn't.

CHAPTER EIGHT

Gloria punched in the numbers of her calling card and relished the sound of the ringing that said her call had finally gone through. She'd spent too much time wandering around the campgrounds trying to find a cell phone signal, and had given up and headed for the payphones at the Lodge.

"Hey, Ma," she said when her mother picked up.

"What's wrong?"

"Nothing's wrong. I can't call you?"

"You send cards. That's what you do. I got your last one, by the way. Lovely, lovely place. But you don't call unless something's wrong. Bear attack?"

"No." Gloria pinched the bridge of her nose.

"Stupid campers?"

"Same as usual."

"Something wrong with the camper? You need to talk to your father?"

"Mom. I'm fine. The camper's fine. Can't I just call to say hi?"

There was silence on the line as her mother processed all of that. Just as Gloria thought she would let it slide, she began to laugh. "No. Your evenings, you hunker down with your work or a book. What's got you worked up enough to find a place to make a call? This isn't your cell. Are you up in Mammoth?"

"At the Lodge, Mom. There are payphones here. The cell coverage is spotty." Gloria rested her back against the building, watching the activity at the corrals, looking for the real reason she'd walked over. She couldn't stop thinking about Kristine. Unanswered questions had been buzzing around in her head, especially during her quiet evenings. Though she realized that Kristine was at the Aspens most days, Gloria still walked over to the Lodge around six thirty, hoping that Kristine might have headed back down for dinner or another campfire gathering.

"You're lonesome," her mother diagnosed.

"I'm fine. I like my solitude."

"Usually when you say that, I believe you. This time, I don't. What's going on?"

Gloria realized she might as well talk to her mother. She had after all called her. "There was this campfire thing a few days ago, after my talk." She shrugged even though she knew her mother could not see her. The line remained quiet as her mother waited for her daughter to continue. "I guess it made me homesick. I move around so much that there's never a group who welcomes me back, no old-timers…" Movement in the yard distracted her. Glancing over her shoulder, she saw Kristine riding in with a string of mules behind her.

Suddenly self-conscious, Gloria swiveled away from looking at the parking lot and corrals.

"Old-timers?" her mother prompted.

"Old-timers," Gloria repeated, kicking herself for not making a plan if she did happen to find Kristine.

"You were saying something about old-timers."

"Oh, right." Curious about what the cowboys were doing, she pivoted back around. She saw Kristine tying her lead mule to a post by a large wooden platform. It looked exactly like a dock she'd expect to see in a lake with a rowboat tied to the side, yet this was on dry land. "Old-timers telling stories about back when I was a teenager just learning the ropes," Gloria said.

"Adam's got those stories, and he's always saying he wished he had funding to keep you at the field office here. I always thought you were kind of relieved there wasn't money for something full-time for you here. I thought you liked being out in the wilds on your own."

"I do like where I am. I love what I do." She kept her eye on the group that had gathered to help unload the mules. "I'm just realizing that it would be nice to have a group." Like the one that she watched working together. They were a unit. The rangers she worked with became units. She'd always been the outsider. Strange that she'd never been so aware of it before.

Her mother laughed heartily. "Does this phone have a record button? I want to hear you say that again. Don't you remember me bugging you to go hang out with people your own age when you were in high school?"

"I remember," she said. Gloria wished she was closer to the work. In a flash, Kristine and Sandy pulled large leather bags from each side of the mule and tossed them onto the dock. Dozer emptied out the bags, stowing the canvas tarps and long ropes in the shed. Kristine glanced toward the building where Gloria stood. Her eyes hit Gloria like an arrow finding its target.

"You sound so blue," her mother's voice brought Gloria back to the conversation she was having. "Not your usual whip-people-into-shape self."

Gloria knew she should respond, but couldn't find words. When they had finished unloading the mules, Dozer and Kristine appeared to discuss something before Dozer took the string and led them away from the dock. Kristine sauntered across the yard, spurs clinking, the fringe of short chaps she wore slapping below her knees. She pushed her rolled-up sleeves back down, concealing her strong forearms, and her black hat shaded her face as she concentrated on buttoning her cuffs. As she entered the store, she glanced briefly in Gloria's direction.

"I'm just in that adjustment period, finding my bearings," Gloria answered. She shifted her position and was able to look in the doorway. Kristine had paused at the counter, chatting with the spellbound store clerk as she rang up an ice cream. As Kristine walked to her truck, the clerk followed her with her eyes until she realized Gloria was watching. She shrugged with a smile of acknowledgment as if to say they'd both been caught. Oblivious to the two women behind her, Kristine climbed into the cab of her truck and pulled out of the parking lot.

"Maybe you should give Meg a call. Touch base."

"Mmm," Gloria mumbled.

"Take care of yourself, sweetie," her mother said, letting her off the hook.

"I will, Mom. I love you." Gloria replaced the receiver in the cradle and paused. Something made her glance in the store again though she knew Kristine was long gone. The clerk smiled brightly.

Gloria didn't miss how the clerk's tight tank showed off her lean figure. She'd swept her dark hair up into a bun that instead of looking messy came off as stylish and cool. She returned Gloria's appraisal with an openness that invited Gloria over. She thought about simply waving because by comparison she felt frumpy in her standard loose-fitting hiking pants, her Department of Fish and Wildlife tee and unexciting ponytail tucked through the back of her ball cap. What she'd said to her mother was true—she was finding her bearings. With the hope that talking to someone would make her feel more settled, she headed toward the store.

"Checking in with the girlfriend back home?" the clerk asked without preamble.

"Mom," Gloria corrected, noting the clerk's reaction, the sport in her eyes.

"I never got to introduce myself the other night," she said. "I'm Ocean."

"Ocean?"

"Daughter of Deadheads and thus destined to be a whaler or marine biologist."

"I know plenty of people whose names match their profession, a Melody in chorus, a baker named Baker."

"Alas, the water is no draw to me." She smiled, her eyes openly assessing Gloria's body. "If you've got some time this evening, I'd be happy to show you what I am drawn to."

In the back of her head, Gloria heard Meg's voice commenting on the wealth of selection Mammoth had to offer. Pushing it aside, she smiled and said, "My evenings are nothing but time."

"Super." Ocean smiled brightly. "You had dinner? I usually grab something at the café."

"That sounds good," Gloria said. Gravitating toward the cards against the wall, she smiled and stepped aside to let Ocean do her job. Though she told herself she should find another photographer's perspective to send to her mother, Kristine's cards still spoke to her the most. She lifted one from the display.

Two backpackers crossed a sheer expanse of granite. The color of the rock, which dominated the image, should have made the picture feel cold, and the tiny backpackers remote. When she studied it though, Gloria felt warmth, felt like Kristine had captured something resonating between the two women and their surroundings.

When the clock rounded to seven, she laid the image on the counter.

"Last sale of the day," Ocean said, slipping the card into a bag for Gloria. She ducked under the counter and motioned Gloria out in front of her. "I could take you there."

Gloria tilted her chin.

"You hike, right? When I'm off, we could take the trail in that picture. That granite pass is on the way to Fish Creek. I hear there's a killer set of hot springs down there. We should go."

Gloria wondered if that's where the women in the picture were headed, if they were going to a romantic natural hot spring. "It sounds lovely," she answered as they settled in at the counter in the café.

"It's on my list of spots I have to get to this summer. It'd be awesome if I had someone to go with." she beamed.

"Is this a second summer for you?" Gloria asked, scanning the simple menu.

"Yeah, it's a pretty sweet setup. I get food and board and a chance to hike on my days off. All of my friends are totally jealous of my summer job."

"You're in college during the winter months?" Gloria asked. Please, please, she thought, let her be working on her master's degree.

"I'm second year at UC Santa Cruz," Ocean said, quickly adding, "I took a few years off after high school. I wanted to do some backpacking in Europe, which my parents totally didn't get, so I worked for two years to have a few months of travel."

"What are you studying?"

Ocean shrugged. "I'm undecided right now. Taking classes keeps my parents quiet, and then I get to play all summer."

Ocean happily described the various kinds of play she enjoyed, requiring very little participation on Gloria's part to keep the conversation going. Had she ever been this young and self-absorbed? She tried to picture a whole day hiking with this woman. Would she ever run out of things to say? Gloria wondered if she was remotely curious about her job or the things that she enjoyed. As they paid the check, Gloria realized she'd be just as content to return to her camper and lose herself in a romance novel, a pastime that she loved and would have enjoyed chatting about, had she been asked. However she found that she couldn't say no when Ocean excitedly suggested that Gloria come to her cabin to see the picture of the bear she'd told her about.

"That's the Dumpster they get into some nights when the kitchen crew forgets to lock the bar across the top."

Gloria resisted the temptation to check the Dumpster to make sure that it was secure. Inside Ocean's room, she chuckled politely at the snapshot. When Ocean offered her a beer Gloria looked for a way to cut out but didn't, not wanting to be impolite. As she sipped, she thought about why being in Ocean's company wasn't taking away her disquiet. She concentrated on not gulping her beer, so she wouldn't seem rude. When she finally finished it, she declined a second and stood to leave but didn't move fast enough to escape Ocean's moving in for a kiss. Out of instinct, she kissed Ocean back, but she found herself unable to move her hands past her shoulders. Ocean's hands traveled freely over Gloria's back, even tucking under her shirt to make contact with her skin. Gloria searched for a reason her kiss and touch did nothing to excite her. It wasn't that her feelings were hurt over Ocean's lack of interest in her career or hobbies. She'd fallen into bed with people she'd exchanged fewer words with, yet the entire time Ocean kissed her, her mind continued to search for a polite way to disengage.

Was she missing Meg? The thought was so foreign to her that she stepped back.

"Sorry," Ocean said, though she smiled. "Too forward?"

Gloria sighed apologetically. "No. It's not that."

"What, then?" Ocean asked, stepping close again and slipping a hand around Gloria's waist.

"I…"

Ocean's thumb traced a path down Gloria's jaw and hovered in front of her lips.

"Did you hear something?" Gloria asked, wondering if the banging she thought she'd heard was only wishful thinking.

Ocean tipped her head to the side, listening. Her eyes opened wide. "The bear!"

They rushed out of the room to see a large brown bear pacing by the Dumpster behind the cabin. It stood on its hind legs bawling at the metal container.

"What's it doing?" Ocean asked.

Gloria clapped her hands together and hollered for the bear to get moving. Instead of fleeing, the bear turned to face Gloria. Gloria knew the stance and looked for the cubs mama was protecting. A moment later, two small faces emerged from inside the bin. Their paws scraped at the walls as they attempted to gain enough purchase to get out, but they both failed and fell back into the Dumpster, prompting mama to turn again.

"We're going to need a truck," Gloria said, relieved to have a legitimate escape. "And a ladder."

CHAPTER NINE

On Friday, the entire crew gathered in the meadow next to the Lodge for the demonstration on how to recondition bears. Kristine's attention was supposed to be on Gloria, but every time Gloria made eye contact with her, she felt awkward. They hadn't spoken since she'd turned Gloria down, but Kristine knew that she'd have to stop by the camper eventually to retrieve her coat. As Gloria glanced in the direction of the pack crew again, Kristine elbowed her brother who was gossiping with Dozer.

"Would you quit and at least pretend to listen?" Kristine hissed.

"Dozer says that hottie bear lady made the moves on Ocean last night."

Kristine scowled at her brother, trying to shut him up.

"Good for her."

"Aren't you mad about it?" he asked.

"Why would I be mad?"

"Because you've got the hots for the bear expert."

"How about you stick to who you've got the hots for. Talked to Takeisha yet?" she asked pointedly.

Gabe's shoulders sank. "Dozer said she's all over Brian. Bear lady's looking your way again, though."

Kristine frowned as she felt stern eyes on her. She didn't feel it fair for Gloria to be the one disappointed. She was the one disappointed. She shouldn't be, she knew. It's not like she expected Gloria to pine away after her all summer after she turned her down, and Ocean was an attractive and fun woman. Still, Ocean just seemed so young. Fun to chat with, sure, but she found it difficult to imagine spending more time with her than it took to ring up an ice cream.

Kristine saw Gloria set her shoulders just as she had during her presentation in the diner. Back to business. "Bears are very intelligent," she said, emphasizing the very, "and persistent. This area has had a jump in reports of human/bear encounters, as illustrated by last night's visit from a mama and her two cubs. We want to shut that down before the little ones learn to associate humans with food. I'll walk you through some of the scare tactics, and we'll wrap up by practicing with the rubber bullets I brought. You can practice with a rifle or a handgun, whichever is more comfortable for you."

While Gloria talked, Kristine watched Ocean. She was full of smiles, but wasn't she always? She tried to discern whether Ocean was watching Gloria any more intently than any of the other employees were. "How do you know they hooked up?" she whispered to Gabe.

"They went up to the corrals last night to borrow a truck. Dozer drove down and helped Gloria drop a ladder into the Dumpster, so the cubs who'd got stuck could get out. He said Ocean made a big deal about how good it was that Gloria'd been right there when it happened, and when he left, he said they were going back into her room."

Suddenly, Gabe's eyes grew wide, and he stood stock straight, looking away from Kristine. She found Gloria's eyes on her yet again.

"I realize you all feel you have experience with bears, but believe me, you have a problem in this valley. It may not seem like that big a deal to you, but a fed bear is a dead bear. If they get food-conditioned, they are destroyed. You might not care about that. I do."

Kristine blushed deeply, regretting her juvenile susceptibility to the barn gossip.

"Busted," Gabe whispered.

Kristine elbowed her brother and tried to concentrate on Gloria's talk.

"I've covered these bales of hay with newspaper," Gloria explained. "Remember that we're shooting to scare, not harm, these animals. We're using bullets that are widely used for riot control. Your store manager will have a gun and ammunition here, and folks who run overnight trips will be equipped as well. Let's start with a backcountry scenario. Sandy? Dozer? A bear is in your kitchen. What's your plan of action?"

"Throw on some jeans and boots, I figure. Them backcountry bears come snooping around our camps when we're still in bed. Should I practice that?" Dozer said.

"That's not necessary." Gloria deflected Dozer's flirtation with ease.

"We prop plates on our tarps, so the clatter of those usually startles the bears off a bit," Sandy said, more helpfully. Her eyes held a warning that Dozer either didn't see or ignored. She ticked off some of Gloria's methods she might try before the rubber bullets. "And if all that fails, we reach for the gun."

"Only if you've got light to see. We're talking dusk and dawn. You don't want to risk missing your target and hitting someone in your group."

"With Sandy's aim, light's not going to make a difference," Dozer said.

Sandy crossed her arms and leveled her gaze in return.

"Besides, big bear's going to send a lady running the other direction."

Kristine could see Gloria's jaw tighten. "I've faced off with plenty of bears, and not your timid black bears. I've convinced some intimidating browns that they don't want to mess with me."

Kristine missed most of Dozer's mumbled retort but heard enough to know that he wasn't defining Gloria as a lady.

"If you do have sight on your target," Gloria said, taking back control of the practice session, "try to hit him in a sensitive spot, avoiding the heavily padded haunches and going for the more tender spot just behind the front legs. Aim for the biggest body mass. Our hay bales represent the barrel of the animal, your most likely hit."

Gloria held the rifle out to Sandy, but Dozer intercepted.

"I'll take the rifle. Sandy's got the kitchen cooking and the cleanup. I protect the camp."

Kristine whispered to Gabe. "What's he trying to prove?"

Gabe shrugged. "You're asking the wrong guy. I think a lady with a rifle is damn sexy. You excluded."

She shot a disgusted look at Dozer and said, "Good thing I don't have a gun right now."

Dozer finally fired at the bale, hitting it squarely in the center.

"That's fine," Gloria said, taking the rifle and handing it to Sandy with new casings. "I'd like to make sure that everyone is equipped to scare off nighttime visitors."

"You folks want to move back from the bale," Dozer called to the kitchen and cabin crew.

"Give me your rifle," Kristine said to her brother.

"Oh, no. Not when you look like that."

Kristine set her jaw. "Then at least aim for our bale. Everyone watching him just feeds his fat ego."

"Don't let him get to you, okay?"

"Something wrong over here?" Gloria asked.

Kristine was getting tired of being on the receiving end of Gloria's disapproval. "No problem," she assured her.

"Don't be a pussy, Teeny," Dozer roared. "It's not even a real bear."

"Shut up, Dozer," Kristine growled.

"Maybe you need the handgun. Do you have enough experience to be handling a rifle like that?"

Kristine couldn't resist. "You want to talk about your experience handling your equipment?"

Dozer sneered and turned back to Sandy and their bear bale.

"Maybe someone should shoot him in the ass," Gabe quipped, loud enough for Dozer to hear.

"Don't tempt me," Kristine said.

"She doesn't have the balls, man," Dozer replied.

Kristine's eyes blazed at his comment, but he offered her his back dismissively. He had always been the most antagonistic of the cowboys. The worst was when they practiced roping the fake cow they had set up by the cabins. While the other cowboys offered pointers on where to stand or how to hold the rope, Dozer sat off to the side shouting that she threw like a girl. He'd finally gotten her to stomp off in a rage one day, but as she made her exit, he quickly threw a loop at her heels and snapped her off her feet. His laughter and "If you want to be one of the guys, you can't complain when you eat a little dirt" still rang in her ears.

"Teeny's always liked to pretend she's one of the guys, but she knows she isn't," he continued to goad.

The others started to look concerned. Those who had been sharing Dozer's bale moved off to the third, out of the way of both Kristine and Dozer.

"You need to leave a man's job for a real man," he said more directly.

Kristine felt her pulse race.

Gabe placed his hand on Kristine's shoulder. "The bale of hay, sis. The bale of hay."

Gloria stepped closer to Dozer. "You've clearly demon-strated you can hit the target. If you'll please locate any bullets we can reuse, I'll set you up with some new canisters you can load for the next shooter."

Dozer tipped his hat at the three of them. "Ladies," he said, turning with a swagger to his bear bale.

Kristine swiped Gabe's rifle, loaded and ready to go. She knew she should listen to Gabe, knew that Dozer was just

Dozer, but she saw the summer stretched out in front of her. Saw herself swallowing all of his bullshit with a smile on her face. She was tired of being polite. Tired of pretending that what he said didn't get to her, so she could be "one of the guys." She slowly raised her rifle and took aim.

"Kristine…" her brother's voice seemed far away.

Everything around her faded away except for Dozer as she pulled her trigger and her ammunition found its target, her aim as true as Gabe had implied.

"What the fuck!" Dozer yelped.

Every head that had been studiously ignoring Dozer whipped to see the large man hopping about the yard.

"Teeny shot me. Fuckin' Teeny shot me. Fuck that hurts," he yowled.

"Ha, Teeny shot herself a bear," Sol said, smacking his thigh with his hat. "My old eyes must be failing me, though, 'cause it sure sounds like a cub crying for his mama."

Everyone guffawed at Dozer's expense as he continued to stomp in pain.

"Suck it up, man."

"Walk it off."

"Let's see it. C'mon, let's see the damage."

Reluctantly, Dozer hitched his pants down, exposing the top of a pale cheek that now had an orange-sized welt with an angry quarter-sized red spot in the middle.

"Oh, that's a beauty," Sol nodded. "It's gonna hurt like a son-of-a-bitch."

"What the hell, Teeny. That fucking hurt. Awe. Fuck. How'm I supposed to ride tomorrow?"

"Let's go, cowboy," Sandy said, taking a swat at his rump, sending him into another hopping fit.

Kristine and Gabe tried to suppress their laughter, though the rest of the crew did not. Even Gloria, after an initial look of shock uttered a soft chuckle before pulling her professional face back into position.

"I think we're through here," Gloria said, shaking her head as she walked away.

Only then did Kristine realize how badly her actions might be viewed. She watched as Gloria strode over to Dozer her professional persona firmly in place. Kristine's rage dissipated, morphing into humiliation.

"I can't believe you shot him in the ass." Still laughing, Gabe punched his sister on the arm.

"Somebody had to shut him up."

"True, he was almost tempting me. And from the look on hot bear lady's face, she was about to take a shot herself."

"I don't know. She didn't seem too happy," Kristine said.

"So you *do* like her."

"Let it go."

Kristine turned on her heel and walked to the truck they'd shared to drive down to the Lodge. She had been interested in Gloria since the first lecture. She saw in her someone who would provide a nice break from the exhausting crew she dealt with daily, an antidote to the guys who thought she was an idiot for going away to college. She'd hoped she might spend time talking to someone who obviously understood being taken seriously her career. However Gloria appeared to be looking for a simple hookup, as demonstrated with Ocean.

She kicked herself when she got to the truck and realized Gabe had the keys. She climbed into the passenger seat and waited for him, bracing herself for more Gabe wisdom. He folded himself into the cab with a smile on his face. "It was a good hit," he said, surprising her. "A nice solid hit. Good to know you could protect us. Truly good to have you back this summer."

Kristine joined him in his laughter, the tension she'd been holding slipping away.

CHAPTER TEN

In the camper, Gloria sat at her tiny kitchen table, now covered with area maps and bear complaints from the prior summer. Feeling like she'd made good progress in both addressing the mama bear and her cubs incident, and training Leo's crew in deterrent tactics, she now planned a trip into the backcountry to check other potential problem areas. She wanted to establish a dominant presence before the bears grew more familiar with humans once the hiking season began. Last year's reports showed that Juanita, the ranger for the Fish Creek valley, had lodged several complaints about an orphan bear cub, so she planned to hike the eight miles in from the Lodge. She wanted to investigate whether exposure to humans had habituated the bear and more importantly whether he'd come to associate them with food.

Her thoughts drifted from the route she was planning to the coat hanging in her closet. She frowned, knowing that she needed to return it to Kristine. At first, she'd wondered if she would stop by for it, giving them another opportunity to chat, but after the Dozer incident, she wasn't sure what to think. Remembering Kristine's shot brought a short bark of laughter from Gloria. Her professional self tried to be angry, and her emotional self tried to warn her about someone with such a short fuse, but her mirth always won out. What she would have given to see how Dozer fared as he set off on his first trip. She was certain of one thing, that Kristine had been successful in taking the cowboy down a notch.

She heard the crunch of tires approaching the camper. A ranger-green truck pulled up.

"Hey, Mitchell. Heading out?" she asked. Scott, the Wilderness and Trail Supervisor had explained that the rangers spent ten days in the backcountry and then four off.

The lanky ranger looked like he spent the winters snowboarding. Despite it being the beginning of the summer season, his face was already deeply tanned with obvious raccoon eyes from wearing shades. His nose was hooked like he'd broken it a few times and his face had that kind of bored look born from persistent risk taking. He took off his ball cap and folded the brim. He had his shaggy brown hair in a messy ponytail. "No, just came in from Thousand. That's generally my area."

"So you haven't been down around Fish Creek?"

"No, usually Juanita has that valley covered. She holds a base camp at Purple. You headed out?"

"There was a lot of activity with an orphan yearling last year. I want to check it out for myself, take some impressions of prints to see if it's just the one or whether there are multiple animals in a small territory," Gloria replied.

"You're going down there on your own? I've got paperwork to file up on the mountain, but I could hike in tomorrow if you want company," Mitchell offered.

"I wouldn't want to make you come all the way back down here from Mammoth when you've just come in."

"It's what I love," he said, his head bobbing. "I usually spend my days off hiking around somewhere. It's time off because I don't have to talk to people. Lose the green costume, and I'm incognito."

"Incognito," Gloria repeated, wishing she could extract herself from where this conversation seemed to be going. She wouldn't say she was in the closet, but she didn't enter a new place screaming that she was lesbian, either. The price she paid was figuring out how to deflect invitations such as Mitchell's. "It's nice of you to offer, but I've got a routine that works for me."

He nodded. "Have you had dinner yet? I'm on my way up to Mammoth now. We could grab something to eat before you head out."

Gloria didn't want to be rude, but she also didn't want to commit to anything with Mitchell. She liked her solitude and rarely sought out social settings, though her indifference to hanging out with Mitchell again made her think of how much she'd enjoyed the campfire with the crew at the Lodge. But she had to admit that it was Kristine who had captured her interest.

As if summoned by Gloria's thoughts, Kristine's white truck swung into the campground, country music pouring out of the open window. Gloria felt a weight lift. Mitchell tensed when he heard the loud rattle of the truck's engine cut out and the heavy door slam against the old frame of the Ford. They both watched her exit the vehicle and approach Gloria's camper. Gloria wondered if Mitchell appreciated Kristine's fluid movements as much as she did. The hat, the belt buckle, the boots. Was this her standard attire, or was she trying to be sexy as hell?

"Hope it's okay to swing by unannounced," Kristine said, her tone light and easy.

"Of course," Gloria replied. She knew Kristine was here for her coat and that she could send her on her way quickly by grabbing it from her camper, but she saw a way out of her awkward conversation with Mitchell and took it.

Mitchell's brows pulled down in confusion. "You pack out of the Aspens, don't you? Your truck's been up there this season."

"It has." Kristine looked from Gloria to Mitchell. She rocked to her toes of her boots and then to her heels.

"Guess I'm on my way," Mitchell excused himself. "See you around."

"Am I interrupting?" Kristine asked as Mitchell slunk off, the hint of a smile playing at her lips.

"Oh, god, no. In fact, your timing couldn't be better."

"You want some more help scaring him off?" she asked.

Gloria couldn't resist. "Are you aiming for some more target practice?"

A burst of laughter escaped from Kristine's mouth before she caught herself and tried to arrange a guilty expression on her face. Watching her take control of her emotions made Gloria realize how different Kristine had been at the shooting practice. The initial outburst of laughter was the Kristine she'd met, but she'd quickly tucked that lighthearted person away as she'd done on their last meeting. Gloria wondered why she was trying so hard to keep her exuberance in check. "It's okay. Remembering it makes me laugh, too. What are you doing in this neck of the woods?"

"Saving you from Mitchell, remember? He doesn't know you're gay…or is the Forest Service that much slower on the gossip?" she asked, her voice heavy with innuendo.

Gloria frowned, trying to figure out why Kristine's attitude had shifted. "Gossip?"

"About your inconvenient bear visitor."

Gloria heard the disapproval in Kristine's tone. "Is that what all the whispering was about at my shooting practice? I'm busting my ass up there trying to make the backcountry safer for my bears, and you all are doing a back-of-classroom high school gossip fest about whether the teacher's getting laid?"

Kristine had the grace to blush and shuffle her feet, admitting her embarrassment. "Yeah, pretty much."

"I have to say I'm surprised you got pulled into that. When we talked after the campfire, it seemed like you were saying you wanted some distance from that."

"That's fair." Kristine's face disappeared behind her hat for a moment when she tipped her chin down, like she was studying her boots. She made eye contact again when she said, "But c'mon. You and Ocean? That's pretty good gossip."

"Really. As if you hadn't been flirting with her, too." She crossed her arms across her chest.

Kristine tensed visibly. "Chatting. There's a difference. I already told you that I'm not here this summer to get distracted."

"Then why are you here?"

Kristine's expression opened to pure innocence. "To get my coat."

Her quip took Gloria aback. She wasn't used to being the one playing catch-up in a conversation. She stepped inside and grabbed the coat from the small closet by the door, remembering that Kristine had said the same thing about no distractions when she'd dropped her off after the campfire. She had felt Kristine's interest that night before she deflected. Trying to figure out Kristine's position, she handed the coat to her and said, "Not to find out if the rumor is true?"

The garment was suddenly engrossing to Kristine.

"Ah, so you do care." She waited for Kristine to say something.

Kristine finally looked up. "I know I shouldn't. It's just that...Ocean's a good kid, but..."

"She's definitely a kid." Gloria stepped toward Kristine leaning forward to put her lips close to Kristine's ear. "I thought I'd made it pretty clear who I was interested in," she whispered, relishing the shiver that ran through Kristine.

"And I told you, I can't." Kristine whispered back, her breath tickling the hairs on Gloria's neck.

She straightened. "Then why leave your coat?"

"It's what friends do."

"Friends?" Gloria stepped away. "You don't even know me."

"My second year of college, there was this girl who sat down behind me in ag class. I'd never seen her before, but when she passed my chair, we made eye contact, and I just knew we'd be friends. I got the same read from you."

"Did you sleep with her?"

Kristine hid behind her hat again.

"Thought so."

"And now we're not friends anymore," Kristine said, regret in her voice.

"And that's what you want?"

"I don't have many that walk on two feet."

Gloria considered the woman in front of her. She'd never met anyone who intrigued her more. She'd been looking to escape from Ocean's place, but here she realized she'd done her best to extend conversation with Kristine. "What the hell. Maybe a friend is what I need," she said, remembering Meg and how homesick she'd been feeling. Maybe instead of distracting herself with a passionate fling, she'd sort through the loneliness that had crept up on her like a cool, damp fogbank.

Kristine's smile looked so relieved that Gloria hugged her, just a *gosh, you're silly, of course I'll be your friend* kind of a hug, but one that surprised her with an intense zing. Her mind might have accepted Kristine's proposition, but her body certainly had not received the memo, humming appreciatively wherever their bodies were in contact. She fought the temptation to run her arms down Kristine's sides, stepping away instead. "I have to warn you…just because we're friends doesn't mean I'm not attracted to you."

"That's a warning?"

"If you keep dressing like that, I can't guarantee I won't flirt with you."

Kristine cocked her eyebrow. "Friends can flirt."

"Just making sure you're up to it."

"Bring it on," Kristine laughed. "I can handle it."

"You have a few days to prepare yourself. I'm headed down to Fish Creek tomorrow morning."

"Oh." Kristine sounded disappointed. "Bear hunting?"

"Yeah. Depending on what I find, I'll be down there from three days to a week."

Kristine looked over her shoulder in the direction of the valley as if she could get a reading on how long Gloria would be away. "I'll keep an eye out for you, then."

"Sounds good."

"You have good stuff to read down there?"

"I've stocked up on lesbian smut."

Kristine rewarded her with her radiant laugh. "I look forward to your book report when you come back." She was still chuckling as she climbed into the cab of her truck. She pulled the door closed by the base of the open window and smacked the door.

Gloria smiled to herself as the country music faded, replaying bits of their conversation. Shaking the memory of their brief hug from her mind, she thought about what made talking to Kristine so much fun. Conversations usually fell at two extremes—analytical shoptalk or time-killing chatter. With her insights and wit, Kristine fit in neither category. She also enjoyed how honest and straightforward Kristine was, that she had no desire to play games and could come right out and say what she thought. Her eyes found the postcard she'd bought before having dinner with Ocean. While she couldn't imagine hiking down to Fish Creek with Ocean, she almost wished for Kristine's company on the trail in the morning.

CHAPTER ELEVEN

Kristine was going to kill Gabe. That was all there was to it. Once again, she reined in Boomerang's brisk walk, the one that would have them at Clark Lakes in two hours. She pulled her camera from the saddlebag. The light wasn't great under the canopy, and if she'd had the pack mules, she could have dismounted to try out her beanbag-based tripod. But she was stuck with the guests, and was forced to shoot from the saddle. The section of the trail before they left the woods had always had a magical feeling for her. She got some decent angles of a tree that had sprouted out of a rock and was making its crooked way toward the light. She also wanted to capture the eerie quiet of a mountain spring, a small pool with no tributary, the water seeping up out of some deep crevasse, the majesty of the light cascading through the canopy.

"Give that horse a kick," she hollered to the dumpy man riding behind her. She should have remembered the outpost trips included guests, rather than carefree days of working with stock.

"I don't want to hurt him," he whined.

"Oh, believe me, you won't," she hollered, though if he'd been closer, she would have been tempted to hurt the rider.

"Is mine a donkey? Is that why he's so slow?" he asked, finally catching up, panting like he'd been the one doing the work.

"You're on a mule, and they travel plenty fast. You just have to remind him who is boss."

"Why did I get stuck with a mule when my friends got horses?"

"Be thankful you have the mule. If we could afford it, everyone would ride mules. They offer a much more comfortable ride."

"So why not breed mules?"

Kristine took a deep breath regretting that she'd initiated the conversation. "Mules are a sterile cross between a horse and a donkey. Because they cannot breed, they are more costly."

"So why not pack horses?"

"Mules are much smarter," she said and because he did not seem to be reaching his limit on questions, she launched into the difference between a mule and a hinny and how offspring take after the mother which is why the cross that included a mare was favored so much of the time. She prattled on about the breeding program she and her father ran explaining the intricacies of their decisions.

At the rest stop, she tended to the stock as she let the riders stretch their legs and complain about how much they ached. Instead of gathering with the guests enjoying the view of Shadow Lake across the valley created by the San Joaquin River, its magnificent waterfall cascading down the rock face to meet the river, she sat cross-legged just off the trail and waited for her brother. She held the shutter down, capturing a quick sequence of him approaching with the party's five mules, ears all askew, packed up neat and tidy and cruising behind him. The guests waved happily, and he tipped his hat, ever the country gentleman. He'd be zipping along at a good clip while she would be stuck reminding her six riders to keep their horses' heads out of the grass and flowers. She gave him a withering look and started planning how to make him pay for taking the choice job.

As she tightened girths on the dude horses, she considered riding at the pace she knew would save her back and her spirits. She wasn't eighteen anymore. What did she care if the horses had to jog or canter to catch up? When had anyone fallen from a trotting horse? She thought hard and could count the number of times her guests had been able to go faster than a walk on the trail. All were times the guests had purposely hung back in order to play cowboy, getting their horses to trot on the trail. Those were the triumphs of her past. Now she had bigger things like where her life was headed after this summer to worry about. She sighed and returned to the task of mounting up the guests.

Back onto the trail, Mr. Chatterbox behind her started in immediately with his game of a thousand questions. She answered questions about the pack outfit, about the mules, the horses, the mountains. Ten years ago, she would have felt like the master guide, batting back every question, a fountain of information and entertainment. Today, she wished he would be quiet. She could use the time to think without the guest's constant chatter.

At the lakes, Gabe had long since finished unloading their gear. She appreciated that he was meticulous and had wound and tied off the fifty-foot long lashropes they used to secure the packs to the animals unlike some packers who flung them aside to get knotted up. When they arrived, she saw that he'd folded and stowed the tarps into the now empty pannier bags. He helped the riders dismount, removed the horses' bridles and tied up the stirrups, so they would not catch on anything on the way back. Maybe she wouldn't kill him, she decided as they sorted the animals into two strings, tying them nose to rump with a tail-tie to keep the animals from trying to pass each other along the trail. They tied the horses to each other first and put the mules at the end because they were more reliable about going around the steep and often tricky switchbacks without taking a shortcut from one level to another.

As she and Gabe mounted up for the ride home, she saw Mr. Chatterbox discuss when Gabe or Kristine would be back to pick them up and hand Gabe a tip. Because the strong man has done all the work of the day. She seethed. She waved to the group and wished them well before glaring at her brother and spurring her horse toward home. Let moneybags eat dust, she thought somewhat testily.

"You know we'll split," he hollered to her on the High Trail.

"Fine," Kristine called back. "Whatever. But you get the guests next time. You can try out being Mr. Entertainment for four hours."

"I thought maybe you'd stopped for a burger on the way in."

Kristine urged Boomerang to extend his stride, putting more distance between herself and her brother. She'd done enough talking for the day. He'd have to keep himself company. Tough for him if he'd been lonely on the ride up.

For the first time that day, she looked around her and remembered one of the big motivators for accepting Gabe's request to come back. The office space couldn't be beat. A ceiling of cumulus clouds chilled her when they obscured the sun. The steady beat of hooves on the trail and the rhythm of Boomerang beneath her brought a song to her heart. She started to hum, then to sing, her mood salvaged from the work of the morning. These were the moments she treasured in the backcountry where she had asked so many difficult questions of the world around her and felt the answers in her core.

These trails had led her to her confidence. Out here it was she, not her father, who was the expert. How often had she heard, "Thank goodness the guide knows the way..." How often had she hidden her fears of the lightning and thunder, so her guests didn't worry about their safety? Enough times that she truly wasn't afraid anymore. She had met those physical challenges and become stronger for it.

And it was the wilderness that had made her unafraid of her sexuality. The vastness of the land around her seemed to quiet the conflict she had about her desires. These mountains had shaped her identity, and she returned this time to ask again for direction. She knew that the longer she stayed at her father's ranch in Quincy, the less likely she was going to ever leave the tiny mountain town. That she excelled at the management side of her father's business only served to strengthen her father's argument that she was meant to take over the ranch someday, especially when it came to their breeding program. As she had proven talking to Mr. Chatterbox, she had an eye for good crosses, and their mules were some of the most sought after in the state, and she was certainly proud of her involvement in training the animals. She had found that to be the highlight of her last six months working the mule farm with her father.

In fact, it was the reward that she felt working with the young mules from the ground and then the saddle that had distracted her for this long. Gabe's pulling her away for the summer reminded her that she did want more from life. She would not be content staying in her small hometown selling homemade cards. She longed to explore and capture new places and people through the lens of her camera.

She thought of Gloria's position as a call-in expert. Kristine felt a twinge of jealousy for the independent, accomplished woman. She'd always been drawn to confident women, so in the past, she would definitely have pursued Gloria. But on reflection, she realized that for too long she had been following rather than setting her own life agenda.

This idea made her think of one of the first backcountry trips she'd been on when she had just started working for Leo. The packer had drawn a map for her in the dirt before she'd left the base.

She'd crossed a creek and was faced with a fork, but couldn't remember if she was supposed to head right or left. The trails were completely new to her, and the horse she'd been riding had been new that summer as well. She'd headed left and had only gone three or four minutes down the trail when her mule, carrying her duffel, sleeping bag and a load of trash from the trip, stopped, nearly jerking her out of the saddle. She'd looked hard at that mule and asked if she'd gone the wrong direction. His head swung around, pointing those long, radar-like ears in the opposite direction. She'd listened to him, and thank goodness, because he'd been right.

In that instance, she'd been smart to follow the mule. But in her life, she was coming to understand that it wasn't always best to accept someone else's notion of what was best for her, although she more often than not had done so. For instance, she recognized the parallel of her graduate program. In that case, she'd spent years fighting against her father's plan for her only to turn and bend to her father's will again when she settled back at his ranch. Kristine could tell in the way Gloria had presented her research that she had a strong innate sense of direction that Kristine felt she lacked herself. Getting involved with someone so driven might be problematic since Kristine felt herself caught at a crossroads again. She didn't want to step off the path her father considered best just to find herself walking on another path behind Gloria. In setting a firm line of friendship with Gloria, Kristine resolved to walk her own path, one she chose for herself.

Gloria was certainly a temptation with an appeal that went far beyond her confidence alone. Her hair swept up in a ponytail highlighted her strong jawline that contrasted with her mouth, seeming always about to smile. That inviting mouth and bright blue eyes might have spelled trouble, but their brief hug had made Kristine feel confident that they could be friends, and she was glad that Gloria had agreed.

* * *

The two strings dropped the five hundred feet down into the outpost yard, the trail snaking back and forth in a tight switchback down the mountain. Content to be through with the day's work, the siblings worked in harmony to put up their stock, stripping the horses and mules of their saddles which they stowed in the sheds. They cleared the pack docks of tarps, panniers and lashropes, leaving everything in order for the next day. Kristine watched her brother work and knew that this was home for him, that wherever the season took him, his life was in the mountains. For him, the trails were livelihood, not metaphor.

In that moment, she felt satisfied with her decision to join Gabe at the Aspens. While her father did his best to dissuade Kristine from returning to the Lodge, her mother offered cautious support as if she could sense what Kristine wrestled with after her brother had called to ask her to help him run the Aspens. Ultimately her opportunity to put things right with Gabe had tipped her into coming back. "You ever want more than this?" she asked, elbows resting on the top rail of the dude corral after they'd turned out and fed the stock.

"Maybe," he said. A broad grin spread across his handsome face.

Kristine squinted at him. "Do not…" she warned him.

"After I'm finished sowing…"

"No, not the wild oats! I know you feel like you want to play the field, but do you have to…" Though she shoved her fingers in her ears and hummed loudly, she still saw his lips move as he continued the sentence. "C'mon. I'm trying to have a serious conversation with you."

"I could tell by the way you had your fingers in your ears. Real grown up."

"Dad wants you back in Quincy after you graduate this year."

"Yeah. And I'll settle there. But you know I'm no good at the broodmares and starting colts. There's a reason you did the ag degree, and I'm in business. Between the two of us, he's got the ranch covered."

The sounds of the night surrounded them, the chomping of thirty animals on sweet alfalfa, hooves stomping flies away. This was the chorus she'd listened to her whole life.

Gabe broke the silence. "And what's so bad about running the ranch with your awesome brother?"

"Nothing at all. After work, we'll go line dancing. It'd be such fun to pick up chicks together."

"Hey, at least one of us has some luck in that category. We could help each other out. Or more specifically, you could send girls my way, let them know why I'm such a catch."

"You are a catch. You know that, right?"

"Catch and release is what I am," he said with uncharacteristic glumness.

"At least you actually have a chance of finding an eligible girl in Quincy. Can you imagine if we did both end up back on the ranch?"

"I could see us double dating," he said, hopefulness in his voice.

"Yeah, that wouldn't be weird at all," she said, needing to change the direction of their conversation. "And pretty soon, the one-screen theater in town might show an independent film."

"We're not that far from Reno, you know," Gabe reminded her.

"Ugh. Gabe. It doesn't take a genius to spot a goat in a herd of sheep."

"Exactly! I'll sow my oats, you go find some goats. Dad will totally understand. Great chat, sis."

Though Kristine hung her head at the remark, inwardly she was thankful to hear his characteristic glibness return. "For that, you cook tonight, my friend."

"You know I cook by driving the truck down to the Lodge."

Kristine wondered if Gloria was back from her trip. She could be at the store getting supplies or having dinner in the café. Maybe she'd run into her by the washing machines. She chided herself for slipping back into such musings. "No. You owe me more than Jorge's chili dogs. You're taking me up the mountain for something good in Mammoth."

CHAPTER TWELVE

Though beat from her all-day hike in from Fish Creek, Gloria's pace quickened for the final uphill push into the yard at the Lodge. She was exhausted, having spent five nights asserting her dominance over last year's orphan yearling which could very easily become a problem bear. The first three nights, she'd chased him out of her camp making as much noise as she could. She'd shot him with rubber bullets so he'd associate pain with humans and start looking for food elsewhere. The gangly black bear was already drawn to her food canisters, which told her that he'd been lucky visiting camps the year before. She was fairly pleased with her progress—he had not visited her camp the last two nights. Maybe it wasn't too late to turn him around. If only she could trust all of his encounters with humans to be consistent.

The ignorant and lazy tourists could very well drive her insane. They were worst in Yosemite. People who covered their food in their cars imagining they could hide the meal from the bear, not understanding that their paws worked just fine as can openers on any vehicle. That big metal box that the state had installed at the campsite? No, please don't use it. Take your chances leaving your food just outside your tent. Better yet, have that late-night snack of an apple or banana and leave the core or peel just outside the door of your tent.

Then, when a bear damages your property, certainly DO freak out and blame the Forest Service or Fish and Wildlife for not doing their job to protect you and your family during your time in the park.

Gloria steamed but tried to remind herself to let go of the frustrations of her job. She tried to see herself as the mediator. She just wished that she could train some of the humans with her rubber bullets instead of turning them toward the bears.

Now she was thinking about Kristine again. Lovely Kristine who refused to bottle her frustration, at least with Dozer. The thought of Kristine's hoot of laughter when they'd recalled her shot again brought a smile to Gloria's face. Then she froze. That wasn't just the thought of Kristine's laughter. It *was* Kristine's laughter, rich and booming, flowing down the trail to her. She slowed as she walked parallel to a corral full of mules and spotted the cowgirl sitting in front of the store. Three young girls sat with her, all laughing, all riveted by Kristine.

She sure has a draw, Gloria acknowledged, wishing she'd heard what made them all laugh so hard. She looked down at her filthy self, days of sweat caked onto her skin, her Fish and Wildlife tee and trousers slept in, scrunched into her pack, pulled back on again, far from how pressed they'd been when she left. She'd hoped to run into Kristine but not before she'd had a chance to shower and change into a fresh set of clothes.

As she dithered about walking across the yard, she noticed the wattage of the smile the girl sitting on Kristine, well practically on, okay, on a closer look, next to, but really close to, more so than a casual acquaintance would sit, next to Kristine. Kristine returned the smile, and Gloria felt a flash of anger. Had she been playing with Gloria with her talk of friendship? She'd seemed so frank about it that it hadn't occurred to Gloria to think that she just wasn't attracted to her.

Gloria scolded herself for the emotional reaction, reminding herself that she had accepted Kristine's invitation of friendship.

Thus, she told herself, no reason to be jealous or angry, and no reason to think that she needed to clean up. Friends didn't need to look good for the other. Chin high, she strode into the yard.

"Gloria!"

Gloria's traitorous heart jumped when Kristine called her name. She was already waving off the three girls and jogging toward Gloria with a smile brighter than the one she'd just seen plastered to her face. Today she wore no riding gear, just her skintight jeans and an untucked tee with The Lodge's logo blazed across her chest. Gloria tried to keep her eyes trained above it.

"Hey," Kristine said.

For a moment, Gloria thought Kristine wanted to hug her. Her arms came up but then she quickly tucked them into her pockets, her thumbs hanging out adorably. Gloria realized she still had her heavy pack on her back. Once she was out of it, she would hate to have to put it back on again. She glanced toward the road leading down to the campground.

"Hope I'm not looking like a creepy stalker right about now. I really did have to come down for hay cubes for a trip that's going out tomorrow." She motioned to her truck parked by a metal feed shed. "I got to chatting with the day-ride crew and thought maybe you'd be up the trail today. Let me take your pack, drive you home?"

Gloria laughed at her babble.

"What?"

"You're the one chattering away like you've been your only company for five days."

"Yeah? Well." That same bright smile swept across her face. "I missed your company."

"Then, by all means, drive me home."

Kristine helped Gloria off with her pack and tossed it in the bed of her truck.

"Either you ate every ounce of food you took in there, or that space-aged food doesn't weigh a thing," she laughed.

"I'm sure it just feels light in comparison to those feed sacks," she said, motioning to the back of the truck. "Too bad I missed you breaking butch. Showing off for the girls?"

"Hardly. More like cracking the whip."

"Are you trying to bait me?" Gloria said, running her eyes over Kristine's body.

Kristine smiled mischievously. "How'd it go down at Fish Creek?" she asked, redirecting the conversation as she pulled out onto the road.

Gloria slumped against the seat, tired to her core. "Touch and go. Whether this bear makes it or not totally rests with the contact he has with humans this season. I really hope we can turn him around."

"Sure he wasn't just hitting on you? Could be he was just noticing the pretty new woman in town."

Gloria swatted her weakly.

"I think I'd better take you home, get some real food into you."

"As good as that sounds, a shower sounds better."

"We have plenty of hot water, and Gabe's cooking tonight. I can't guarantee it'll be good, but I can tell you it'll be better than your camp food."

Gloria's head rolled to the side. "I'm too tired to argue."

"Good."

"But I'll do dinner next." That was what friends did, she told herself.

"Sounds good to me."

Gloria couldn't help closing her eyes as Kristine drove to The Aspen Outpost down the road. Kristine kept a steady conversation on the short drive, full of details about her various trips, the stock, her guests. She had no shortage of material and masterfully shaped it into a fun narrative. Gloria relaxed and listened, enjoying how good it felt to be in her company.

"What's that smile for? Are you laughing at how much I talk? I can stop anytime."

"No, please don't. I was just sitting here thinking about how much fun you must make the overnight trips with your storytelling."

"Yeah, used to."

Gloria's brows creased in confusion. Kristine's answers were rarely so brief. "But..." she prompted. Kristine's pause before answering sparked Gloria's curiosity again. She looked like she was at a fork in the trail, considering which direction to take.

"But that's not our job at the outpost," she said with a little hesitation in her voice. After a brief silence, she seemed to recover and launched into her more typical delivery. "We'll occasionally help a longer trip, like packing in food for the stock. That's why I had to make the run into the Lodge for these hay cubes. There's a base camp up at Garnet, and they lost a bunch of their stock the first day…"

"Lost them?" Gloria sat up, alarmed.

"Not lost, lost. They came home for supper. Gabe will run the stock back in tomorrow and set them up with feed, so the packer out there doesn't have to worry about keeping his stock from running home again."

Gloria noticed that Kristine's answer was centered on another story about this season, rather than explaining why she no longer took overnight trips out. "Don't you miss those trips? The overnight trips take you further back into the wilderness, don't they?" Again, Gloria saw Kristine tense when she steered the topic back to overnighters. Their easy flow of conversation had hit a snag again. Kristine smiled at her as if to apologize, and her eyes, in the flash that they connected with Gloria's, expressed both sadness and discovery.

"I do," Kristine answered simply.

Before Gloria could even consider pushing the subject further, Kristine pulled into the outpost which looked to be roughly a third of the size of the setup at the Lodge. It had a similar layout to the larger outfit: stock corralled in several paddocks by the side of the road, a saddle shed in the center of the yard, tie-rails on either side. Their pack dock sat between the saddle shed and a cabin, which she assumed Kristine shared with Gabe. She smiled at its placement, tucked at the edge of a lovely grove of aspens. An evening breeze made their silvery leaves dance.

"It's so tidy," she observed as they walked through the working area to the cabin. "Is it always like this?"

"Being so close to the road, Leo has a thing about the yard being spotless. Trying to make a good impression and all." Her hand paused on the doorknob of the cabin, and she turned and wiggled her eyebrows, "But this is where it ends."

Gloria couldn't contain her gasp at the contrast when she stepped inside. Kristine kicked her boots off at the door and hung her hat on some antlers mounted on the wall. A sock-footed, hatless Gabe stood at the small stove, spatula in hand, and what looked like every dish in the place stacked on the counter behind him. He waved the spatula at Gloria.

"Ms. Fisher, what a surprise!" Gabe said. Gloria read the twinkle in his eye and saw him look from her to Kristine and back again.

"Hope you made enough for three," Kristine said, swatting her brother's attention back to the stove in front of him.

Gloria removed her own boots and took in the living space that was littered with piles of clothes, clean or dirty she couldn't determine. Her survey stopped at a pile of shoeing gear and horseshoes that took up an entire corner. "The stock has to take off its shoes, too?"

The siblings laughed in stereo, Gabe from the kitchen and Kristine from the hallway.

"Of course. They're just in the bathroom cleaning up," Gabe offered.

"I'll shoo them out, so you can have a turn," Kristine said, disappearing.

Gloria smiled again at Gabe, at the picture of the cowboy at home in the absurdly disheveled kitchen. "I hope I'm not putting you out by joining you."

"Oh, no. I was all set to head over to the Lodge for the evening, but…" A surprised look crossed his face, and Gloria caught Kristine's glare out of the bathroom door. She glanced back to Gabe, and he whispered, "Insurance."

"Oh?" Gloria asked, surprised. Remembering the charge between them when she'd hugged Kristine, she wondered if Kristine was having trouble sticking to her own resolve to be just friends. She picked up an apple from the kitchen, polishing it above her right breast as she approached Kristine. As they passed in the hallway, she handed the apple to Kristine.

Kristine held her eye contact as she accepted the apple. She spun it a few times, pressed it to her lips and inhaled deeply. She arched an eyebrow and lowered the apple without taking a bite. "Wouldn't want to spoil supper," she said, a smile playing at the corner of her mouth. "I left some clean clothes for you."

Again, Gloria felt the heat between them and couldn't understand Kristine's reluctance to explore their spark. It had to be more than overcoming her past reputation. She shut the door, stripped down quickly, and stepped into the gloriously warm shower.

She scrubbed quickly and furiously, feeling self-conscious showering so close to where both Gabe and Kristine worked. She felt vulnerable out of her clothes and away from the siblings who, no doubt, were talking about her. Neatly folded sweats and a tee sat on the bathroom cabinet next to the towel which Gloria grabbed. Gratefully, she slipped into them and emerged from the bathroom. As she figured, Gabe and Kristine grew silent at her approach. She continued to stare at Kristine, willing herself to look away, but unable to do so. Kristine didn't break their eye contact either, just stayed in an all-too alluring pose leaning up against the counter.

"Feel better?" It was Gabe who finally snapped them out of their staring contest.

"Much. After five days in the backcountry, I really needed that. I think I used all your hot water."

"That's okay. I'm sure Kristine's ready for a cold one now," Gabe quipped, earning him one of the many swats of the evening.

"I apologize for my brother," Kristine said. "He's the type to think that just because two ladies play for the same team, they'd like to play with each other."

The two of them continued to needle each other good-humoredly in between questions directed at Gloria about her trip. They found the perfect balance, never making Gloria feel pressured to fill the silence but never making her feel left out, either. After dinner, Gloria volunteered to do the dishes. Kristine took up her maddening pose next to her under the pretense of drying the dishes, and Gabe played a few songs on his guitar. She wanted to stay longer but when she couldn't deny that her eyes refused to stay open any longer, she let Kristine drive her home.

"Sorry I'm such lousy company," she said, watching Kristine's hands on the wheel as she handled the curves of the road.

"You're great company," Kristine said, her vibrant smile directed at Gloria.

"It beats hanging around with your cowboy friends?"

"That and then some," Kristine said.

Gloria leaned back against the seat and shut her eyes momentarily, comparing this to other times a woman had driven her home. Instead of running through scenarios about whether they would kiss and how far things might go, she found herself thinking about the value Kristine obviously placed on company. Good company. When was the last time she'd heard someone talk about good company? She had to admit that Kristine was good company, and it felt nice to share an evening with someone who asked questions about her, listened to what she had to say and shared her own ideas. Suddenly, Kristine's warm hand was on her shoulder and quiet surrounded them. She didn't remember falling asleep and hadn't even noticed when Kristine cut the engine. When her eyes snapped open, she asked how long she'd been asleep.

"A few minutes. You looked too peaceful to wake, but it's getting colder," Kristine said.

Gloria shivered, the temperature in the cab suggesting it had been more than a few minutes. "Thank you. I can't tell you how nice it was to hang out with you and your brother."

"Anytime," Kristine replied.

"Careful," Gloria said, turning to get out of the truck. "I might take that literally."

Kristine laughed her valley-filling laugh. "I hope so. You do owe me supper."

No awkwardness, she jumped out of the truck, promising to fulfill her promise soon. Inside, she scurried straight to bed, still wrapped in Kristine's borrowed sweats, shivering as she waited for her bunk to return her heat. Her body startled awake by the cold, she thought about when she'd return the dinner and what they'd find to talk about, whether Kristine would tell her more about why she wasn't in the backcountry when she seemed to miss the longer trips. She had to laugh at herself, wondering if her finding more pleasure in talking to Kristine than fooling around with Ocean was a sure sign of her getting old. She knew without a doubt that had she turned down Kristine's offer for dinner and sought out Ocean that she'd be naked in a different bed, her muscles humming from an uncomplicated sexual workout, her mind only replaying sensory details.

Yet, she'd been honest with Kristine about how much she had enjoyed the evening, way more than many dates she'd endured. Her thoughts circled back to the shower, and she allowed herself a fantasized version without Kristine's brother in earshot. She pictured Kristine's toned body naked in front of her as she ran her hands along her own flat belly. Her hands would be more thorough, curiosity guiding them as she learned the curves of Gloria's body the way she obviously knew the curves of the mountain road. Gloria's own hands paused at her breasts, and she felt her nipples grow hard. She pictured Kristine's hands following the path that the water had taken earlier and let her own hand find its way.

CHAPTER THIRTEEN

Kristine twisted around in her saddle again to assess Scooter's pack. She watched the red crisscross of the sawbuck saddle between the mule's ears, and as she feared, they did not return to center. Instead, they rocked steadily to the right. She swore under her breath at Nard. When she agreed to take on the Aspens with Gabe, she had forgotten about how many of Nard's trips left out of the outpost and how often that meant she would see him.

From the moment Kristine had stepped out onto the porch to a brilliant orange-hued sunrise, the day had taken an ominous tone. She heard Sol's adaptation of the old sailor's adage the cowboys used, "red sky morning, packer take warning." It felt even more foreboding to have one of Nard's trips leaving from the outpost that morning. It didn't help that her head was swimming with images of Gloria emerging from the bathroom pink and flushed. The way Gloria had glanced in her direction and held her eyes, Gloria must have known or guessed how Gabe was teasing her about how it would be fine with him if she wanted to wash up before supper, too. As if her own mind hadn't stepped into the bathroom with Gloria. As if she hadn't second-guessed asking him to stick around. She certainly didn't need Gabe pointing out the possibility available to her. She needed him to help her keep her resolve.

In the truck, she'd limited her touch to waking Gloria, knowing how easy it would be to linger and explore. She loved how easy it had been to convince Gloria to let them take care of her after her long hike in and how well she'd fit into their evening. Around the cowboys, she felt the constant need to be on her guard, and that was certainly true this morning with Nard "helping" her pack up her animals. He'd been too close, putting himself right where she needed to be, so she'd have to step into his space to complete her ties, touching her hand when she threaded the lashrope through for a diamond hitch. With Nard, she felt like she was being stalked; with Dozer, she felt she was being judged and criticized. With Gloria, she felt none of that. Though she barely knew her, she knew she could simply be herself.

She glanced at the listing load again, resigned that she would have to deal with it before they got much further. She waited until they had reached the bottom of the steep, rocky descent into the valley and were on the River Trail where she'd have a chance to tie up her horse. Had it been Boomerang, who she'd been riding for weeks, she would have felt fine messing with the pack with the leadrope tucked into her belt, but today she had Nard to thank for having to ride one of the outfit's new horses, so she'd play it safe and tie him to a tree to rearrange the pack.

"Sorry for the holdup folks. I just need to make a quick adjustment to this pack," she explained to the family riding behind her mules. She tied the Appaloosa to one of the aspens by the trail, glancing at the many initials carved in the tree's trunk. The backcountry graffiti had never made any sense to her, but she'd always ridden by it framing pictures in her head. She wished she could afford the time to pull her camera out of her saddlebag but knew with the limited light that she'd get better results with her tripod. She made a mental note to pack it the next time she traveled the River Trail with empty mules before attending to the leaning pack. Grabbing the lashrope, she picked up her feet, letting the weight of her body pull the pack back to center. As she worked, she listened to the young blond boy decked out in his Western duds complete with red checked neckerchief. He was worried about his horse. Last year, he'd been allowed to ride with his mom, but this year, he was on his own horse, and she knew given his tiny stature that the horse she'd chosen intimidated him. He was scared. The doubt she read in his round freckled face relayed how little faith he had in her explanation that big horses are actually easier to control and calmer than small ones. Each parent had begged him to listen and trust the guide. When that failed, the dad explained how he was a big boy, too big to ride double, and his mom tried threatening to cancel the trip if he could not be reasonable. The boy had yet to settle into the ride, and stopping to adjust the pack hadn't helped anything.

"He wants to buck me!" he cried as his horse stomped a hoof.

With a tired voice, his father explained that the horse was trying to scare off a fly, not try to toss his son off.

Kristine had had enough. "Malcolm, right?" His little head turned to her. "I need your help, buddy. See this red X here?" she pointed to the back of the saddle. "It holds the two bags on the mule, but the bags aren't quite the same weight, so the heavier one is tipping the saddle farther and farther to the right instead of rocking back to center. See, your horse can count on you to stay in the middle, right?" He nodded. "But this pack isn't like you. We need to get it to sit right on the mule like you're sitting on your horse. Do you see a rock about this big?" She held up her hands, and he scanned the area around them.

"How about that one?" he pointed.

Kristine picked it up and studied the weight of it, about five pounds. "Should work. You think it's been wanting to see Rosalie Lake?"

The boy nodded earnestly. "Just like me! I'm going for my birthday!"

"How old will you be this year?" Kristine asked, tucking the rock between the tarp and the lashrope on the left side of the mule.

"Six," Malcolm answered proudly.

Kristine pulled lightly on the pack and asked her young rider if the X came back to line up with the mule's tail. He nodded. "Then we're all set. I'm going to give you an important job, okay? You keep your eye on that X, and if it starts to tip funny again, you tell me."

He nodded and kept his eyes firmly on the mule's saddle. Kristine approached her little Appaloosa and groaned again. In front of him was a large hole he'd dug during Kristine's pack adjustment. *So that's why your name's Digger*, she thought to herself, quickly kicking the dirt back into place and swinging onto the horse, holding him steady as her mules and then riders fell into place.

"You must've majored in child development," Jack, the boy's father, called once they were back on the trail.

"Just giving him a job to do." She motioned to her horse and said, "Like this guy, he'll be happier with a task. It's a matter of directing energy."

"Well, you clearly love what you do."

Kristine nodded. She couldn't deny it, couldn't ignore how being out in the backcountry on horseback made her heart sing. Nard's behavior in the yard had reminded her all too vividly why she had stayed away from the Lodge for so long. A shiver went down her spine remembering how she startled when she heard his voice that morning.

He'd called her Teeny again, refusing to bend and use her full name. He'd unsaddled her horse and was holding the heavy roping saddle by the horn like it weighed nothing. "I need that Boomerang horse in the backcountry."

She'd moved to take her saddle, realizing that there was no easy way to take it without touching him. "Throw it on the rail," she'd said. Though she liked Boomerang a lot, she let it go. She couldn't argue with him for not wanting to have a new horse on an overnight trip. It wasn't his choices, it was the way he stood there waiting for her to challenge him. He'd been testing her, she was certain, seeing how far he could push her, his watery blue eyes intent on her reaction.

He'd pushed again. "There's a number of people who can help your brother here. Dad's having to send a cook from the café on this trip. After this, I've got the photography trip. You should cook it."

"I'm a packer, Nard, not a backcountry cook."

He'd pulled at his mustache with his bottom lip, a habit that had always made her skin crawl. She'd been proud of herself for the unemotional reply, for shutting him down.

Though she'd tried to tune him out and stay on task, the expression on his face as he lurked around her pack dock this morning had made her rush to get out of the yard. Now Scooter was stuck with the extra weight of the stone she'd added to his load, carrying it up the rocky staircase that switchbacked beside the Shadow Lake waterfall.

She paused halfway up the hill before the climb got more intense. Her riders halted on the switchback below her.

"How's Scooter's pack riding?" she asked the boy.

"Great!" he chirped. "I've been watching it the whole time!"

Kristine winked at the boy's parents, knowing they were all glad that he'd stopped complaining about being on his own horse. She glanced ahead of her, aware that the next part of the trail would test her young rider's bravery.

"I'm really going to need you to watch it closely until we get to the lake, okay?"

His nod and his lowered brows matched her serious tone.

"You can help out your horse by holding onto the horn of the saddle and leaning forward. We're going to climb some pretty steep stairs, and I want that pack riding just like you are. Ready?"

"Ready," they all agreed.

She nudged her horse forward and onto the steep staircase. The Appaloosa struggled with the uphill climb, making her even more aware of the small burden she had added to her mule. A burden much like the one she had carried since she'd left the Lodge unexpectedly, one that Nard had handed her and that she had carried ever since. As they climbed the steepest part of the trail water thundered from the lake in the valley above them, drowning out even the sound of her horse's hooves scrambling to find purchase. She felt herself slipping back to the panic of refusing Nard, the feel of his hands around her wrists and her inability to make any noise at all, the only sound her heart thrumming in her ears.

And then the silence.

The vast, calm lake before them.

She released the breath she'd been holding and assessed the guests and the mules. All fell into line behind her. She had made it to safety. She was in control. Malcolm gave her a big thumbs-up. Kristine's tension eased as the seven animals snaked silently along the trail, their hoofbeats now muffled by the soft earth. She gave Digger his head, liking how he'd dug into his challenge and smiling at how it fit his excavator tendencies.

Her senses still heightened, she methodically unloaded the mules and tended to the dude horses. She stood letting Peacock rub his head on her when Malcolm's father, Jack, came to find her. "Will it be you picking us up?"

"Hard to say," she answered truthfully.

"We all enjoyed the trip up so much. Thank you for working with Malcolm. The gentleman last year got us to Emerald, but he certainly didn't have the gift you have. I thought you'd like to know that Malcolm invited you to his party. We'll try to save you a cupcake."

"Just promise me you've got your bear containers and won't be attracting any other guests," Kristine joked.

"We know the drill." He smiled. "Hope to see you in a few days."

"Me, too." She strung up the horses but detoured to the lake before starting her journey back. She took a deep breath, standing on the rocks at the shore of the crystal blue lake, the dramatic backdrop of rocky mountain with sporadic pines growing from crevices. She rolled the rock from Scooter's pack in the palm of her hand, feeling the weight of it. With all of her might, she threw it as far into the lake as she could, standing on the shore until the ripples reached her toes. She smiled, then, feeling lighter than she had in years.

CHAPTER FOURTEEN

"Gloria!" Mitchell's voice startled her out of her chore of poring through years and years of ranger reports, collecting data on the local bears. "Anything I can help you with?"

"No, but thanks." She bent to her work, grumbling inside when he sat down across from her.

"Boss man says you're picking up camp."

"I just moved the camper to the Aspen Grove Campground. I want to talk to the campers and hosts at both campgrounds, get a read on whether the Lodge is attracting more problems." Gloria left out that being at the Aspen camp would mean she could easily walk over to the outpost at the end of her day. More days than not, she found herself joining the Owenses there, if not for dinner, then to share a few beers out on the pack docks, listening to the valley settle for the night.

"Doing any research in the backcountry? I cover the Thousand Island section, and my camp up there is suh-weet. You're welcome to stay anytime. Plenty of room in the tent for you, so you don't have to carry that in. I've got a bear box, the works."

"I'll be doing some day hikes into the backcountry to set up some barbed wire to collect hair samples. We check the DNA back at the lab in Sacramento to determine whether it's the same bear turning up at multiple camps. If I end up needing to stay out there longer, I'll keep your camp in mind."

"I just finished my report for Scott, so I'm a free man for the next four days."

"Great." Gloria was starting to feel uncomfortable with his continued conversation given that she had done her best not to encourage him. He certainly smelled like he'd come in from his ten days out, and she was anxious to have the workspace back to herself.

"I was thinking of driving out to Mono. Have you been?"

"Nope."

"It's truly awesome. How can I describe it?" He tipped his head back, his scraggly Adam's apple protruding and bobbing as he swallowed. "The lake's full of these weird-shaped spires that make it look like an alien landscape. The saline content is so high that you float like you're sitting in a chair. You want to check it out?"

"No, thank you. I still need to settle into my new camp."

Mitchell studied her. "Is this a PhD thing?"

"Sorry?"

"I'm a lowly seasonal employee, and you're this expert research scientist. Is that why you're blowing me off?"

Gloria set down the reports she'd been reading and took a deep breath. "I've dated plenty of rangers," she said.

Mitchell's eyes lit up.

"Female ones," she said.

"Oh, dude. I'm sorry."

"You're sorry?"

"That came out wrong. I just meant…ugh. I just feel so stupid. I just assumed…It's not like we get much gossip to key us in."

"No sweat, Mitchell. As long as we're clear, we're good. We're good?"

"You're still welcome up at my camp by Thousand. While you're here, you should see some of the backcountry. It would be a shame not to. And Mono really rocks."

"Thanks, Mitchell. If I do decide on some sightseeing, I'll track you down."

After he left, she'd tried to get back to the reports again, but she couldn't get her mind off her move. Being able to get to and from the outpost on foot instead of having to rely on the shuttle and Kristine's kindness was certainly the main motivator for her move, but she was also thinking about how one-sided the arrangement felt. She wanted to be able to reciprocate dinner casually.

She checked her watch and decided to head back home. She'd found the perfect campsite located between the outpost and the trailhead for the River Trail. She was certain Kristine would often pass through there on her way home when she wasn't using the High Trail. Though it was early, she couldn't concentrate on her work, only on what she'd planned for dinner and how much she hoped to be able to share it with Kristine.

Back home, she threw some steaks in a marinade, chopped veggies, sliced and buttered bread and built a fire for coals. She grabbed a novel from the camper and settled in to wait for Kristine to come through, hoping that her assignment for the day would bring her home through her campsite. She paused, wondering whether Kristine would read her presence as a come-on which wasn't her intention. She simply enjoyed Kristine's company, Gabe's too, for that matter. The more time she spent with the Owenses, the more she admired Kristine's pursuit of her goals. Kristine came alive talking about her dreams of traveling as a photographer and the places she wanted to explore through her lens.

The sun was starting to set, and still no sound of hoofbeats. She felt disappointed, like a girl stood up for a date, which was totally unfair given that she hadn't even made one. Resigning herself to the fact that Kristine must have used the High Trail, she set aside her book. Time to cook. Probably for the best, she decided, ducking into the camper to get her trays of food. She didn't want to cook in the dark.

Of course as soon as she stepped away from the grill, she heard stock crossing the road. She panicked. In all of her preparation, she had not considered what she was going to say to Kristine. She dove out of the camper in time to see the packer's approach. She looked damn sexy riding up on a spotted horse, a string of horses and mules stretched out behind her. She couldn't keep her eyes off the figure covered head to toe in dirt from the trail. And Kristine hadn't even looked at her yet, hadn't graced her with that exuberant smile that welcomed her each time they saw each other. She could not deny how much she still craved Kristine.

"Thought your crew didn't like to be called late for dinner," she called out.

"Gloria?" Kristine asked in the dim light, pulling her horse to a stop. "What in the world?"

"Lovely thing about a camper—it's mobile."

"Lovely thing, indeed," Kristine said, trying to control the squirrely horse she rode. "He's anxious to get home. Give me some time to unsaddle? I need to make sure Gabe's back to put up my stock."

"Absolutely." Gloria was set to return to her task but couldn't resist watching Kristine continue down the trail.

"You watching my ass?" she called from the front of the line.

"I thought those were mules," Gloria hollered back. She smiled hearing Kristine's laughter mix with the sound of all of the horseshoes ringing on the pavement, enjoying her ability to draw forth that sound.

* * *

"And that, in short, is why there are days I spend the entire time in the saddle thinking about how long it would take to pack my shit and leave," Kristine said, finally releasing her wadded, crumpled napkin on the table. "Ugh. I'm sorry. I hate to complain about Nard taking my horse, but I've had a string of bad days since he stuck me with that Appaloosa horse."

Gloria frowned in sympathy. She had enjoyed every minute of Kristine's account of the problems she'd had with new stock. The details of her job fascinated her, and Kristine's animated delivery captivated Gloria even more. She found herself staring at Kristine's mouth trying not to think about kissing her. This, she realized, was why they kept hanging out at the cabin. Without Gabe's presence, she was more acutely aware of her attraction to Kristine. Without the conversation to distract her, Gloria couldn't think of a reason not to kiss Kristine. She searched for the topic. "I wondered why I didn't recognize any of your animals." Kristine looked relieved, and Gloria wondered if she also felt like the dynamic between them had shifted now that it was just the two of them.

She leaned back with her beer. "Nard has this thing about big mules, but he's cheap, so he won't buy them trained."

"I thought Leo bought all their animals from your family."

"All the good ones." Kristine quirked her eyebrow.

"Of course."

"But that's Leo. The big babies are Nard's idea, his attempt at establishing himself apart from Leo. It wouldn't be an issue if he knew how to train them, but he has no idea and would never admit it. He works them 'til they're real screwed up and then leaves them in the corral as the last option. And these two, Beetle and Bailey..." She grimaced. "They could kill someone with their stupidity. It's a good thing I wasn't up on the rock steps by Shadow when Bailey set back the way he did. He'd have pulled Digger straight off the trail. There's a sobering thought."

"Do you run through your head what you'd do if that happened?"

"Of course," Kristine said. She drained her beer and stared at it much like she had at the campfire at the beginning of the summer. Finally, she answered, "'Never quit a wreck' is what my dad always said."

"I don't follow."

"Say your horse slips. It's more dangerous to jump off because you might mess up their balance. They might end up falling right on you."

"If you stay in the saddle you have more control."

"Exactly. Even if you end up getting thrown, you're at least going to clear the mess."

Gloria nodded, processing. "You guys should call that pair Thing One and Thing Two with the trouble they cause."

"Gabe's going to love that." She smiled, but her voice sounded distracted.

"Is that why you took off before? You got fed up with…" she searched for a word to describe what she read in Kristine's eyes.

"Partly," Kristine supplied without answering the question. She stood to clear the dishes.

Gloria rose quickly, worried that her question had spooked Kristine. She took the plates. "Please don't worry about the cleanup. I've got my system." They stood so near to each other in the small space that it would have taken nothing to lean forward and capture the mouth that she'd been watching. Kristine surrendered the dishes and sat back down at the small table. Silence filled the space as Gloria took care of the dishes. She was trying hard to maintain the easy conversations that had become the norm when they were with Gabe, and Kristine seemed aware of that too. She glanced over her shoulder to see if Kristine still held a defensive posture and saw her holding a greeting card.

"You bought one of mine," she said, meeting Gloria's eyes.

"A bunch, actually. I've been sending my mom's letters in them."

"I'm flattered," Kristine said. "This is one of my favorites. I was on one of my first solo spots down to Island Crossing, and my horse had a loose shoe. I didn't want to risk it on the granite pass, so I was trying to pry it off. These women came up and chatted with me, wanted to know about the animals, about my job. It hit me the minute I saw them that they were a couple. Didn't say anything, you know, no secret handshake, no rainbow sticker, but there was this energy between them, this sense of happiness that they just radiated. I couldn't help but feel it. You can't tell in this shot," she shrugged, studying the picture of the two hikers on the blasted out trail along a sheer granite cliff, "but I think about that every time I look at it."

"It's funny, but I sensed that about them too, the first time I saw the card. I couldn't put my finger on it, but I sensed that they were together." She was tempted to add how she had pictured herself happily following Kristine on the same trail and how often her thoughts had been occupied by Kristine when she had been camped at Fish Creek. There it was, again. A patch of silence in which to grow her desire.

Kristine set the card back down on the counter where she'd found it. She seemed to be grasping for something to say, as if she was safer when her mouth was moving. "All the stuff in the store is so old. I have other pieces with me at the cabin if you need more. It's not all from here, but you're welcome to have a look."

"I like your work, the angles you find. They've got a really personal feel to them."

"I used to have my eye on the landscape all the time. Now I find myself drawn to people."

Kristine's words surprised Gloria. She turned, wiping her hands on a dishtowel, studying Kristine, worried that it was her own thoughts that had her reading more into Kristine's words than she intended. Kristine quieted, too. They stood nearly opposite each other in the small quarters. Gloria wondered if Kristine was aware of her provocative pose. She leaned back against the counter, her elbows bearing her weight. Her long, jean-clad legs stretched out in front of her and crossed at the ankles. Gloria took a deep breath, finding it difficult to keep her eyes off Kristine's breasts, the fabric of her sweatshirt pulled taut by her posture. She decided Kristine's last statement needed clarification. "You're drawn to people in terms of photography?"

Kristine's eyes were on Gloria's mouth when she answered. "Yes."

"Not drawn to as in interested in…"

"No." Gloria tried to hide her disappointment by turning back to the dishes, but Kristine grabbed her hand, stilling her. "Not to people. Just one person. Just you."

Relief that she wasn't alone in having difficulty managing Kristine's request flooded through her. "Good. Because it's getting harder and harder not to kiss you," she said, putting a foot on either side of Kristine's crossed boots.

"Is that so?"

Gloria's breath caught when Kristine took hold of her hips and pulled them to her own. She straightened, surprised by Kristine's action and needing to see her eyes. The hesitation she usually read there was replaced completely with desire. She waited a few heartbeats, giving Kristine ample time to move away if she needed to, before she leaned forward and kissed the lips that she'd been dreaming about for weeks. She lost herself in the give of Kristine's lips, in the inviting warmth and softness.

Kristine's lips parted, summoning more. Gloria ran the tip of her tongue along Kristine's bottom lip, smiling at the groan her movement elicited. She tested again and met Kristine's tongue with her own. With a sharp intake of breath, Kristine pushed away from the counter, standing to reclaim her height advantage. Her right hand swept behind Gloria's neck, fingers playing with the wisps of hair that had escaped Gloria's ponytail as she hungrily deepened the kiss.

"I've been thinking about the way that would feel since the last time we stood in a kitchen together," Kristine said.

"And?" Gloria said, tilting her chin up.

"So much better." Kristine kissed along Gloria's neck before reclaiming her lips.

Gloria reciprocated and ran her own hands into Kristine's thick hair, pulling her closer and losing herself in the rush of pure pleasure as Kristine's hands explored her contours. She loved Kristine's playfulness. Her kisses changed quickly, like an unfamiliar trail where every turn brings a new and wonderful view. Gloria felt as if she was running to keep up. Reluctantly, she pulled away to catch her breath. She regretted her decision immediately when she felt Kristine's hands leave her body.

She grabbed for Kristine's hands, holding her put. "Don't go."

"If I stay one kiss longer, I'll be here all night."

"And that's a bad thing," Gloria said, wanting Kristine to know she didn't want to push her.

"Not bad," Kristine said. "There are just things…" her voice trailed away.

"That you're working on. I know," Gloria said, when the silence lengthened.

Kristine nodded, pulling her into a tight embrace. "Trust me, you're making it very difficult to leave."

Gloria grabbed onto Kristine's belt buckle to make it even harder for her. She ran her thumb across the twenty-mule team printed on it. "What is it with cowboys and their belt buckles? They're kind of ridiculous."

"But sexy…" Kristine purred, kicking up one eyebrow and cocking a hip.

Gloria laughed at Kristine's pose and swatted her away. If she wasn't staying, she didn't get to tease. Kristine's eyes grew serious again, and she cupped Gloria's face with both hands to give her a gentle goodnight kiss. With an audible sigh, Kristine stepped away from Gloria. "Dinner tomorrow?" Gloria asked.

Kristine smiled. "Absolutely."

Gloria watched the cowgirl disappear into the darkness, wishing she could have convinced her to stay longer. But Kristine had proven herself not one to linger. Knowing that had made Gloria feel safe in moving her camper because she knew Kristine would never overstay her welcome. In fact, Gloria found herself wishing Kristine had stayed longer.

CHAPTER FIFTEEN

Kristine fixed a worried eye to the lightning snaking across the black sky. The thick cloud cover almost made the early afternoon look like sundown. It felt like a reprimand for the slip in her resolve. The entire summer had rolled along with bright skies until she gave in to her desire to kiss Gloria. As if the storm wasn't signal enough, she was also stuck in the backcountry for the afternoon helping Dozer set up his camp above Shadow Lake. He was so sick that morning throwing up repeatedly that he'd barely been able to load up his animals. He had asked Leo to send her in until he had his camp under control. Dozer never asked for help, especially not from her. The feeling she got when she was headed the wrong direction on an unfamiliar trail crept into her belly.

She carried an empty leather pannier, half of one of the sets they used for packing much of their gear into the backcountry, from the kitchen. She walked by Dozer chopping on an old log to gather wood for his party and listening to the thunk of the ax succeeded by a string of swearing. Suddenly, she stopped, hearing a familiar voice, a voice that zinged a delicious shiver through her body. She closed her eyes remembering the feel of the speaker's lips against her own.

"Dozer?"

The chopping stopped. "Hey, Ms. Fisher. Lookin' for bears?"

"Sounded like you were losing a fight, so I thought I'd investigate," Gloria answered.

Kristine smiled reflexively and bounded up the last hill to join them. "If I scream bear, will you shoot him in the ass?" she teased.

Dozer scowled at Kristine. "You going to carry more wood or do some more sissy chopping, Teeny?"

"Keep calling me Teeny, and I'll shoot you myself," she said, snatching the ax from him. She aimed at the log in front of her, trying to avoid looking at Gloria for fear of betraying the guilt and disappointment she felt. It was challenging, as she looked irresistible in her official uniform, her hair pulled through the forest-green cap. The original plan was to get in earlier and be the one to cook dinner for them both, but that was before she'd been sent out to Dozer's camp. "I'm not exactly sure how late I'm going to be tonight," she said in what she hoped was an offhand voice.

"That's all right. I don't mind cooking again," Gloria said with much too much pleasure in her voice. Clearly, she was remembering the advantage she had on her home court.

"Again!" Dozer inserted. "You and the bear lady, huh?"

Kristine shot Dozer a look that silenced him. "We've got wood to stock, the horses to put up," Kristine pulled the ball cap she was wearing down on her forehead, wiped her palms on her jeans and swung again at a thick branch in front of her.

"Tarps to string up," Dozer wheezed, rubbing at his beard. "But she'll still beat your ass out traveling without mules or guests."

"Fat chance. You underestimate how fast I travel," Gloria said.

"Yeah, I'd be hightailing it if I saw Teeny on my trail, too," Dozer retorted. Before Kristine could insert that she wasn't chasing Gloria, he growled, "Give me that ax before you chip it all to hell."

Kristine loaded up the pannier with her chopped wood, and tipped her chin toward the kitchen, inviting Gloria to follow her. They passed the stock tied in a cluster of trees, unbothered by the storm, heads down, ears pointing at loose angles. Gloria first smelled and then heard the pop of the campfire and stopped short when they emerged at the kitchen Sandy was in the process of setting up. Behind two tables set together in an L, she shelved pots and pans in pack boxes she'd stacked three high. Her produce was neatly arranged in an expanding net shelf hung from a tree.

"Think you'll be cooking in the rain tonight?" Kristine asked, dropping the wood by the cooking fire.

"I hope not." Sandy dug in a different bag. "Oh, good. Here's my camp slippers." She sat on one of the coolers and pulled off her boots to replace them with sneakers. "Where's Mooch?" she asked Gloria.

"Mooch?"

"The ranger we usually run into out here."

"Oh, I'm not checking permits. I'm out here collecting samples. Leo said you guys had a bear visit, and the ranger's reported more encounters too. I want to see if see if it's one animal or if there's a high concentration of bears. That might push them to compete for natural food and turn to campers to supplement."

"Well, I packed extra chicken for tonight. The ranger always seems to show up right around dinner time."

"With the spread you've got going, I don't blame him." Gloria smiled.

"Help yourself. Like I said, I've got plenty." To Kristine she said, "Three more bags should get us through breakfast tomorrow, and I can chop for dinner. Usually Dozer won't let me touch his gear, but he's sure not up to it."

"What's wrong with him?" Gloria asked. "He sounds like he's dying."

"He says it's food poisoning. I made him take me up the mountain for dinner in town. Says I'm trying to kill him by not cooking for him."

"How many days are you out?"

"Just five. We'll do two days here, one at Ruby, then a few at Shadow."

"Will he make it?"

"He'll be fine. Luckily, this is a base camp. We'll be here the whole time because this group wants to fish along Shadow Creek."

"You need a hand?" Gloria asked.

"That's okay," Kristine replied. "I've got it."

Gloria shrugged out of her knapsack. "If I hike in now, I'll be home early enough that I'll have to do my own work. I don't mind pitching in."

"You sure? If you're truly game, I'll show you where Dozer wants the animals picketed." Kristine grabbed two lashropes, and they tromped back through the trees to where the animals stood. "You really want to give up your head start?"

Gloria wrapped her arms around Kristine's waist. "What if my motives are selfish? What if I'm just trying to get you back to the Aspens earlier?"

Lightning zigzagged through the sky, lighting up the blue of Gloria's eyes. Her gaze dropped to Gloria's lips, and she remembered how good it felt to kiss them and how easy it would be to close the distance and kiss her again. She stepped back abruptly.

"Are you okay?" Gloria asked.

"Fine," Kristine lied. Why hadn't she stepped away last night and kept her focus? "Just thinking of how much work there's left to do." She showed Gloria how to loosen the latigo on the cinch and pull the saddle off. Gloria continued while Kristine strung one of the lashropes high between two trees. "I'd better get some more wood to the kitchen. You're okay unsaddling the rest?" she asked once she'd tied the animals to the picket. She needed to put some distance between herself and Gloria who assured her that she was up to the task. Kristine jogged back down to the kitchen and swiped the pannier, wishing she'd remembered to take it when they went to set up the pickets. She tried to dodge by Sandy unnoticed.

"What've you got going on with Gloria?" Sandy asked. "Who volunteers to unsaddle sweaty horses?"

Kristine shrugged. "I make this work look glamorous?"

"You're totally sleeping with her, aren't you?" Sandy whispered.

"No," she answered honestly, ignoring Sandy's calling after her that she wasn't going to get off that easy. Her escape faltered when she met an equally pushy Dozer taking a rest from his chopping.

"Jesus, Teeny. I'm dying here, and you're screwing around?"

"I'm not screwing around," she answered, quickly filling the pannier with wood.

"Right."

"I'm out here busting my ass to help you out," she snapped. The mountains echoed her tone with another rumble of thunder.

"Like you were helping Nard?" He shook his head and went back to his chopping.

"What's that supposed to mean?"

"C'mon. Everyone knows where your mind is and what you do when things get tough."

"I…" She started to say that she'd never screwed around on any of the backcountry trips but realized she couldn't honestly say that. A flash of lightning lit up the sky. Kristine balled her fists and bit her tongue to keep from saying he didn't know her half of the story. No point in telling him when he'd probably side with Nard anyway. He clearly held the same opinion of her that he'd always had. They all believed that sex was the only thing on her mind, that she was easy. In the past, she'd always gotten by at the Lodge by ignoring the guys, their taunts and attitude. She realized that maybe that was part of the problem. "I'm not some backcountry ho." He ignored her, his slow, steady swing taking bites out of the log he was splitting into kindling. Kristine felt the first drops of rain, bringing her back to her work. She stomped to the kitchen, dumping her load, still fuming over Dozer's comments.

"What's wrong with you?" Sandy asked.

"Nothing," Kristine said, seeing that Gloria was on her way back to the kitchen too.

Sandy looked in the same direction. "Your girlfriend is an angel. We've got enough wood if you want to take off," she said with a wink.

"She's not my girlfriend. Where's your tarp?"

Sandy furrowed her brow in response to Kristine's clipped tone and fetched the tarp. Kristine worked in silence, brewing over Dozer's words.

Gloria returned, her eyes still full of sparkle. "All the saddles are piled up. Do you want to cover them with something?"

"I'll throw a tarp on them when I go for more wood," Kristine said, watching Sandy observe them.

With a sly look, Sandy said, "Thanks again for the warning about the bear and your help. You know, you two should just stay for dinner, wait out the storm."

"Oh, thanks," Gloria said. "But I think I'll head out. You close to wrapping up?"

Kristine knew from Sandy's satisfied smirk that she understood that Gloria was anxious to get Kristine out of the backcountry. "I still have the stock to help with and probably a few more camp chores."

"Take some snacks with you," Sandy prompted impishly. "You want to keep your strength up."

"I'm off then," Gloria said, grabbing a handful of trail mix. Her eyes asked for assurance, so Kristine gave her what she hoped was a convincing smile. Gloria hesitated for a moment, and Kristine willed her not to comment on her shift in behavior. "Thanks for the snacks," she said to Sandy before turning back to Kristine. "Don't get lost," she said, shouldering her pack and hitting the trail.

"I know the way."

Lightning lit the sky quickly followed by the ground-rumbling boom of thunder. The storm was almost on top of them. Dozer wheezed back to camp with the last of the wood. "Itching to take off?" Dozer said, his eyes on Gloria as she disappeared down the trail.

All business, Kristine refused to look in that direction. "Let's get the tarp up." Dozer's accusation about where her priorities were made her realize how instead of dealing with the past as she had resolved to do, she was hiding out with Gloria. She dug into the remaining chores, ducking in and out of the tarp as the rain picked up to a pour.

She stayed past dinner and helped Dozer put up the barrier on the trail that would keep his stock from returning home when he turned them out for the night. Leaving on the cusp of nightfall, she was almost tempted to huddle up under the saddle pads, spend the night and head home in the morning, but she trusted Digger to get her home in the dark. The storm had moved through the valley, leaving the sky bright with stars. She kept wondering what she'd do if she found Gloria still on the trail. However as she'd argued, Gloria set a good pace and had beaten Kristine back.

Her light shone in her small camper. Kristine rode past.

"Hey," Gloria called out, swinging her head out of the door. "I was starved and already ate, but I saved a plate for you."

"I'm going to get this guy home. Then I think I'll wash up at home. Stay warm," she added lamely. "I'll see you tomorrow, okay?"

Gloria wasn't letting her off that easily. She shoved her feet into sneakers and jogged over. Kristine could read the concern in Gloria's eyes. She put her hand on Kristine's thigh, sending a bolt of electricity through her body. "No, not okay. I know something happened out there."

"Nothing happened," Kristine lied. "I'm just beat is all." She nudged her mount forward, feeling Gloria's hand slip away. When she hit the road, the last stretch before home, she put her own hand on her thigh where Gloria's had been, missing the warmth of it. She unsaddled without hurry, working another internal dialogue about her ill-fated trip with Nard so long ago, this time with Dozer. In this version, she told him everything. She turned out her stock and went inside to shower, barely saying anything to Gabe.

As the water ran over her, she remembered when she threw the stone into Rosalie Lake and vowed to stop carrying the past.

Despite being given the chance to do just that in her exchange with Dozer that afternoon, she had not let go. Emotions washed over her: anger at her inability to tell Dozer the truth and guilt for blowing Gloria off. She threw on a pair of sweats, long-sleeved tee, sweatshirt and jacket.

"Forget something out there?" Gabe asked when she emerged from her bedroom.

"Gloria held supper for me. I'll be back later."

"I haven't eaten yet," he said, balancing on the back two legs of the chair, angling for an invite.

"So go scrounge something down at the Lodge."

"Why is it I suddenly feel like a third wheel? I thought we were all buddies."

"Girl talk tonight."

He let the chair slam back down to the floor. "In that case, the Lodge it is. I'll drop you, if you like."

Kristine opened her mouth to turn down the offer but then thought of how much harder it would be to chicken out if Gabe dropped her off. The sooner she got there, the better, before she talked herself out of it.

CHAPTER SIXTEEN

Her table strewn with reports, Gloria tried her best to put Kristine's weirdness out of her mind, but she kept circling back around, trying to figure out when things had shifted between them, how Kristine could have gone from steamy promising kisses to aloof so quickly. She glanced at the clock, wondering if she should walk down to the Aspens and demand an answer. Kristine's rebuff stung, and she found it hard to ignore. Exasperated with her inability to let it go, she scooped up the reports and dropped them into a drawer hoping she could lose herself in a novel. She gathered up her toiletries and made a run to the bathrooms to get ready for bed.

When she returned, she found Kristine sitting on her step. She rose as Gloria approached. Gloria was tempted to say that she was beat and send Kristine home but accepted that Kristine had come back and invited her into the camper.

"Do you want the plate I fixed for you?"

"No, thanks," Kristine said, sitting down at the table. Gloria sat down across from her. "You don't have to tell me what happened out there. I didn't mean to push."

"No. I do. It's just…it's a long story, and one the people here don't know. I'm not sure where to start."

Gloria reached for Kristine's hand. "This isn't about today."

"No. It's about Nard."

Kristine's statement didn't make sense to Gloria, but she waited, guessing that Kristine needed to work up the courage to talk about what clearly haunted her.

Kristine continued, "When I first started at the Lodge, I didn't even notice him. He was in the backcountry most of the time, and I was at the corrals. The day-ride girls used to make fun of how every summer he had a new girlfriend and take bets on how much any one of them would know about horses. So many of them were such bimbos. My last summer, he didn't have a girlfriend. All of a sudden he zeroed in on me. Every time he was in from a trip, he'd try to convince me to sleep with him, said that if I would just give guys a try…"

Gloria rolled her eyes in sympathy.

"I got good at avoiding him when he was in, but then he started pulling me out on his trips. Out there, I'd always get the cook to say she needed my help guarding the kitchen because I didn't trust having my bedroll out near the stock where he slept. I always stayed near the guests. That only helped a little. He'd still find ways to get in my space when we were saddling and packing, those were the hardest." Her voice took on a hard edge.

"And you couldn't get out of the trips?"

Kristine shrugged. "Everyone wants to be on the overnighters. I'd been fighting to get out there and pack for ages, but all the cowboys were like Dozer. They didn't want me around, so I kept taking the trips with Nard, thinking he'd eventually get the message that I didn't want to sleep with him. That last trip was big enough that Leo made me second packer and sent Gabe as the helper.

"We had a new cook, too. She'd been doing day rides but wanted to try to cook, and since I'd been hanging around the kitchen on other trips, I shared some tips with her. She was probably my age. Since Gabe was the helper, he rode with her and the guests and did the kitchen chores. The three of us got on really well. It's the only time I remember being in the backcountry and being relaxed, having fun without watching my back.

"But Nard was watching. He saw what I didn't, and on the third day out, when we stopped to camp, he saw Nicole follow me down to the river. I don't know what I was thinking. I shouldn't have. I knew better than to fool around with anyone on trips, especially with Gabe out there. But that night after everyone had turned in, I slipped off to her tent." Briefly, she looked guilty, but before Gloria could comment, Kristine's expression darkened. "I was on my way back to the kitchen where my bedroll was when Nard grabbed me." She looked down, like she was embarrassed and sounded apologetic when she said, "He caught me off guard."

Gloria hated Nard for putting that tone in Kristine's voice. She stroked the veins on the back of Kristine's hand, admiring the strength that it took to come back to the Lodge.

"He said he was tired of me being a tease and accused me of going after Nicole to turn him on. I told him to stop. I was *very* clear about not being interested him." Her eyes sparked anger before fading with the memory that had to be playing in her head. "But he said I was in no place to argue, not as the campfire slut."

"At the beginning of the season everyone seemed to know that you had that reputation," Gloria said softly.

Kristine looked away. "I crossed a line in the backcountry. I knew it, and he knew it, and when I refused him…he got so angry. I thought I could shake him off, but his hands were everywhere. He was so much stronger than I thought. I…" She swiped tears from her eyes. "I couldn't get away from him. I tried, but I fell backward, and then he was on top of me. I tried to kick him, and he struck me across the cheek, telling me not to fight him. I was dazed, stunned. He laughed." Her voice caught. "He laughed and said, 'That's right. I knew you wanted it.'"

Gloria didn't know what to say. She feared that she knew what came next and squeezed Kristine's hand, willing her to feel the strength she was offering.

Kristine wouldn't meet her eyes. After a long silence, she continued. "I hated myself trapped there underneath him. He made me a helpless girl."

"You weren't helpless," Gloria argued. "You were overpowered. There's a difference."

Kristine stared at her hands. "You don't understand. He took everything from me, everything I'd been trying to prove. I felt so small."

Gloria ached for the woman sitting in front of her. Questions she wanted to ask buzzed around her brain, but she didn't want to ask something insensitive, something that would worsen the memory. "Wasn't there anyone…?" she risked.

"Of course. Everyone was within shouting distance. If I could have made a sound. But I was so shocked, so rattled. By everything. I couldn't get my thoughts unscrambled enough to make any noise. I would have been in real trouble if one of your friends hadn't shown up."

Gloria blinked, confused. "He didn't…?"

"No." Kristine looked away, retreating into the memory. Gloria watched as Kristine seemed to search for what to say, her gaze darting everywhere but back to Gloria. She couldn't understand why Kristine seemed more upset after she clarified that Nard had not raped her.

Kristine cleared her throat and continued, "The cook started screaming her head off because a bear was in the kitchen. Everyone for miles around must have heard her. Nard crushed my mouth with his hand and said, 'Don't even think we've finished this.' There was no way I was going to give him a chance to finish anything, so I bailed. I was pretty banged up, but I rode out that night and became their joke. Dozer said something today about how I was too busy screwing around to help him, just like before. He doesn't know. None of them know. To them, I'm just a flake. I'm still the one who was wrong."

"But you didn't do anything wrong."

"But I did." Kristine's eyes blazed.

Gloria didn't understand her adamance and sought to reassure her. "You did what you needed to do. You took care of yourself. There's nothing to be ashamed about there. And you're here now. I think that takes an amazing amount of courage."

Kristine slipped her hand away from Gloria's. She sat folded in on herself and looked so vulnerable, so completely different than Gloria had ever seen her. "Yeah, look at me, so courageous. For two months, I've been trying to earn back some respect, but there's no way they'll forget what they think they know."

"Why didn't you tell Dozer the truth today?" Gloria asked gently.

"What was I going to say? I got scared and ran. I quit the wreck. I bailed and lost control." She swallowed hard.

Gloria hated the resignation she heard in Kristine's voice. "He attacked you and if it weren't for the cook calling him, he would have raped you. That's assault," she insisted.

Tears began to stream down Kristine's face. Gloria grabbed a box of tissues and scooted around so she was sitting next to Kristine. "None of this is your fault." She put an arm around Kristine and held her while she cried, wishing that words could fix the hurt she was feeling. She stroked Kristine's hair and touched her lips to her forehead, using her chin to pull Kristine closer. "You are the victor here. You came back. That earns you my respect."

Kristine nodded against her chest. "Can I stay here?" She whispered so softly Gloria almost missed it.

"Absolutely," Gloria answered, honored that Kristine would trust her to ask. She wanted Kristine to know that she understood why Kristine had stepped away from her that afternoon and that she wasn't expecting anything more now. "Whatever you need. This folds into a bed if that's what you'd like."

"No…if it's okay, I'd like…to be next to you."

"Of course."

She gave Kristine a spare toothbrush, boxers and an old tee, changed into similar sleep attire and crawled into bed. Kristine's confession explained so much, the tension between Kristine and her colleagues and her reluctance to get involved. She sensed Kristine's need to not let anything distract her.

Kristine returned from the bathroom and locked the door. "Lights out?"

"I'm good," Gloria replied.

Kristine crossed the short space between them and crawled under the covers. Gloria wasn't sure what to do with her body. She wanted to hold Kristine, but she didn't want her to think that she was pushing for something sexual. She didn't want any of her actions to come across wrongly, so they simply lay next to each other. Gloria wondered what Kristine was thinking about, and then she felt her move, shift just enough so that her hip and thigh touched Gloria's.

"Do you want to turn?" Gloria asked. "I could hold you if you'd like."

Instead of turning away from Gloria, Kristine rolled to her side to face Gloria. It was too dark to see her, so Gloria had no insight to what she wanted. She was about to scoot to her hip when she felt Kristine's hand slip into hers. Silently, she lifted Gloria's arm and nestled her head on Gloria's chest. "Is this okay?"

"Yes," Gloria answered, happy to open her arms and let Kristine in. It still amazed her to see such a vulnerable side to someone who typically exuded such strength and confidence. "Thank you, Kristine. Thank you for trusting me."

Kristine nodded but said nothing, and Gloria guessed she must have been emotionally beat because her body soon relaxed into sleep.

Good thing she's snuggled on my right side, Gloria thought, certain that the pounding of her heart would have kept Kristine awake had she been on the left. She willed her breathing to slow, her heart to calm. When had she ever held anyone like this? Post-sex, she'd tangled limbs with women but quickly drifted to sleep. Holding Kristine, she felt far from sleep with the range of emotions she felt, still angry at Nard and all of the cowboys for what happened, sad for how wounded Kristine was, and surprisingly protective of the woman she had known for such a short time. Strangely, she realized that though she'd had sex with plenty of partners, she'd never experienced intimacy that could compete.

CHAPTER SEVENTEEN

Eyes closed, legs and arms outstretched to gather as much sun as possible, Kristine sat in a skimpy tank top and shorts trying to absorb the morning sun that shone brightly in the outpost yard. Since the scheduled all-day ride was a no-show, she'd decided to get a little sun. Typically, she spent the whole day with only her lower arms exposed which had already given her a pronounced farmer tan.

In the quiet, she felt utterly content. Even Gabe's comments about her not coming home had not soured her mood. She'd left Gloria's at first light to ready her stock for the day and worked beside him in the yard all morning without a word about the previous night. She couldn't believe she'd told Gloria. Telling her felt as good as throwing the rock into Rosalie. Now she could be less guarded and know that Gloria would understand.

The mountain air was crisp enough that the moment a shadow fell across her body, her skin erupted in gooseflesh. She opened her eyes to find Gloria blocking her sun, startled to be caught staring. "I'm working on my tan," she said in response to Gloria's befuddled expression.

"It needs a lot of work," Gloria laughed, pulling another lawn chair out of the shed and joining Kristine on the pack dock.

Kristine smiled at the woman next to her. Gloria leaned back and closed her eyes, immediately falling into a comfortable silence. Something about her manner inspired a confidence that Kristine had never felt before.

"Do you have to stick around here today?" Gloria asked, finally breaking the silence.

"No. I guess not. Why?" Kristine tilted her head to the side.

"You really need a beach for proper sunbathing. I say we head out to Mono. Mitchell said it's not to be missed, and it shouldn't take much more than an hour to get there."

A broad smile spread across Kristine's face. "You don't have work to do?"

"I have reports to pick up from the office in Mammoth."

"In other words, you want to borrow my truck."

Gloria elbowed her playfully. "No. I want to borrow you."

Kristine pursed her lips. "Are you asking me on a date?"

"If I did, would you say yes?"

Kristine thought about her promise to herself. And she thought about how much she enjoyed Gloria's company and how very long it had been since she'd been on a date. She didn't date at home. Once in a while, she thought about checking out a gay club in Reno, but for the most part, her life consisted of turning down invitations from eligible cowboys in Quincy. She could go on a date with Gloria. In trying to avoid falling into the empty and distracting flings as she had in the past, she had unknowingly allowed herself space to move into something more serious. Quite unexpectedly, with Gloria by her side, she felt supported. "Yes," she finally said.

"Whew. I'm glad I won that internal battle," Gloria laughed. "Come on a date with me."

"Do I need a swimsuit for this date?"

"Absolutely."

"Give me a few minutes. I'll pack us a lunch and grab a change of clothes."

"Perfect. I'll need to swing by my place for my suit, too."

"And something nice, right? If this is a real date, I figure you're taking me to a nice supper in town."

Gloria's lovely laughter filled the yard.

"What?" Kristine asked, perplexed. She liked that she had that effect on Gloria but would like to know for future reference what delighted her so.

"'Supper in town.' I feel like I just asked Laura Ingalls out."

"Small-town girl to the core," Kristine agreed. "Go get your stuff. I'll pick you up in fifteen."

They chatted easily during the drive, comparing taste in music and other topics that kept the conversation light. They stopped briefly at the visitor's center and learned about the tufa that emerged from the lake when water levels dropped because of water diversions to Los Angeles in the early 1980s. Driving to the South Tufa Grove where most of the strange porous rocks were clustered, the barren, treeless landscape around the vast and shallow lake felt foreign after spending so much time under the forest canopy. They found a small beach to soak in the rays and tried out the water, sharing the odd sensation of floating in the salty body of water. Kristine quickly abandoned the cool water, less icy than the mountain streams, but still not warm enough to feel comfortable in on the breezy day. She picked up her camera and took some shots of Gloria's head and toes poking out of the brine. She looked as if she were sitting in a recliner, buoyed by the high saline content. She, too, quickly abandoned the strange tickly water for sunbathing.

Before joining her, Kristine stayed at the water's edge shooting frames of the strange foam at her feet and the tufa that rose up to ten feet out of the lake. Once Gloria lost herself in her work, Kristine focused her frame on Gloria's fierce look of concentration on her new reports. When Gloria felt Kristine looking at her and raised her head, Kristine snapped a few more photos of her in repose, her expression clear and open for an instant before she became self-conscious.

She joined Gloria on the beach towels and sat back to admire Gloria's toned body. The blue bikini top and board shorts made Kristine smile. The bathing suit reflected exactly who Gloria was, feminine and sporty. She'd pulled her hair up into a messy ponytail that showed off her long neck. Gloria continued reading, making notes as she went. Kristine pretended to take a snooze but kept peeking over at Gloria, thinking about how appealing each curve of her body was. Gloria's long fingers caught Kristine's eye. The way she perched her index finger poised to turn the top of the page made her body tighten in response.

"Stop," Gloria said, catching her staring again.

"What?"

"Staring at me like I'm an ice cream cone."

Kristine quirked her eyebrow. "What's wrong with that? You getting a little drippy over there?" She traced her finger down Gloria's stomach, stopping at her trunks.

Gloria's quick intake of breath tempted Kristine to go further. "You're very distracting, you know that."

"Good. It's mutual." She shoved off her chair, pulling on a tee and shorts over her black one-piece suit.

Gloria shaded her eyes, frowning. "You're leaving?"

"I'll quit distracting you. I'm going to explore the tufa a little more before you take me on my fancy date."

Kristine pulled out her camera and marveled at the tufa on the shore. Alkali flies buzzed around her, and she heard a Mountain Chickadee's distinctive call. They had read all about how the limestone spires form when calcium rich spring water mixes with the carbonates in the alkaline lake creating the bizarre dribble-castle-like landscape around them. She crouched down, accentuating their height, some towering thirty feet. She changed lenses to explore the coarse and knobbly forms up close. She added a polarizing filter, amazed at the contrast of the white pillars reflected in the dramatically blue lake. She easily lost track of the time climbing about taking shot after shot.

Once in a while, she glanced over to the beach to see Gloria still hard at work. Kristine admired Gloria's concentration.

She'd always been drawn to women with determination and drive, and Gloria certainly had both, keeping herself on track with her grant project. Kristine wondered what her next career goal was, if she planned on staying at the Fish and Wildlife office in southern California, or if she was investigating new opportunities.

When she saw Gloria start to pack up her things, she headed back, hundreds of images later. They headed to the Mono Lake campground showers together, Kristine feeling nervous about the dinner part of their date. She had only packed for the backcountry, so a newer pair of blue jeans and a tight black tank were the best she could do for dinner in Mammoth. She was finished before Gloria and waited anxiously by her truck. When Gloria emerged, she sighed in relief to see that her idea of dressing up included jeans too. She wore a form-fitting white camisole with a silky blue overshirt, unbuttoned to just below her breasts.

"That shirt makes your eyes look amazing," Kristine said.

Gloria blinked in Kristine's direction. "Without a hat and plaid shirt, I hardly recognized you!" she laughed.

"I've got a hat if you like that better," Kristine said, a little embarrassed, tousling her hair nervously.

"Are you kidding?" Gloria ran her own fingers through Kristine's short waves, tucking a strand behind her ear. "I love being able to see your whole face. You've got nowhere to hide from me." She ran a hand down Kristine's arm. Kristine reacted with a shiver. "You clean up nice. Up 'til today, I couldn't picture you away from the horses and the trail."

Kristine drove them back to Mammoth Lakes thinking about Gloria's words. Though she doubted it was intentional, Gloria's comment about seeing only the cowgirl version of her renewed the hesitation Kristine felt about getting involved with someone who was okay with a summer fling. When the summer came to a close, would she desire something more with Kristine?

They found a small steakhouse and were tickled to be seated right in front of the stone fireplace. They took the waiter's suggestion and had the buffalo burger and Mediterranean shrimp and talked about the aspects of Mammoth they'd miss when the summer was over, both agreeing that it was sometimes nice to be the tourist, unrecognized by everyone in town. While they waited for their food, Kristine scrolled through some of the photos she'd taken to distract herself from the question of what would happen when the season closed in just a few weeks.

"I like the close-ups the best," Gloria said. "The texture is really something, isn't it?"

"That, in contrast to the still, clearness of the water is really fun to play with. I can't believe I've driven by the lake so many times without stopping to shoot anything."

"I'm really impressed," Gloria said. "I was with you all day, but I don't feel like I saw half of this. You have a way of finding the coolest angles. I'd love to see how you would capture the places I love. What you'd do with the fog in the redwoods or when it settles in on the coast like a blanket. There are all these great gnarled trees that hang onto the rocky cliffs."

"I saw a collection of prints from a place called Fern Canyon. That area is definitely on my list of places to visit."

"Well consider yourself invited. I'll be your tour guide."

The day had made her feel close to Gloria, closer than she'd been to anyone in a long time, yet she couldn't shake the feeling that they were spending time together out of the convenience of being in the same place. Kristine, herself, was a tour guide to hundreds of people in the backcountry during the summer. There was no intimacy there, just a professional courtesy. She wanted to ask if that was all Gloria would be, but instead she said, "It sounds like you miss home."

"I'll be happy to wrap up this project and get back," Gloria admitted. "I enjoyed fieldwork a lot more when my folks could join me. When I was little, we used to take family vacations every year, a different state park that my mom would research the whole year. When I started working with Fish and Wildlife, it was kind of continuing that tradition, only we went where the job took me instead of the park my mom chose."

"They can't join you here?"

"No, my mom has leukemia. At first it just meant no hiking. That's when we got the camper. That made it a lot easier on my mom. But it's gotten trickier to manage—more medication, more doctors' appointments. She's more comfortable at home."

"And this is why you send her pictures," Kristine said. "Because she can't make it."

"You remembered."

"Of course. You sent her my stuff. I was really flattered." They ate in silence, Kristine appreciating a salad after months of chicken and ribs. "Is it easier for your mom when you're home?" she asked.

"Yes and no. I really enjoy her company, and my dad is always telling me how much better she does when I'm around. He keeps urging me to get something full time in town. I want to be there, but at the same time, I don't want her to feel like I'm hovering. Like when I'm away, it's because I have faith that she's doing well enough that I can be away."

"So, she's doing well now?"

"Well enough, thanks." Gloria's eyes were warm. She reached across the table and traced her finger along the back of Kristine's hand. "What about your parents? Are you close?"

Kristine sighed, pushing her plate away. "They're good people, and we get on fine if I follow their cues."

"So the pun on your logo is intended."

Kristine was impressed that Gloria had noticed what she'd implied on the Suzy-Q Card logo she used. The disagreements with her father always stemmed from Kristine trying to go in a direction that didn't match his plans. "My father would very much like it if I would be more dutiful and grateful for the ranch he'd like to hand over to me when he retires. I love the ranch, and I love Quincy, but I cannot spend the rest of my life there."

The attentive waiter returned and offered dessert. Gloria waved him off easily, and Kristine agreed that she had no room for it, but the way Gloria kept her gaze on Kristine made her wonder if she had a different kind of dessert in mind. Back in the cab of the truck, Gloria leaned over and pulled Kristine into a deep kiss, an *I have plans for you* kiss. Her lips tempted her down a very appealing trail, one she knew offered all sorts of wondrous views and experiences. Reluctantly, she broke away from the kiss.

Her attention back on the road, her father's parting words as she'd left for the Lodge came back to her. He challenged her about whether she had a concrete plan for her future because unless she did, he figured she'd stick to his plan for her on the ranch. Kristine did have a plan of sorts, which she hadn't told her father. It was to extract herself from the ranch. Whatever came next she didn't know, but she knew she would never return for an extended period ever again. Instead of forging out on her own after she graduated, she'd made the mistake of going home and had found it almost impossible to leave. Gabe's last-minute call had given her a toehold to the freedom to make her own choices.

Kristine held the hand Gloria put in her lap and wondered where this woman might lead her. At the beginning of the summer, she'd been drawn to Gloria because she seemed to see Kristine for who she was, not as the girl she had been as everyone else did. Now, since she'd spent more time with Gloria and shared the conflict about her past at the Lodge, she knew for certain that if they slept together it would not be a transient thing, at least for her. She still worried about the comment Gloria had made earlier in the summer about casual sex not being a problem for her.

"You're not staying," Gloria stated when Kristine pulled up next to Gloria's camper and put the truck into neutral.

Kristine kissed her, trying to convey with her actions how very much she would like to stay. "I had the best day."

"I did, too."

"I'm sorry, I…" What could Kristine say? It wasn't that she didn't want to stay or that she wasn't immensely attracted to Gloria. "You are so beautiful, so sexy…"

"It's okay." Gloria kissed her again, her tongue dancing playfully against Kristine's. "I know you've got a lot going on in here." She massaged Kristine's temple.

"You're not disappointed?"

"I was disappointed at the beginning of the summer when you said no."

"I never meant…"

"No." Gloria kissed her. "I wasn't trying to make you feel guilty. I was disappointed because from the moment I saw you, I wanted to kiss those lips, I wanted to get you out of those sexy jeans you wear. I wanted what I always wanted. Your wanting to be friends changed things..."

"You don't want me so much anymore?" Kristine said, lacing her fingers with Gloria's.

"If you're getting that impression, I need to try harder to show you that *everything's* different." She squeezed Kristine's hand. "What I wanted always burned bright and quick, but now...You told me you're not into that anymore."

"No." Kristine hadn't expected the idea she'd been struggling with all night to turn into a conversation with Gloria. But then, she hadn't expected saying yes to a date and finding herself wanting the more-than-casual relationship that they now seemed to have. She wasn't even sure what kind of relationship that meant.

"As it turns out, neither am I."

"What are you into now?"

"Whatever this is with you. I want it to be more than friendship, but I know that you need to do what feels right to you. I'm following your lead."

"That could be trouble if I don't know where I'm going." Kristine leaned forward, and their mouths met again. Kristine was aiming for a thank-you-for-understanding kiss, uncomplicated. Succinct. Her lips betrayed her though, parting enough that Gloria teased her tongue past them in invitation. Kristine could not resist, opening her mouth further, losing herself in the caress of Gloria's lips, the playful dance of their tongues. Their kisses quickened, luring her in deeper. This, she realized, felt right. She'd be crazy to drive away knowing Gloria felt the same way. She threw the truck in reverse, and Gloria pulled away, confused.

"You told me to do what feels right. I'm listening." She eyed Gloria's camper. "But your camper seems a little cramped. Is my place okay?"

"I wasn't trying to pressure..."

Kristine stopped her with a kiss. "Do you need anything, or can I drive?"

"I just need you."

For now, Kristine thought, that would be enough.

CHAPTER EIGHTEEN

"What about your brother?" Gloria asked as they pulled up in front of the cabin.

"Down at the Lodge. They'll keep him out late."

"You hope," Gloria teased, joining Kristine inside.

"I hope," Kristine said low and throaty, her eyes dancing.

The short walk to the front door left Gloria out of breath. Admitting to Kristine that she was emotionally involved had intensified everything she was feeling, the anticipation, the nerves. She stood inside the cabin door, wanting Kristine but also wanting her to see that she cared so much about her. "You are so beautiful," she said, taking Kristine's hands and holding them against her hips. Gloria ran her hands down Kristine's arms, admiring the muscling before tucking her hands beneath Kristine's shirt, finding an equally tight abdomen underneath her fingertips. "So strong," she whispered at the nape of her neck, smiling as she felt Kristine's skin flutter underneath her touch. She'd wanted to touch her for so long and intended to savor the body in front of her.

"Sure you're not talking about yourself?" Kristine said, leading her back to the bedroom. She kicked her door shut behind them, her hands immediately on Gloria, unbuttoning her shirt and skimming over the top of her exposed breasts. Gloria shrugged the overshirt from her shoulders, but before Kristine could work off the camisole, she pushed her in the direction of her bed. Usually she was the one to let her partner take the lead, completely attuned to what she wanted to feel. Tonight, she wanted her hands on Kristine. She needed to communicate to Kristine that what they were doing was more than just sex.

Gloria kissed her way up Kristine's neck, taking an earlobe in her teeth, enjoying the hiss it produced from Kristine. "Someone likes her ears kissed?" she asked, tracing Kristine's ear with her tongue. "Keep showing me what you like, what you want. I want to make you happy." Kristine's arms tightened around Gloria in response. She pulled Gloria to her, groaning as it brought every part of their bodies together. Gloria felt the closeness go beyond the physical contact and ran her arms up Kristine's back and wrapped them around her neck thinking how absurd it felt to want to protect a woman who felt so strong to her.

Gloria pulled back and studied Kristine's eyes, dilated with desire. Slipping her hands under Kristine's shirt, Gloria swept up the curve of Kristine's sides, removing her black tank, reveling in the feel of her smooth skin. Slowly unfastening her bra, she found already budded nipples which she teased slowly, making Kristine gasp. Kristine unfastened the button of Gloria's jeans and lowered the zipper before she eased them from Gloria's hips. When they caught at Gloria's knees, Kristine lifted a foot and stepped down, pushing the pants to the floor where Gloria stepped out of them.

"Nice trick," she said, returning to Kristine's lips, kissing and pulling, gently taking Kristine's lower lip between her teeth.

"Stick around. I've got a few more," purred Kristine.

She closed her eyes as Kristine's strong hands grazed her now naked form, exploring every surface. Kristine stepped closer, guiding her backward until her knees hit the bed. She kissed Gloria to a seated position, but Gloria did not let her push her on to her back. Instead she took in the sexy body standing topless but still in her tight jeans. She traced a line from Kristine's clavicle to her belt. "Not this ridiculous thing again. Off. Now."

Kristine laughed and shucked off the offending belt along with the jeans it held up, before returning to the bed, hiking a knee up on either side of Gloria and settling into her lap.

"So much better," Gloria said, running her hands over Kristine's now bare ass.

Kristine kissed her deeply, tipping her back to rest on the bed. Gloria groaned into the kiss as Kristine's breasts swept up her belly and met her own. Her center begged to be in contact as well. Her right foot braced on the bed, she levered her hips and swung Kristine to her back, quickly scissoring their legs and meeting Kristine's hot, wet center with her own.

Kristine gasped at the contact as Gloria ground into her, rocking her hips rhythmically. She moved one hand to Kristine's nipple, teasing, and at the same time maintaining her thrusts. Kristine felt so good beneath her. Their lips met again, and Gloria nearly came with the intensity of Kristine's tongue dancing against her own.

Suddenly, Gloria shifted, running her hand down Kristine's thigh. She needed to feel her. She needed to be inside her. Her fingers dipped into Kristine's wetness and pulled it to her clit, stroking in quick motions wringing a surprised cry from Kristine. She slowed only to slip inside Kristine, relishing the feel of her walls clamping against her, speeding up and playing Kristine's clit with her thumb. She listened to the song of Kristine's climax building, the moans mixed with gasps, the catch of her breath and pant that guided Gloria to the strokes that would bring release.

She captured Kristine's nipple in her mouth, feeling Kristine push her upper body up off the bed to meet her with a long low moan.

"You. Feel. So. Good." Kristine panted.

"You do," Gloria said, her thumb slowly circling Kristine's clit.

Still moving against Gloria's finger, Kristine surprised Gloria by shifting her hips and rolling her over. "Not so fast," she whispered, tipping Gloria's head to the side, kissing the down behind Gloria's ear. Gloria shuddered and arched into Kristine, wanting to feel her again. She withdrew from Kristine and pulled their groins together. Kristine sped up for a moment and then paused, her hand drifting down Gloria's side.

"Don't stop. I'm so close," Gloria whispered. "Please don't stop."

"But I want to touch you," Kristine said. "Let me touch you."

Gloria pulled again on Kristine's hips and captured her lips in another searing kiss. "No time," she said, demanding compliance by rocking her center against Kristine.

"This?" Kristine asked, returning the pressure.

"More."

"Just this?" Kristine teased as she ground faster.

"Yes, just you," Gloria cried out as her climax overtook her. She raked her nails up Kristine's back, enjoying the arch of response, then tickled fingertips around in circles, finally stopping on Kristine's butt.

"Are you always that fast?" Kristine teased.

"Hey, I've been waiting a long time for that," Gloria murmured, smiling.

Kristine traced Gloria's body, and her lips echoed their course, switchbacking lower and lower until Kristine settled between her legs.

"Come back here," Gloria said, trying to pull Kristine from her destination.

"I want my mouth on you. I want to feel you come."

"But I already—" The rest of Gloria's sentence disappeared as Kristine slipped fingers past her wet folds at the same moment her hot mouth closed around her clit. "Oh, Kristine." Kristine's moan of reply amped her body's response. Kristine's mouth felt too good to fight. She rested back against the bed, unbelieving as she felt a second climax building. Hands buried in Kristine's hair, her back arched off the bed, a second orgasm crashed through her body, ripping cries of ecstasy from her throat.

"That's a bit better," Kristine said, resting her cheek against Gloria's thigh while her fingers continued to play in Gloria's slick folds.

"Up here, now."

"Oooh, sounds like I'm in trouble." Humor filled Kristine's voice as she climbed up Gloria's body, hovering infuriatingly above as she planted feathery kisses on Gloria's abdomen and chest. Her upper body strength made it impossible for Gloria to pull their bodies together. Frustrated, Gloria changed tactics, slipping her hand between them and finding Kristine's center even wetter than she'd remembered.

"You're so wet."

"Because you're so incredibly sexy," Kristine whispered, gasping as Gloria slipped her fingers back inside.

Kristine ground her hips deliciously against Gloria. "More." Gloria obliged, loving the feel of Kristine's walls tight on the two fingers she buried inside. Gloria held tight as Kristine's rhythmic thrusts quickened until she tumbled into her own orgasm, shuddering on top of Gloria, her thrusts slowing as she rode out the waves of her pleasure. She pulled away from Gloria's fingers and collapsed next to her on the bed.

"That was incredible," Kristine said.

"I knew it would be. But someone was a little stubborn."

"Mulish, I've been told."

"I can't move," Gloria said sleepily.

"I wasn't asking you to. I was hoping you'd help keep the bed warm tonight."

"Oh, is that what I'm doing?" Gloria finally managed to turn on her side, so she could get her hands back on Kristine, petting lazy circles along her hip. Given a job, she reached down and pulled a comforter over their bodies. She settled down easily next to Kristine's body, not feeling her typical anxiety about extracting herself after sex. The time she'd spent with Kristine made it feel more natural to be together than apart, making it easy to drift into a deep sleep.

CHAPTER NINETEEN

Kristine ignored her brother's raised eyebrows the next morning as she shut her bedroom door and slipped into the bathroom.

"I already caught up your stock," he said when she emerged.

"You didn't have to do that," Kristine poured herself some coffee and popped some bread in the toaster.

"Might as well cook for the two of you."

She whipped around.

"You pee a lot during the night, but not twice in a row."

She couldn't help the smile that crept to her lips.

"Better wipe that look off your face. Sol and Brian have some huge spot leaving out of here. I'm aiming to get out of here before they can rope me into helping."

"Thanks for the heads-up."

Kristine popped in two more pieces of toast and poured a second cup of coffee, carrying it back to the bedroom. Shutting the door behind her, she set the mug down on the old rope spool that served as her bedside table and buried her face above

Gloria's shoulder to kiss the naked skin. Gloria shifted in the covers and the smell of their combined sex wafted out. Kristine felt a surge of wet between her legs and fought the urge to crawl back in next to Gloria.

"I have coffee here and toast coming up. You want it back here or by the table? Gabe's already up."

Gloria shot to a seated position, her hair adorably mussed from sex and sleep. "I forgot about your brother. I'd hide out here, but I already have to pee so bad."

"Forget about trying to hide. He's already read my rubber legs and deduced what we've been up to." Kristine leaned over to kiss her. "Good morning, by the way."

"Good morning." Gloria smiled into the kiss.

"What?" Kristine asked.

"You smell like me."

Kristine moaned into the extended kiss Gloria delivered. "Don't tempt me. If I don't haul ass, I'm going to be stuck in the yard forever."

"So the quicker I let you go, the shorter your day is?"

"Exactly."

Gloria frowned with disappointment. "Then you'll have to make it up to me."

"That's an easy promise to make," Kristine said. She handed Gloria a pair of sweats to throw on and left before she lost her resolve.

Gabe didn't comment when Gloria emerged, disappeared into the bathroom and then joined them, her face washed and hair pulled back. Kristine pointed to a plate of toast and eggs on the breakfast table in front of an empty chair.

"Thanks for the offer," she said, setting her coffee cup on the counter. "But I'd better get out of your hair. Sounds like you have a busy morning."

"Sit," Gabe said. "Everyone's having breakfast over at the Lodge. You've got time to eat and then sneak off."

Gloria looked guilty.

"C'mon. Eat. I'm sure you worked up just as much of an appetite as Kristine."

He ducked away from Kristine's crushing look. "Sorry," she said, waving a half-eaten piece of toast. "I was famished. Sit. He's right. You have time for breakfast before the truck gets here."

They ate in silence, stealing glances and smiling after Gabe ducked out. Kristine finished quickly, dropped her plate in the sink and splashed water over her face.

"You don't have to sneak off. Stay for a shower if you want. I'm sorry I've got to get my stock ready."

Gloria stood and slipped into Kristine's arms. "Meet you back here?"

"Not soon enough." Kristine kissed her with the promise of another wonderful night and then reluctantly slipped into a thick flannel overshirt and nestled her hat onto her head, joining her brother in the yard to get ready for their day. The sky brightened clear of any clouds, the sun quickly taking the edge off the brisk morning air. She aimed for nonchalant when Gloria discreetly slipped out of the house and headed down the road.

"So you finally smartened up?" Gabe asked, grabbing his saddle from the shed.

Busy saddling her own mount, Kristine jabbed a finger in his direction to silence him. "Not a word."

He settled the saddle onto his horse and held up his hands in defense. Kristine tried to concentrate on her own task without giving in to the smile that threatened to take over her face. The crew from the Lodge was soon with them, as were their guests, piling load after load of boxes from their SUV to the pack dock.

"See why I suggested we get out of here?" Gabe asked, fetching his mount.

"I've never seen such a ridiculous amount of gear on a dock before."

"Don't I know it." He swung aboard and held his mount for a moment, pulling on his bottom lip like he had something to say. "My advice is to get out of here before they spoil that grin you've been trying to hide all morning."

With that, he spurred his horse up the trail, his stock falling in line behind him. For his being the younger of the two, his protectiveness touched her deeply. She took his advice, wanting to hold onto the first equilibrium she'd felt in a long time.

CHAPTER TWENTY

Back in her camper, Gloria attempted to work, but her mind kept slipping back to the breathtaking night she'd spent with Kristine. She wished she could have pulled her back into the warmth of the bed to continue her research of Kristine's body and what her touch did to her. The two-way radio Scott had given her when she'd checked in with the local Forest Service at the beginning of the summer crackled to life, interrupting her review of all the night's lovely details.

"Gloria, you within range?"

"I'm here, Scott. What's up?"

"Just got a call from Leo. Seems there's been an incident down at Fish Creek with a horse of his. He was calling to let us know he's got a carcass he's got to haul out of camp."

Gloria hesitated, wondering how the horse involved her. "Okay...?" she said, prompting him to continue.

"Normally, I'd just let Leo deal with moving the animal as far away from the camp as possible, but he said something about a bear attacking the animal, so I thought you'd better have a look before they quarter the carcass and drag it off. Leo's sending someone down from the Lodge this morning to clean up the camp. I've notified Juanita since this is her area, and she is on her way to assess the scene."

"I haven't seen anything in Juanita's reports about him being a problem. I'd like a chance to check the scene, too."

"Of course. That's why I'm calling. You'll need to get down there today. Leo agreed to let you ride in with the packer if you can get down there within the hour."

"Done."

Thinking about the bear, Gloria threw together a pack. This late in the season, he would be moving beyond grazing the grass, looking for game, but he was much more likely to fish than take on a horse. She couldn't imagine the scenario, especially picturing the scrawny excuse for a bear she'd been de-conditioning at the beginning of the season. She felt sick. Was this horse's death the result of her leaving the valley too soon? Had she misread the animal's potential for danger?

She swung back by Kristine and Gabe's place to leave a note explaining why she'd had to head down to the Lodge. She included what little she knew and how she hoped she wouldn't be gone long. She paused before signing the note, opting for a simple "see you soon" instead of anything more explicit. She had no idea who might return to the outpost first, and she knew what kind of fun Gabe would have if he found it first.

Down at the Lodge, Frank, the packer assigned to clean up the camp, grabbed her pack and pointed her toward a dude horse. A full goatee hid the tall cowboy's mouth, but she could still see that his lips were pursed tight in annoyance. She hoped it wasn't from having to take her along. Gloria could ride well enough, and although Kristine had shown her how to work the cinch in reverse to remove the saddle, she allowed one of the day-ride girls to tighten the latigo on the horse and help her aboard. Frank ambled off, his striped shirt taut between his broad shoulders. He made quick work of securing her pack on the smallest of his three mules, acknowledged her with a nod and swung aboard his own mount. Gloria's mount fell in line on autopilot down the trail, and they spent the hours it took to get to Fish Creek riding in silence.

From Scott's briefing, the campsite was how she'd expected: all of the food opened and scattered everywhere, the tent ripped to shreds and clothing unstuffed from the duffels like a disemboweled…horse. She wondered if Kristine had known the animal that now lay at the base of the tree.

"Fuck me," Frank said, a look of disgust on his face. Obviously, he hadn't been prepared for what he saw. He offered Gloria an apologetic look. "Sorry about that. I thought I was just moving a carcass and picking up their stuff. They didn't say anything about the mess. This is easily five mule loads of stuff."

"How many people were here?"

"Three. A fifty-year-old woman, her dad and a friend. Nard dropped them off yesterday, and they were supposed to camp here two nights."

"And they had this much food?"

Frank shrugged. "Like I said. I didn't pack them in. And now I'm stuck packing all this crap out."

He hiked back to fetch the tools he'd brought to tackle the cleanup. Sensing trouble, the stock had refused to move any closer to the camp. Gloria studied the mess, noting how thoroughly the bear had gone through all the campers' things. But it was odd. It had ripped open cans of beans, yet had left their contents untouched. She moved to the horse carcass. As terrible as the gaping wounds were where the bear had gnawed, it had not made a significant meal of the animal. It was not a hungry bear.

"Frank?"

"Yup?" he said, joining her and setting down his tools.

"This horse doesn't seem to have been attacked. All of this looks like a scavenger taking advantage of an easy meal."

Frank ran his hand affectionately along the dead horse's neck, shaking his head. "Yeah…this horse hung himself. See here? He got his foreleg hooked over the lead. I don't know who tied this knot, but whoever it was killed 'im. Suffocated when he couldn't get his head up. It's why we usually have the animals tied to the picket." He motioned to the line tied above them between the two trees.

The breeze shifted, and Gloria covered her mouth.

"Do you know why they kept the horse unattended down here?"

"The woman who booked the trip was worried about her father. Wanted to be able to get him out quickly if he had problems with his health."

"And after the horse died?"

"He hiked out on his own, no problem."

Gloria bowed her head, fuming inside.

"You seen enough? Can I haul him off now?" Frank asked.

"Yeah. I've seen enough." She left him to his grisly task and set to finding some good paw prints to cast. Though she was fairly certain it was the yearling she'd worked with, she wanted to gather what she could. She would also search the trees for claw marks or hair he'd lost brushing against the trees, so she could compare it to what she'd gathered during her first trip down in the valley to verify that it was the same young black one she'd done her best to scare away from humans.

The longer she worked, the angrier she became. Everything about the situation felt like such a waste to her: the loot that would potentially turn a habituated bear into a food-conditioned bear and the dead animal. She couldn't believe that Leo would be foolish enough to leave one of his animals in the care of such inexperienced campers. By the time Juanita reached the camp, she was about to come unglued.

"Leo has got to be held accountable for this," she barked, gesturing at the mess Frank had barely made a dent in despite the hours he had worked. "This is simply unacceptable. Talk about managing human stupidity. I said at the beginning of the season that this animal would be okay if the hikers in the area could keep food away from him. And here someone's set up a bear buffet. Look at this!"

"Leo is being held accountable," Juanita said in an infuriatingly reasonable voice. "He's aware that he has to clean up this mess which is why he sent in the packer. It's unfortunate that the bear got into so much of the human food, and we'll have to keep an eye on him."

"The horse is dead," Gloria said.

"I thought you were concerned about the bear," Juanita said. This was the quality Gloria had assessed from the beginning of the season when she'd first met Juanita. All efficiency, an emotional appeal would have no effect on her. She looked at Frank and then back at Gloria. "He understands that accidents happen in the backcountry. Stock is lost, and we do our best to remove the carcass from areas hikers or campers would stumble upon it. This is not an isolated incident."

"This is not an accident. This is stupidity," Gloria seethed. "Leo killed this horse by leaving stupid people alone in the backcountry with a horse and no employee. This is the Las Vegas strip of stupid right here, and my bear will take the rap."

"We'll do our best to warn campers to use another campsite until the scavengers have taken care of the carcass."

"You obviously can't be out here every day, or you would have advised this party on how to store their food. When you have such a large area to patrol, you can't possibly ensure that this bear will have some breathing room, and you and I both know that the more contact he has with people, the more likely it is that he'll end up being destroyed."

"I do my best," Juanita said, her tone more clipped.

"How come the locations Leo uses frequently for spot trips don't include a bear box? They're often packing in more inexperienced people and should take responsibility for maintaining a habitat that encourages distance between human and wildlife by making sure food is stored in a bear-proof container. Clearly it is not enough to rely on people to tie their food out of reach, especially when they're bringing in food in this quantity. At the very least, the amount of food packed in should be regulated," Gloria emphasized.

Juanita shrugged. "You'd have to talk to Leo about those ideas. We've made our own suggestions, but he's under no obligation to comply. And you know as well as anyone that even when the state installs bear boxes, there is no guarantee that people are going to use them correctly or use them at all."

Gloria wanted to hit her. The more calmly she spoke, the more irritated Gloria became. Ignorant people she dealt with every day. But these particular guests had been brought in by professionals. She'd come into this project to ensure that the overnight packers were diligent in keeping their food away from bears. Her anger, she realized had built because she was at fault for not seeing such a huge hole in the spot trips the Lodge did on a daily basis.

"They should be responsible for the people that they escort out into the backcountry. They bring in all this food. They should incur penalties when a situation like this occurs."

"Why don't you start with your girlfriend, see if she agrees," Juanita answered, unfazed by Gloria's tirade.

Gloria blinked, confused. She had to mean Kristine, but who would know they were more than friends? She, herself, didn't call Kristine her girlfriend. Mitchell, she supposed. Juanita moved on, unaware of Gloria's musings.

"I'll let Scott know I don't see a problem with bear aggression here."

"Thanks." Gloria watched Juanita and Frank unemotionally discuss the details of removing the carcass. They did their job of monitoring people and livestock well, concentrating only on the immediate task. Gloria, on the other hand, worried about the growing number of reported contacts between bear and human. Her bears kept coming last, and she felt like she was their only advocate.

Knowing Frank would remove all of the human food and that the bear would naturally scavenge on the horse carcass once it had been hauled away from the campsite, she resigned herself to a long hike home with a heavy pack. Her anger made it feel like a daypack as she charged up the trail, working out what she wanted to say to Leo.

CHAPTER TWENTY-ONE

After reading Gloria's note about the problem with the Fish Creek bear, Kristine seized the opportunity to take some pictures of Sol when he returned from the huge trip he'd helped pack in. Hearing hoofbeats on the road, she stood poised to capture him.

"Put that goddamn camera down and make yourself useful," Sol spat at Kristine as he rode into the yard. It was close to dinnertime, hours after the packers normally returned.

She stole two more frames of him hunched in the saddle, leadrope stashed under his armpit, both arms resting on the horn of his saddle. The leadrope he tossed at her almost pegged her before she could swing her camera out of the way. All summer she'd been trying to take pictures of the old cowboy, and he'd been pulling similar stunts to thwart her.

"When I'm famous, you'll be happy I took the time."

"I'll be happy when people stop being idiots."

"Who's got you so worked up?"

"Damn group we packed in today. Pissheads, all of them. Wish I could throw 'em all on the ground and piss on their heads, make 'em wish they were dead." He squirted a line of chewing tobacco juice through his teeth to punctuate the remark.

Kristine had been relieved that she had a scheduled pickup in the backcountry and left the yard before the chaos of the morning could come into contact with her. She'd been mounted and out of the yard with her three mules before the other packers had even made a dent in figuring out how many loads to pack.

"How many mules did it come out to?" she asked, untying the mules from the string.

"Twelve."

"TWELVE! How many people in the party?"

"Eight."

Takeisha, the gregarious day-ride girl who had come over to help out with the massive ride, didn't appear to be put out in the least. When she began the season, her gear had all been stiff off the rack, and Kristine had thought the yellow kerchief she wore tied around her neck was hokey. After two months of saddling and riding, she fit right in with the crew with their frayed-at-the- cuff jeans and shirts that were never going to come quite clean because of the oil and dust that had been ground into them. Kristine had grown used to the kerchief, admiring how good it looked against her ebony skin. "I'm glad. It was fun to lead a ride over here, and bringing the string in was totally cool," she said.

"Are they out there for a week?"

"Four nights," Brian said. He'd been roped into helping with the giant party.

"What in the world did they bring?" Kristine asked.

"Five mules alone were alcohol."

"You're shitting me."

"Watch your mouth, girl," Sol warned.

Kristine had to laugh. He could swear up a storm, but she was never allowed to follow suit. "What are you doing tomorrow? Going out of here? Should we put up your stock for the night, or is everything going back down to the Lodge?"

"Overnighter leaving out of the Lodge tomorrow. Leo said he'd be here with the stock truck."

"You want a beer while you wait?"

"Sure, he might be a while."

"Takeisha? Brian?"

"No. If it's all the same to you two, we were thinking of catching the shuttle down to the Lodge. We're hoping Frank's in to tell us more about the bear mauling."

"Bear mauling?"

"Gimme a beer. I'll fill you in." Sol waved Takeisha off.

Kristine brought two beers from the fridge, and Sol unfolded a couple of lawn chairs on the upper dock and lowered his crooked body into one. He took a long pull from the bottle before he leaned back. "We lost that Cisco horse down at Fish Creek."

"In all the years I've worked here, I've never heard of a bear mauling a horse," Kristine said.

"Weren't no bear mauling. Just Leo being stupid and listening to his pocketbook first. Sent that old horse down with some greenhorns. I bet you anything that's what killed 'im."

"And Frank gets to clean him up?" Kristine asked, wondering if Gloria was down with the crew. Even though the topic was gruesome, a flutter went through her stomach thinking about the night they had shared.

"The cleanup is sure to be the shits, but I'd sure take a dead horse over packing in assholes like today's group. It's a goddamned tailgate party up there."

"You said that Leo shouldn't be working with this group. What's that about," Kristine asked, settling in next to Sol.

"Last season, they had a trip out of the Lodge. Wanted a base camp out at Second Crossing."

"That's a long ride for a spot. I thought Leo only used that for travel trips."

"Like I said, Leo listens to his pocketbook. He'll agree to anything, even if the packer is riding home in the dark after supper. Didn't even make them change their plans when they rolled in late and had way more gear than they'd reserved mules for. It was late in the season. Everything was out except for the babies. Instead of telling those fools to cut back, he adds the two babies to the string. Barely got them out of the yard with them bucking off the loads.

"So they finally get on the trail. This packer named Pat's got the string. Heather's leading the guests. They're complaining the whole way about how their stuff's been treated, getting bucked off the mules, saying they should get a discount, bitching about the saddles, about that granite pass being dangerous. It's the backcountry, not a goddamned hotel.

"When they get to Second, Pat's ready to drop them at that nice camp right by the meadow, good fishing up and down the river. Great established camp. No. They want to be on the other side of the river. Heather says no. The river's too high. They go back to bitching about their 'experience' not being what Leo promised when they booked. Said Leo assured them a more private campsite off the main trail. Pat..." Sol shook his head. "He was new that summer, didn't know you can't cross anywhere near that camp. Just plunged right into the river."

"Gabe said the runoff was huge last year."

"Yup," Sol said. "Swept those mules right away. Panniers filled up with water and pulled them down."

"I never heard any of this. What did Pat do?"

"Tried cutting them apart to see if they could swim, but those damn bags were so heavy that they couldn't make it. Not one animal made it out of there. And you know what those goddamned people said?"

"Where's my stuff?"

"Where's my goddamned stuff. No sorry. Not one blink of the fine animals that got killed on account of their stupidity."

"I can't believe they're back this year," Kristine said, shocked.

"Free trip. Why do you think they brought so much crap? Leo's doing this for free because of what they lost." He spit in disgust. "They're trouble. Cursed. He should never have let them back in this valley."

"How do you get over losing your whole string like that? Those new babies, too."

"Oh, Pat didn't." Sol drained his beer. "Took off that night. Never saw him again." He stopped, looking pointedly at her. For a moment, she thought he'd ask, bring up the parallel, but he took a deep breath and continued. "Heather's back this year, but she's smart. Wouldn't have anything to do with this group. That's why Takeisha was up here today."

A few of the mules on the tie rail started braying. Kristine tipped her head back, looking up the trail. "Here comes Gabe."

Gabe came in with a string of two mules and four riders. A large black duffel rode across the horn of his saddle.

"Someone lost a top pack," he said, tossing the bag to his sister.

"Son'bitch," Sol grumbled. "I told you that group was trouble. Had to be one of Brian's loads. He was the last one out. If it had fallen after we passed the riders, they sure would have bitched about it right then. They're just waiting for us to make a mistake. I'm sure they'll start bitching about that the minute we get back in there to haul their asses out."

"I think there's an all-day ride scheduled out of here tomorrow," Kristine said. "If they're at Shadow fishing, the guide can swing it up to Rosalie pretty easily."

"I wouldn't touch that bag," Sol said. "Just leave it here for them. They've already gotten more than they deserve."

Kristine looked at Gabe. He rolled his eyes behind Sol's back and shrugged. Kristine tossed the bag into the pack saddle shed. The three shared stories on the dock until Nard pulled in with the stock truck.

"About time," Sol barked. "I was beginning to think you forgot about me over here."

"Dad's a little tied up with that bear lady. She's pretty worked up about that bear down at Fish Creek."

Kristine's ears pricked at the mention of Gloria, but she concentrated on loading Sol's mules into the truck.

"Jump in, Kristine. I'm sure you'd appreciate the show," Nard said.

"I've got plenty to keep me busy here, thanks."

"Hope that involves getting ready for the photography trip."

"I'm no cook. I told you that," Kristine said.

Nard pulled on his mustache, waiting longer than polite to answer her. "Maybe not. But you are a photographer."

"Nan's much better than I am."

His lascivious smile turned Kristine's stomach. "I told my dad how much you've been missing the backcountry and reminded him about that photography degree you've got. I thought he'd have told you, so you could start thinking about your lessons. Better get crackin'. We leave in four days."

Kristine almost asked when the trip was leaving and whether it left out of the Lodge or the Aspens. She stopped herself, kicking herself for automatically accepting his orders. She didn't have to go. He was messing with her.

"It's going to be like old times," he said, pulling himself into the cab and firing up the engine.

Kristine spun on her heel, overwhelmed. Her mind returned to the strategizing that had gotten her off Nard's Horse Heaven trip at the beginning of the season. Sending someone else wasn't going to work, not if he'd really canceled Nan. They had to have a photographer. She waved off invitations to join the crew for a campfire down at the Lodge. Gabe promised to join them but lingered, wanting to know what it was that wiped her smile off her face, asking what Nard had done to turn her mood so thoroughly. She studied his concerned eyes, on the verge of telling him why she dreaded working with Nard, but she knew he'd blow. She thought again about how angry he would be if he found out. The summer was almost over, and she thought there was a real possibility that she could finish up the season without confronting Nard. Proving to him and the whole crew that she was not a quitter would be enough to allow her to put it all behind her once and for all. Even though Gloria had argued that what had happened was serious, from the cowboys' perspective she knew it would seem like she had run away without reason.

Plus, when Gabe took over their father's ranch, he'd still have to work with Leo and Nard. She didn't want to jeopardize that working relationship. She waved him off with the rest of them, steeling herself for the trip ahead of her, seeing it as the real test of getting back on the horse, completing a trip in the backcountry without letting Nard scare her away. This trip would be the final proof of her strength.

CHAPTER TWENTY-TWO

Gloria's voice was already hoarse from trying to talk to Leo. She'd had to leave because she relied on the shuttle back to the outpost and knew the last one was about to leave the valley. She didn't want to be stuck at the Lodge, and she certainly couldn't bum a ride from any of the people she'd just been calling idiots for the last hour.

At the outpost stop, she tossed her backpack out of the shuttle, taking deep breaths, trying to calm down and convince herself to go all the way home. She could just walk past the Aspens and keep on going. She should cool down, sleep on the events of the day. She was in no shape to talk to Kristine. It wasn't her fault the horse was dead. She wasn't the one who booked these trips, made the choices. Her pack settled onto aching shoulders, she trudged down the road trying to ignore the outpost, thinking it better to get back, take a shower, and relax before she saw Kristine. However, Kristine stood at the corral watching the stock, one booted foot hitched up on the rail, the picture of cowgirl charm.

She stopped and closed her eyes, struggling to be rational. When she opened them, her eyes immediately found Kristine's. Wave and keep walking. Tell her you need to clean up, and you'll be back later. Something in Kristine's gaze kept her rooted. She must know already, she thought. In all the evenings she'd walked over from the campground, she'd never found her out at the corrals watching the stock.

"Hear you had a hell of a day," Kristine said, breaking the silence.

"You could say that."

"Hungry?"

"No. Actually, I'm not," Gloria responded crisply.

Kristine nodded. "Understandable after seeing Cisco out there like that. Want to talk about it?"

Did she want to talk about it, Gloria seethed. No, she didn't want to talk about it. She was finished talking. She wanted to do something about it. "I'm pretty pissed about it."

"Why don't you take that ridiculous thing off. You look like a pack mule standing there. Come on in. Have a beer, at least." Kristine walked to the road and held the pack. Gloria let her take the weight, slipping out of the shoulder straps.

"Heavy," Kristine observed.

"I thought I'd be down there a while, but with that carcass, there's no point in trying to do any conditioning with my bear." Once inside the cabin, she sat down and accepted the beer.

"Sol said he'd bet anything your bear didn't kill that horse."

Gloria couldn't help it, she exploded. "No, your idiot boss killed that horse, sending it down there without any kind of instruction. How can he be so stupid? How can you people take these idiots out into the backcountry, take in food no backpacker would ever carry and just offer it up to these animals. Do you bother telling them how to tie up their food? Do you do anything at all to try to maintain the wildlife?"

"Wait, wait, wait," Kristine said. "How is this about me?"

"You pack people in every day. How prepared are they to coexist with the wildlife when you leave."

Kristine looked like she was trying to choose the right words. "Leo made a bad call with Cisco. But I'm sure the packer who left him down there tried to teach them how to deal with him."

She'd been prepared for Juanita and Leo to disagree with her, but hearing Kristine defend her boss crushed her. "So it's their fault. Not your boss's."

"He always thinks about profit first. Hell, we used to joke that if he could get a saddle on a deer, he'd call it a mule and send it down the trail. He's running a business."

"I can't believe you're defending him. Don't you at least care about the horse?"

"You learn to not get attached to stock."

Gloria shoved her beer back into Kristine's hand and got up to leave. She'd heard enough.

"Where are you going?" Kristine said, setting both bottles down on the floor.

"I can't talk to you right now. I just spent an hour being ignored by Leo, and, I don't know, I thought maybe you would really listen to me. How is this not bothering you?"

"He keeps the Lodge going. He manages to care for all this stock, all of his employees. He's providing a service to people who wouldn't be able to see the backcountry if not by horseback."

"You ask about my bear research like you're interested in what I'm trying to do, yet you don't have any problem with how your boss works when he makes my job a hundred times harder."

"What happened down there wasn't the bear's deal," Kristine insisted. "Accidents happen, all part of the 'rugged backcountry experience.' They'll get it all cleaned up, and everything goes back to business as usual."

"It's negligent the way he sends these people out," Gloria shot back.

"Maybe the bears pay your paycheck, but they don't pay ours."

Gloria felt like she'd been sucker-punched. Her body radiated with heat she was so angry. "You don't care at all."

"Can you prove that what Leo's doing caused the mess down there?"

"What the hell do you think I'm trying to do here this summer?"

Kristine frowned. She looked at her, looked away, and then began laughing.

Gloria could not recognize the woman in front of her. "Do not laugh at me," she said, a hard edge in her voice.

Kristine quieted, and her expression grew serious. "Go to Rosalie Lake and check out the trip from hell that's camped there. If you've got a problem with what Leo allowed down at Fish Creek, what's going on up at Rosalie will make you shit yourself. I'm sure you'll find a dozen guys drunk off their asses paying no regard whatsoever to the backcountry."

By the time Kristine was finished relaying all the details Sol had given her, Gloria felt physically ill. She stood again, shaking. "How can you laugh? How can you sit there and do nothing?"

Kristine stood and walked to Gloria. She put her hand on Gloria's forearm. "I'm sorry. I know that it's the world to you. And believe me, I worried about it once. I used to fight them. I had all of these ideas. They dismissed every single one of my 'college' ideas. I stopped fighting, stopped trying. It's so much easier to just do my job."

Gloria pulled her arm away. She couldn't take it. Her intuition about needing to cool off had been right. Trying to talk to Kristine had just taken her beyond boiling. Without looking back, she picked up her pack, shrugged into it and walked out of the door. She was fired up enough that she actually considered walking past her camper and straight out to Rosalie. Exhaustion won that fight, however, and she stopped to sleep in her own bed. She left at first light, dressed in the same clothes she'd slept in and worn the day before.

CHAPTER TWENTY-THREE

Kristine expected to see Gloria a few days later at Rosalie on her way to pick up a trip due to come in from Gladys Lake. While they hiked home, she would pack in their camping equipment and remaining supplies on the mules. She only needed two mules for this, so she'd left the yard much more quickly than the team that was packing out the cursed group. She'd already passed her group hiking out, and was nearing Rosalie. Kristine was ready for Gloria's anger, but she was in no way prepared for the scene at the Rosalie camp.

The team coming to pick them up was at most an hour behind her, yet two campfires still burned, all of their tents were still assembled, and garbage lay strewn all over the camp. Although it wasn't her problem, she reined Digger in.

"Hello!" she hollered.

A scruffy face poked out of the nearest tent. "Is that all the mules you've got? They sent us in with a lot more."

"I'm not your packer. He's on his way, but I wanted to let you know, he's going to expect you packed up. You have a lot of work to do here."

The man surveyed the mess of food. "This isn't our fault. This huge-ass bear came through here and tore up all of our food."

"Well, you'll have to clean it up. Bulk up those campfires and burn it. When you drown the fire, you'll need to pull out the trash, but it'll be a lot easier to pack up than this is."

He emerged from the tent to face her. "Didn't you hear what I said? This isn't our fault. A grizzly bear did this. Let him come back and finish up."

"We only have black bear in the area."

"This bear was definitely not black. He was brown, and he's been in some fights. One of his ears is all messed up."

"Black bears can be brown in color. In any case, it's your responsibility to keep food away from all bears, although to a grizzly, you are the food." She smiled tightly. "You will have to dispose of this before your team will take you out."

"She's the one who allowed this to happen," the man said, jutting his chin past Kristine.

Kristine looked over her shoulder and found a very tired, very angry Gloria staring at her. Kristine's stomach clenched. The softness of their intimacy was long gone. At their last meeting, she'd responded to Gloria's rant poorly, having been in turmoil from Nard's bombshell. Gloria's anger still radiated from where she stood. Gloria's expression held her responsible for the mess because she had defended the work practices at the Lodge. She returned her head to her job. "More likely, she's the reason your tents aren't in shreds. No one leaves until this campsite is picked clean." Though she was curious about how the bear had managed to trash the site, she thought it best not to linger. She aimed an apologetic smile at Gloria and tipped her hips in the saddle, setting Digger's feet into motion.

She'd heard enough about this group to be grateful that she didn't have to spend the day working with them, and she'd already meddled enough in sending the duffel and Gloria their way. Her own work went smoothly at Gladys Lake, as she found her campers' gear neatly stacked by a campsite that showed no evidence of their stay, following the backcountry creed: Leave only footprints. She soon found herself heading back down the trail toward home. Stopping at Rosalie was nowhere on her agenda. Her own party was well on their way to the outpost and would be expecting her, but she couldn't help assessing the other team's progress as she rode back through. What she saw made her slam to a stop.

"You're not riding doubles on those horses," she shouted across the campsite.

Takeisha stepped away from the rider whose stirrups she'd been adjusting. In front of the rider sat a young boy.

"This is how we came up," she explained. "Both boys rode double with their dads."

Kristine clenched her jaw in anger. The boys were at least eight years old and certainly big enough to handle their own horses.

"Well, he's not riding home that way. Dad, you can walk and let your son ride. I'm sure he can handle Grumpy. But it's way too dangerous for you to go down the switchbacks like that."

"I'm riding. I didn't pay to have to hike," the man said.

You didn't pay at all, Kristine thought. Last year's mules, and your stupidity paid. Now you want to add more to your tab?

The man Kristine had spoken to earlier agreed. "We were fine on the way up, and I'm not letting my kid ride alone."

Kristine swore under her breath, trying to figure out how to talk some sense into the group.

Brian was mounted up with one string waiting, Beetle and Bailey full of their typical nervous energy at the back of the line.

"We've got this, Teeny," the new guy called.

Kristine gritted her teeth, wondering who she had to thank for that. Glancing in his direction, she saw that he already had most of his mules loaded and ready to go. He wore a gray felt hat so tall-domed that he had to have chosen it for the height he thought it added. She felt petty to let his appearance bother her but noted that he would have been better off getting his lift from some good cowboy boots instead of the soft-soled work boots he wore that were completely inappropriate for the saddle.

She swung off her horse and quickly tied him to a tree. "You have not got this," she growled. "I told you this morning those two babies need to be split up."

"Everything's fine, just fine," he insisted.

He sounded exactly like Nard. Steaming, she looked for help from Brian and Takeisha. Having worked with both before, she hoped they would listen to her. "Takeisha, you can't take doubles down that big switchback. Make someone walk, the dad, the kid. Make them both walk and loose herd them down, but don't let them go doubles. You're asking for trouble if you make them carry that much weight. And Brian, I'll take the babies. I've got a short string."

"They're good," he insisted, looking to the other packer. "The guests are already all worked up over their camp getting trashed. Just let us get them out. We've got this."

"And you are?" Kristine asked, pinching the bridge of her nose, feeling the frustration Gloria must have felt the last time they'd talked.

"Judd."

"I hope you're as right as you are stupid, Judd." As she walked back to her own horse, she stopped by the two men riding double with their boys. "Look, if I were on this team, you'd be walking out of here. Takeisha, here, is nicer than I am, so she's going to let you ride. But when you get to the end of Shadow, one of you walks down that staircase. You boys," she said to the little ones, "you're old enough to ride on your own, you hear? I want you to be safe, okay?"

Digger stood in his signature hole when she returned. She took her time kicking the dirt back into place, hoping that Brian would change his mind about his string. He didn't, so she swung aboard and spurred Digger down the trail, hoping to put a good distance between herself and the group. She let the horse have his head, enjoying the feel of him pounding down the trail. Smoke and Scooter kept up with him until the short stretch of granite trail along the tributary of Shadow Lake. Hearing the clatter of their hooves on the granite reminded her to take care and not be rash. She reined Digger in.

The quiet around Shadow did its trick again, smoothing out the anger she'd felt up at Rosalie. She recalled what she'd told Gloria, realizing that her argument about money holding the highest priority held true in this situation as well. Of course Leo would have the boys ride double. He wasn't making any money from this trip, and the two horses that should have been carrying the boys were for sure earning him money on another ride today. No use in letting her own blood boil over his business thinking. At the switchbacks, water roared past her on its way from Shadow Lake down into the canyon to join the San Joaquin. As she came to the end of the switchbacks, she glanced up over her shoulder wondering how far back Takeisha was with her riders.

Brian and his string of five mules were roughly two hundred feet up already halfway down the switchbacks, and Takeisha had just crested the top of the trail with her riders. Kristine took a deep breath, trying to control her anger at the sight of the doubles sitting atop their horses looking smug and entitled. She wished she was closer where she could yell at them to stop their foolishness, but now that they were on the rock face, there was no stopping, no getting off. The trail was too narrow.

Digger danced in place, anxious to keep moving, but Kristine kept him reined in, watching with dread. Her heart lurched as one of the horses tripped on the steep stairs. Even from a distance, Kristine could see how hard the little horse was working and how the rider was making his job harder. "Give him his head," she whispered to herself. Shouting would have done no good. The horse stumbled again and fell to its knees. The boy pitched forward on the horse's neck. "Give him his head and stay put. Stay put! Stay put!" she yelled in vain, hearing her father's voice telling her to never quit a wreck.

Struggling to regain his footing, the horse lurched forward, pitching the boy off onto the rocks. As his father attempted to dismount on the downhill side of the trail, his horse scrambled on the sharp rocks trying to keep his balance, but he lost his footing and pitched off the switchback, taking the rider with him.

Kristine leapt from her own saddle and began scaling the switchback, climbing from pass to pass like a ladder.

The horse rolled down a switchback, landing on the rider. She saw his momentum leaning for another roll. "Brian!" Kristine screamed. The cowboy whipped his head around to look above him as the horse rolled, losing his rider but continuing down the mountain. "Move, move, move!" she shouted as the horse tumbled right at Brian's string. But he was frozen, his mules all in a line on the trail when Grumpy smashed into them.

Tied together, the mules scrambled to take the impact of the horse, and Brian held tight to the rope he'd looped around his saddle horn.

"Let them go!" Kristine shouted. "Drop your lead! Drop your lead!" She pulled her knife out of her belt as she reached the mess of animals writhing frantically between levels of the trail. She sawed at the leads that connected them. As they came free and rolled, she prayed that they could find purchase on the trail and that they wouldn't reach her own stock. The third mule in line lay on the trail, and without the weight of the babies pulling from behind and below, stayed put. She cut his lead and swatted the second mule, hoping he and the first mule could make it back to the trail above where Brian sat, stunned.

"Dismount on the mountain side and leave your horse. See if you can get those two up onto the trail." She slipped on the rocks. On blood. She didn't know who was cut or how bad it was. She didn't know whether to pull packs off or try to get the animals to the trail with their loads still on. Below her, she saw gear. One of the baby's packs must have come undone on its own, littering the hillside. She continued scaling the mountain in between the switchbacks to reach the rider. He groaned, which was good. He wasn't dead. But bones poked through ripped jeans. Kristine stood stunned for a moment at a loss for what to do. They needed help. That was clear. She wasn't going to get this rider out on a horse. She hollered up the mountain, "How's the boy?"

"He's sitting up now," one of the riders answered. "But he's bleeding. Can we get down to help him?"

"I want off the horse," the boy's friend called from his perch in front of his father.

"Stay put!" Kristine ordered. She held up her hand, trying to think. "Not yet. It's too dangerous. Sit tight for a few minutes." She shut her eyes, sorting out all she needed to do and prioritizing it. The roar of the waterfall behind her did nothing to help her plan her next move. "Brian, you got those mules up?"

"They're on the trail, but their packs are falling off."

"Leave them. Cut the switchbacks down to my horse and ride like hell back to the Aspens. We're going to need a chopper for a busted leg and maybe a concussion."

"Got it," he hollered back.

"How far behind is your other string?" she asked Takeisha.

"He said he'd be another twenty getting the last mules ready to go."

"Do you have any emergency training?"

"No," Takeisha answered meekly.

"Okay. Who's got enough of a level spot to get off their horse safely?" she called up to the riders.

"I think I could get off," the rider at the turn of the switchback said.

Kristine went to his side and held the horse until he was off. "We need an emergency kit. I think Gloria, the woman who was lecturing you about bears, carries one. Head up to Shadow and tell the packer to get her here as quickly as he can." He carefully inched past the horses, stopping briefly to whisper something to the crying child on the rocks before he continued up the stairs. Kristine pointed his horse down the switchback and slapped him on the rump, making him skip a switchback. She led each of the other riders to the wide section of trail and helped them off. The riders rushed to the boy and his father.

"How bad is it?" one asked. "Is he going to die?"

"He's not going to die," Kristine said. She thought about what they needed to do for the injured as well as the stock. "We shouldn't move them, but it's likely to take a while to get help in here. Some of you stay here with them, keep them talking.

Takeisha, let's go try to round up the stock, and a few of you come with us to get some food and sleeping bags."

Two men quickly volunteered to go down the mountain and gather supplies from their bags. "Just tell us what to do. We want to help."

Now they're ready to listen, Kristine mused. "Yep, we've got this," she mumbled under her breath, leading the way down the trail.

CHAPTER TWENTY-FOUR

Gloria hadn't liked the situation at all down at Fish Creek with the bear scavenging a dead horse. As she had hiked the trail to Rosalie, she kept replaying the talk she'd tried to have with Kristine. At that point, the issue of balance had felt like the key point to her, and balance could be managed. Limit the number of trips taken into the backcountry or at least to certain sites. Control the amount of food brought in or packed in and require guests to use bear boxes. In Yosemite, her colleagues had made great progress with bear boxes in the areas most saturated with tourists. She knew they didn't solve all of the problems, but they at least acknowledged bears as the local wildlife, acknowledged that people had a part in their own safety.

But now here at Rosalie she had a problem much bigger than the one down at Fish Creek. This group had brought another issue to light. The group that Leo had packed in was a miserable mess of chaos and overkill. Their attitude appalled her. Not only did they ignore the way their presence attracted wildlife, they insisted that the wildlife was an inconvenience.

She'd highlighted Leo's part in that by packing people in with no limitations on what they brought with them. Campers like these contributed to the problem of balance by tempting bears with an easy meal, eventually making them reliant on a diet of human food and putting campers in real danger. Once food-conditioned, bears became territorial and confrontational, learning that humans were happy to drop and abandon their food when rushed.

She'd approached the Rosalie camp with all this in mind. When she'd reached the group, the long hike had tempered her anger. Though they reported no bear visits, she camped near them, expecting to be on duty during the night when their food supply would be more vulnerable to bears. However, she still kicked herself for taking a day hike to collect evidence of bear activity in the area. She had returned to a trashed camp.

The party said the old bear had lumbered in and had not responded to their efforts to scare it away. This alarmed Gloria. Wandering around during the day wasn't completely out of character when a bear was grazing on berries or even taking the opportunity to root around in an unsupervised campsite to bulk up on calories. But human presence should have acted as a deterrent. Even habituated to humans, unless someone was holding an item it had claimed as its own as a food-conditioned bear would, the bear should have had zero interest in the people and run when confronted. It troubled her enough that she decided to spend another day in the backcountry hoping that the bear would return.

Though the bear disappointed her, she'd been pleased to hear Kristine defend her and light a fire under the campers to clean up the area. The Kristine she'd stormed out on hadn't seemed to care about such things. She'd been the complete opposite of the indifferent woman who'd blown off her concerns. It occurred to her that the response that had pissed her off so much was the one out of character, yet she had been too upset to discuss it with Kristine. Chagrined, she knew she owed Kristine an apology. Unfortunately, she had no time for that now. After the group finally left to return to the Lodge, she packed up her things, stringing up her large backpack from a tree limb out of reach of bears. She only needed her daypack with her while she hiked around the area to talk to other campers and see if they had encountered the animal. If there were other reports of such aggressive, atypical behavior, she'd need to talk to Scott about the possibility of relocation for the animal.

She'd been on the trail about a half hour, stopping to question the campers along the way, when she heard thunderous hoofbeats approaching. She couldn't remember hearing an animal moving on the trail so quickly and stepped off it to avoid a collision. The rider, one of the men from the team that packed the group from hell out that morning, slid to a stop in front of her.

"Gloria?" he asked.

"Yes," she answered, confused.

"We've got a situation on the switchback below Shadow. Some riders went down. They sent someone up saying they need first aid. Teeny thought you might have a first-aid kit."

"How serious is it?"

"Don't know. The guy said a kid took a tumble, and his dad's got a nasty fracture."

Gloria quickly shrugged out of her pack and pulled out her radio. "Glad I've been lugging this around," she said, hoping Scott was right about the radio being able to bounce off a repeater and reach the office in Mammoth. "Scott, it's Gloria," she said, relieved when he answered. "There's an accident on the switchbacks below Shadow. All I've got right now is possible concussion and a fractured leg."

"Any idea how bad the break is?" he asked.

"No. The rider from the Lodge who found me was already relaying a message."

"How long until you can assess yourself?"

"I'm probably..." She directed her question to the rider. "How long till we can get to them?"

"Twenty, thirty minutes."

"I'm a half hour from the scene," Gloria said.

"I'm going to go ahead and radio for a chopper, but update me once you're there."

"Absolutely."

"I'm Judd," the cowboy said. "Hop aboard. I'll get you down there in no time."

Gloria stared at him. "It sounds like that's the thinking that got everyone into this mess."

"Look, ma'am. I'm a professional. I can get you there safely and in half the time."

She would have trusted Kristine's word more, but Kristine wasn't in front of her. Judd was. She stowed the radio back into her daypack. Judd hung the backpack from the horn of his saddle, gave her his left stirrup and showed her how to link her elbow through his to swing aboard. As soon as she had her arms around his waist, they were moving down the trail.

Her mind jumped back four years, hearing her father's voice full of fear, urging her to come home as soon as possible. Her mother was in the hospital with complications from her last treatment. He'd called Gloria in Tennessee where she had picked up a research opportunity in the Smoky Mountains. Hours had already passed when she returned to her camper to find the message. All of the unknowns had crunched her stomach into a knot as she put herself into motion to get home. She'd worried the entire time that she wouldn't make it. The drive to the airport, the flight, getting a car to make it home…she was suspended in time, as she was now on the trail, at the mercy of the transportation to deliver her but void of control of the situation, at the mercy of what she would find when she arrived. That trip had indirectly brought her here to the High Sierras. The thought of arriving home to find her mother already gone drove her to select her next projects more conservatively.

Judd let her off at the crest of the waterfall. Running down the switchback stairs, she quickly spotted the fallen riders. Her brain tried to unscramble the words she heard them hollering. Then she realized they were not calling her. They were letting Kristine know she'd arrived.

Gloria reached the boy first. He sat in another rider's lap resting against the man's chest.

"I hope it's okay that we moved him. He seems mostly scared. I couldn't let him sit on the rocks any longer."

"Should be fine. What's your name?" She asked the shaggy-haired boy. He grimaced, and his recently-cut adult teeth that pinched his lower lip accentuated how small his face was.

"Sammy. I want to see my dad. They won't let me go see my dad."

"It's important we know you're okay first. Can you follow my finger?" she asked, moving it from side to side in front of him. His eyes tracked her finger, and his pupils dilated. She felt his hands and asked the man holding him to lift the shirt that he held to the boy's head. Blood matted the boy's head but the pressure seemed to have stopped active bleeding. "Looks like they've taken really good care of you. Now let me check on your dad, okay? Sit tight for just a minute longer."

She found Kristine standing on the trail. Those eyes catching her off guard again. No matter what her expression, Kristine always managed to give Gloria pause. Gone were the indifference, anger and hesitation. The woman looking at her was fully in her element, calm and in control.

"We did okay by him?" Kristine's eyes darted to the boy.

"Yes, he'll be fine. His father's in worse shape?"

"That's where we need your help. He was bleeding pretty badly out of his thigh. I've got his buddy applying pressure up in his groin. I'm so glad you got here as fast as you did." Kristine cut the switchback, and Gloria did the same.

"Good chance he's in shock," Gloria said, settling next to him, taking in his pale coloring. "Smart to cover up the wound. What did it look like before you started applying pressure?"

"Like I said, he was bleeding. I saw bone but still figured we needed to try to stop the blood loss."

"Are we talking bright red spurting blood or darker, seeping blood?" Gloria asked quietly.

"I'd say seeping."

"Let's have a look, then." She nodded at the man applying pressure, and he sat back, giving Gloria access. As she peeled away the towel, her patient wailed in pain. She placed a hand on his shoulder. "I know it hurts, but I've got to have a look before I radio the Forest Service." She nodded as she examined the wound. "Well, the good news is the blood isn't from a major artery, so we'll just need to stabilize the leg to travel."

"What do you need?" Kristine asked. "A belt? Boards?"

"Let me call Scott and see what the EMTs recommend doing. For now, keeping him still should be enough."

"Could we move his son down here? They've both been asking to see the other."

"The boy can come down here for the time being." Instead of calling to one of the guests, Kristine cut the switchback again, climbing to the boy. Gloria saw another side of Kristine as she bent over him. He listened attentively to whatever it was she said, nodding in agreement when she sat back with her hand on his shoulder. She swept him up in her arms and carried him down the trail, setting him gently by his father who immediately wrapped his arms around his boy.

Her eyes went to the father and son and then returned to Kristine. "You're good with kids. What were you saying to him?"

"Just some stuff about helping his dad out."

Knowing how upset Kristine had been with the party, Gloria was surprised by the gestures that went beyond managing the crisis. Kristine's tenderness made Gloria want to wrap her arms around her. However, she reminded herself that they were professionals and there were still a lot of things to address before they could evacuate.

"The boy'll be okay to ride, won't he?" Kristine asked.

"I expect so. My guess is that they won't take him out by air," Gloria answered.

"You know what they say about getting back on the horse."

"Why do you cowboys make such a big deal out of that, anyway?"

"Keeps him from associating riding with falling. Always stop on the positive."

Gloria saw Kristine retreat into the thoughts that so often distracted her and realized that she was probably thinking about how she'd left the Lodge on a negative. She wanted to ask about it, but Kristine had already pushed the thought away, telling Gloria to let her know when the boy was ready to travel, her mind back on the task at hand.

Gloria nodded, and as she put in the call to Scott, she watched Kristine coordinate a crew to gather the dunnage spilled in the fall. She admired how Kristine controlled the scene and knew that her calm had been a big part of managing what could have been chaos. That she did so without letting the past distract her impressed her even more.

"You two work together a lot?" the wounded man's friend asked when Gloria ended the call.

"No. We've crossed paths a few times this summer, but we're not colleagues."

He looked puzzled. "The way you work together, it seems like you've done this before."

Gloria smiled. "I'm just following Kristine's lead like the rest of you."

"Well, we would have been sunk without you two." He nodded from Gloria to Kristine, who stood catching her breath from hiking back up the trail.

"Do we need boards to make a brace?"

"No. Scott says we don't want to risk nicking the femoral artery, so we'll just bind the broken leg to the good to keep it stable. A few belts will do the trick."

"You heard her. We need some belts here," Kristine said with authority. Gloria enjoyed watching the guests scramble to comply.

Gloria accepted the belts and snugly bound the legs just above and below the protruding bone.

"Can I snag some of your gauze?" Kristine asked when she'd finished. "One of the mules has a nasty gash I need to wrap before he can travel."

"Make sure the injured guy stays still. Give a holler if the wound starts bleeding again or he passes out." Standing, she said to Kristine, "Let's see how good I am at doctoring a mule."

"Thank you for helping us out," Kristine said when they reached the stock. "The way you talked about the Lodge before, I wasn't sure…"

Gloria waved off Kristine's thanks.

"What?" Kristine asked.

"You're here," she pointed out. "What makes any part of this mess your deal?"

"I'm just doing what needs to be done," Kristine answered.

"Cleaning up a mess very similar to Fish Creek?" Gloria ventured.

Kristine ducked her head, the brim of her hat hiding her face. "I'm surprised you weren't ahead of the party this morning on your way to chew Leo out again."

"Good thing I wasn't ahead of you."

"And now you've got more to add to the mile-long list you had this morning," Kristine tossed over her shoulder as she tromped down the trail.

"That so?" Gloria smirked, trailing the clink of Kristine's spurs. She wondered what Kristine would think of her original litany of worries about the bear. Though the accident had taken precedence, that problem still weighed heavily. She had been planning what to say to Leo, and thought again about how much Kristine's blowing her off had bothered her. She'd anticipated Leo's response but had thought she would have had Kristine's support.

"That's so," Kristine said. She met Gloria's eyes. The challenge she'd had when they'd spoken about Fish Creek two nights ago was gone. Gloria hadn't even felt like Kristine had seen her during that conversation. This time, Gloria's body flushed hot under the intense stare. "And this time, I've got a few things to add."

Gloria read so many things in Kristine's eyes, apology, anger and frustration. But now she knew that they were on the same side, angry for the same reason. "It's a good thing you sent me out, though."

"Lucky," Kristine said, continuing down the hill.

Gloria considered her words. It didn't feel like luck. It felt like fate. Fear for her mother had brought her back to California. But fear of death had kept her away from home. Anger at Leo and Kristine had pushed her away from them into the backcountry. And now she followed Kristine, unable to peel her eyes away from the way Kristine's chaps highlighted her ass.

After a few steps, Kristine stopped and swung about, catching Gloria midstare. Her eyes twinkled in response. "What's the holdup?"

"You," Gloria said. "I'm sorry I took my frustration out on you."

"Oh." Kristine looked down the trail and then back to Gloria. She smiled. "You can make it up to me when we get home tonight."

Gloria liked the sound of that very much.

CHAPTER TWENTY-FIVE

Kristine stood in the stirrups and craned her neck around to see if she could spot the chopper coming into the valley. Not wanting to risk spooked stock on top of all of the other excitement of the day, she'd left with her mules after Gloria had helped her bandage Ramsey's leg. Judd was on his own for the cleanup but lucky to have only the big mess and no casualties to manage. She was happy to leave it all behind. She should have been fuming about the accident. She should have been worrying about her upcoming trip with Nard.

Instead, her thoughts were full of Gloria. She admired her skill and had found it difficult to pull herself away from watching her confident hands moving over the rider's body to assess any damage. Her own body responded to the memory. They'd been professional, and as that guest said, they made a great team. She was one who usually preferred to work alone, typically finding that people got in her way. Yet Gloria didn't get in her way. They had worked together instinctively. Kristine flushed hot remembering just how well they'd worked together in the cabin…

Instead of leaning on her when her old fears returned, Kristine realized that she had pushed Gloria away, regressing to her I-have-to-tackle-this-on-my-own mentality. The irony suddenly hit her. She trusted Gloria enough to share her past but not enough to risk her future. Their night together was far beyond casual, and that scared Kristine. She didn't know what the end of the summer meant for Gloria. Instead of risking that discussion, she created a distance at the first opportunity. That way she didn't need to acknowledge her own fear, something she'd have to fess up to Gloria when she came back in.

While she waited, she put up her stock. Since she didn't want to miss Gloria, she couldn't head down to the Lodge to do proper laundry. Instead, she dragged a pile of dirty jeans to the porch and began thwacking them against the railing to see if any could be salvaged.

"What in the world are you doing?" Gloria asked, appearing as Kristine started in on the third pair.

"Laundry," Kristine said simply.

Gloria's wonderful laughter filled the yard. Kristine had missed that laugh when Gloria was out in the backcountry, undoubtedly stewing about how insensitive Kristine had been. "You know they have machines for that. Water. Soap."

"That's not very Western. We aim for authentic around here." Kristine beat the pair of jeans in her hands against the railing a few more times, held them up, nodded and folded them to add to her pile. "That'll do."

"You're a puzzle, you know that?" Gloria said, her head cocked to the side studying Kristine.

"That sounds like a bad thing."

"Who is the authentic Kristine?" she asked, her eyes searching. "I don't know that I've seen her."

At first Gloria's words seemed confrontational. Kristine felt like marching into the cabin, but she could hear that the words were not delivered with malice, just confusion. She fought the urge to run. She recognized that it was Gloria who had remained steady throughout the summer while, true to her form, Kristine had swung wildly from flirtatious to detached, from confident to unsure. She took her time gathering the jeans to take inside, feeling Gloria behind her. She shut the door gently, and Kristine could see how tired she was. The long day they'd shared had shaved off some of the radiance Gloria usually brought to a room.

Tentatively, Kristine set down her clothes and crossed the room to wrap her arms around Gloria. "I have to be honest with you. I don't know that I know the answer to that question. I'm kind of working on it."

"That confident woman on the mountain, the one who backed me up. I'd like to believe that's the authentic Kristine."

Kristine smiled and ran her fingers down Gloria's neck, cupping her hand around her face. "Believe me, I'm trying to stick with that one." Her hand slipped down Gloria's shoulder and arm and intertwined with her fingers. "You look like you could use a shower and food."

Gloria simply nodded, so Kristine pushed her toward the bathroom, leaving her to undress while she found clean clothes for her.

When she stepped back into the steamy bathroom, she could see Gloria's naked form silhouetted behind the glass door. One thing she knew for certain: she wanted Gloria. Quickly, she stripped and slipped into the shower. She took in the beautiful, toned body that stood before her, water running off Gloria's nipples, cascading down to the blond thatch between her legs. Gloria pulled her head from the stream of water. Her eyes were waiting for Kristine's when she made her way back up the tour of her body. She handed the bar of soap to Kristine, increasing the heat Kristine felt stepping into the shower.

Gloria turned, covering her chest with her hands, tucking her chin over her shoulder to block the hot spray of the shower as Kristine lathered the soap. Her hands traveled freely over Gloria's shoulders, back and hips. She pulled Gloria's hips back into her own, her body warming in response to the moan that escaped Gloria's throat. Gloria lowered her hands, reaching behind her to pull Kristine closer. Kristine took advantage, running her hands around Gloria's hips, up her belly and over her breasts, loving how Gloria arched into the cups of her hands.

The rise and fall of Gloria's chest matched Kristine's own. Gloria reached out to brace herself between the walls of the shower, her head bent forward in the spray of the shower.

Kristine sputtered when Gloria tilted her head, spray hitting her directly in the face. Gloria spun around. "I'm so sorry!" she said, wiping water from Kristine's face.

They laughed together and circled to let water rinse soap and weariness away. "I have to admit that I've never gotten very far in a shower," Kristine said, kissing her way around Gloria's collarbone, reaching around her to shut off the water.

"Me neither." Gloria closed her eyes, as Kristine's hands traced the droplets of water cascading down her body.

They grabbed towels, drying off enough to tumble into bed, so they could get wet again in different and wonderful places.

* * *

Later, Gloria lay with Kristine's naked form draped over her belly and legs. "I don't want to move, but I'm hungry."

"I don't know if we have any food," Kristine said. "Good in that it got Gabe out of the house…"

Gloria swatted her playfully. "I don't care if it's PB&J. I need some sustenance."

Kristine rolled out of bed, grabbing clean tees and sweats for both of them. They scrounged together soup and grilled cheese sandwiches. Though clothed, they touched frequently in the small space of the kitchen. Each time she felt Gloria's hand at her waist or brush past her butt, she again felt the energy of their connection surge.

"You're never getting food if you keep that up," Kristine said.

"What," Gloria asked, running her hand along Kristine's ass again, "I thought it was important to let you know I was behind you, so you wouldn't kick me."

"Ah, so you do think I'm an ass." Kristine had meant it as a joke, but she could tell that her words had taken both of them back to the last time they'd stood in this kitchen, fighting instead of touching.

"I am sorry I took out my frustration on you."

Kristine carried their food to the table. She paused before sitting. "No. I'm sorry. I was awful to you because of this photography trip."

"Trip?" Gloria stepped closer to Kristine, taking her hand.

"I'd just found out that Nard put me on his photography trip. Five days, four nights."

"No. Since when?"

Kristine couldn't meet her eyes. "Since you were down at Fish Creek."

"And when does it leave?" Gloria insisted.

Kristine sat and bit into her sandwich, instantly regretting it because her suddenly dry mouth made it hard to chew.

Gloria sat next to her. "Tomorrow morning? That's why you were doing laundry before?" Kristine nodded.

"Well that explains a lot. I wish you'd told me."

"Kind of hard to get a word in edgewise."

Gloria shot her a penetrating look. "You still could have shared that with me."

"I know." Kristine's mind spun. She considered telling Gloria it just wasn't her instinct to reach out when she got scared. Instinct told her to protect herself, and she'd felt particularly vulnerable. She knew, though, that Gloria would have argued that was all the more reason to tell her, to let her help or at least offer support. Kristine blew out a breath, feeling lost. "I don't have a lot of practice telling people stuff like that."

Gloria traced the back of Kristine's hand. "Maybe that's something we could work on."

Kristine smiled and tipped her hand over to hold Gloria's. "That's fair. As long as we can work on other stuff, too." She arched an eyebrow.

"Food. Quit trying to distract me." Gloria's expression had finally softened. She spooned up some soup. "So where will you be for this photography trip?"

"Starts out at Rosalie. We'll base camp there for a few days and then head across to Thousand." Having just cleared the air, Kristine was surprised when Gloria's spoon reversed direction and plopped back in the bowl. "What?"

"Can you start out at Thousand and go somewhere else?"

"What's wrong with Rosalie?"

"I have a really bad feeling about that bear up there. After you left, I talked about it with Rick. He's had some experience with the bear in past seasons, but this season his behavior has changed, dramatically in the past few days. He recalled a hiker talking about a weasel acting weird. He's going to see if he can track down which report it's in for me."

"Why do you care about a weasel acting funny?"

"What we're looking at doesn't sound like a food-conditioned bear. It sounds like a rabid bear. And if that's the case, I'd have to prove myself wrong before another big party enters his territory."

"Bears get rabies?" Kristine asked, not wanting to argue but also shocked. When she'd been in the valley last, no one was even talking about food-conditioned bears, much less sick ones.

"Not very often, in fact it's quite rare, but I'd be negligent if I didn't issue a warning and follow through on my analysis."

Kristine wondered if she was being more cautious than she needed to be because of the Fish Creek bear that had been attracted to the campsite by the dead horse.

"You think I'm crazy," Gloria said, breaking the extended silence.

"I think it wouldn't hurt to talk to Leo tomorrow morning." She held Gloria's eyes. "I doubt he'll move the trip on such short notice, but at least you'll have someone there who's backing you up."

"I like it better when you're on my side."

"Sorry that was in question before," Kristine said, and she meant it.

CHAPTER TWENTY-SIX

A few of the Lodge employees acknowledged Gloria when she stepped into the employee dining room, but she didn't see Leo. She'd headed over first thing to see if she could convince him to redirect his trip.

Nard stood with his plate and coffee cup and glanced out the window. "Teeny with you?"

"She let me borrow her truck. I'm looking for Leo."

Nard swigged the last of his coffee and appraised her, his lips pursed under his scraggly mustache. Gloria met his gaze and did not blush or offer any explanation. He gave up the glaring contest first, sucking some of his breakfast from in between his teeth.

"Dad's up at the corrals. Dude animals are out of water."

Gloria thanked him and strode up to the corrals, locating Leo easily with his grunts and mumblings. He wore his typical plaid shirt, jeans and suspenders, though the suspenders had lost the fight to keep his jeans up over his rear. Gloria cleared her throat.

Leo rocked back onto his heels next to the trench he'd dug, wiping sweat off his forehead with the back of a grimy hand. "Miss Fisher. Does Sacramento back up your assessment that I'm causing in the backcountry?"

"I've only had the chance to check in with my boss in Ontario who was going to contact the Director in Sacramento. I haven't had a chance to hear what he said yet about the Fish Creek problem, sir. I've been up at Rosalie Lake. I'm sure you heard about the bear up there?" She hoped her tone conveyed that the number of incidents involving bear and human contact alone suggested that he should listen to her.

"Oh, yeah. Heard all about the mess it made before my guys got in there to pack them out."

"Two encounters with two different bears in less than a week warrant a re-evaluation of your policy to pack whatever a client wants into the backcountry."

"They know they're headed into the wilderness. What they choose to bring is their business. Far as I know, backpackers have that same right."

But backpackers actually have to carry what they take in, which gives them the common sense that many of the Lodge clients lacked, she thought. That lack of common sense raised her ire when she was in Fish Creek. It was certainly magnified by the Rosalie trip he'd allowed. However, that wasn't why she was standing in front of him now. "Unfortunately, what a group takes into the backcountry isn't my only concern anymore. I didn't have a lot of time up at Rosalie, but I have talked to the ranger in that area, and we are both worried about that animal. We cannot ignore his unnatural behavior at the campsite."

"Isn't this where you get your rubber bullets out? Give him a good spanking?"

"That might work if the bear were merely habituated or food-conditioned. In those cases, the precautionary measures I discussed at the beginning of the season might be effective. We fear, though, that this bear is no longer sane."

"You're suggesting the bear is crazy?" He did not bother to stop his work as she talked.

"Sir, food conditioning happens with exposure and opportunity. Nothing in the ranger's reports indicates that the bear has been taking advantage of humans for food this season."

"You see how much crap that group hauled in, and how bad they were at securing it? My bet is that's what attracted the bear."

"Yes, but if that were the case, the campers should have been able to scare him off easily. I'd like some time to study the animal before you put more parties in the area. The ranger and I suspect that the animal may be rabid," she said frankly.

Leo finally paused and tipped his battered straw hat back on his head. "Never heard of no rabid bear. I've worked down here just about my whole life."

"It's not common for an animal that large to contract rabies, but it's not undocumented."

"How many?"

"None documented in California, but nearly a dozen in North America."

"None in California," he repeated, turning back to his tools.

"You already have the incident with another bear down at Fish Creek. The horse carcass is likely to be pretty attractive to bears for some time. Juanita assured me that she would be warning campers to avoid that area for weeks, and I would hope that your staff isn't dropping any other campers there. I'm asking that you do the same with the bear at Rosalie. At best, he's food-conditioned which already presents a risk to your guests. At worst, he's sick and dangerous. The Rosalie bear disturbs me much more than the scavenger down at Fish Creek."

"Then feel free to keep an eye on it. But that's your deal. Mine is keeping this place going, and I trust my staff to keep food away from all the animals they encounter." He loosened a screw and pulled the line apart. Water sputtered from the pipe above. "Here's our problem. Damn pumice gums up the works." He fiddled with the screwdriver and blew through the lower part of the tube a few times. When he hooked it back up again, water sputtered into the bathtub.

Gloria wasn't to be dismissed so easily. "Sir, there are three stages of rabies. Prodromal comes with behavioral changes and lasts anywhere from one to three days. What happened out at Rosalie three days ago qualifies as behavioral changes. I'd guess he's moving to the next stage, the excited, or since we're talking a large animal, the furious stage. You're sending a trip back into the area at the very time this animal is most likely to have increased activity, and more importantly, no fear of its natural predators. It's already demonstrated some of that. The next encounter that animal has with a person could turn deadly."

"You said three stages."

"The last is paralytic. That's when you'll see the frothing associated with a rabid animal."

"And the timeline?"

"Sometimes a week for the second stage. Once they hit the third, they usually die fairly quickly, within a matter of hours."

"You're asking me to keep trips out of there for a week?"

Gloria felt a glimmer of hope. Leo had stopped working and had been listening to what she'd said. She wanted to say at least a week, but she didn't want to push her luck. "A week, yes."

Leo set down the tools and rose to his feet awkwardly. He kicked pumice back over his lines to bury them and wiped his hands on a bandana. "I've got a lot of trips going out. Don't know where else I'd send that photography trip. If you're worried, you're free to keep an eye out."

"There's no way for me to police his entire territory. My last trip out, I wasn't able to locate a den."

Leo shrugged. "Maybe Scott has some manpower. I'll make sure Nard is aware of your concern."

He limped back to the tool shed, dismissing Gloria and raising her ire. She already knew Scott had no other rangers to send up to the Shadow area. Nothing to lose, she flipped open her phone. Grateful she had signal, she called the Ontario office hoping to catch someone working early. She met less resistance than Leo had given her, but the same conclusion. There wasn't enough evidence to force Leo to change his plans, or mobilize a bear hunt. She got the bureaucratic response of their being happy with her reports and trusting that she could handle the situation. Snapping the phone shut and grumbling about the lack of help, she headed back to the Aspens.

Driving back, she remembered Kristine's assessment that the fiasco at Fish Creek had stemmed from the way Leo prioritized money above reason. Leo made decisions in his office without thinking about how they would play out in the backcountry. She felt that same kind of disconnect herself, unable to understand why those in control refused to listen to the people in the field. She was the one putting herself in danger. She was the one immediately assessing the situation, yet from their office everything looked fine. They were impressed with the data she had gathered and it would be "very helpful" when considering the effect humans had on bear activity, blah blah blah. But when presented with something outside of routine information, when asked to take action or change policy, well, sorry. Keep an eye on things, and we'll get back to you.

Kristine had argued that all decisions tied back to money and resources, and she knew how thinly stretched state resources were and just how low they registered on priority for funds. What would it take for her bosses to register the changing dynamics of the backcountry and do something about it? A bear mauling? She grimaced. One injured rider hadn't changed Leo's policy on riding double, something that clearly upset Kristine. Would one person injured by a bear even register in Sacramento?

She needed people to hear and understand what was happening. The research she was doing needed to be put to use, not simply stamped and filed. It was easier to change the behavior of those who stayed in the campgrounds with hosts who could monitor how they stowed their food. She'd discovered just how hard it was to manage what people took into the backcountry and how they kept it from the wildlife, especially in the case of the guests the outfit simply dropped off without guides.

If she were in charge… She pulled up at the outpost. Now there was an idea. If she were in charge, she'd remember to listen closely to the people in the field, not just politicians and money.

CHAPTER TWENTY-SEVEN

Kristine sat with her back pressed against a Jeffrey pine enjoying her lunch with Shadow Lake a picture in front of her. The forested area that surrounded the lake provided a quiet like nowhere else in the backcountry. Across the lake, the jagged mountain range of the Minarets juxtaposed the deep blue calm of the water's surface. Her guests were scattered around the lake, their assignment to "capture the tranquility." Kristine would introduce various techniques later. Though she had spent the last three nights preparing lessons for them on nature photography, what they brought back to her after this first stop would give her a good idea of their skills base.

One of the pale Midwestern brothers approached her hesitantly.

"What's up, Gary?" she asked the heavier-set of the two.

"I didn't want to bother you on your break."

"It's no bother. Did you run into trouble?" She waved him over and invited him to sit.

"I did, actually," he said, lowering himself down. "Oh. This feels so good I may never get up again."

Kristine laughed. "Takes a while to get used to being on horseback. About the time you get stretched out, we'll be home."

"You're not afraid to tell the truth." Gary smiled.

Kristine paused for a moment thinking of the many truths she had kept to herself. She thought of the rock she'd thrown in Rosalie Lake at the beginning of the summer, how it had broken the surface of the water. She needed to reveal these truths, and they would cause their own ripples. More like waves in this case… She brought herself back to the moment, jutting her chin toward Gary's camera. "What've you got?"

"I'm trying to get the creek up here feeding into the lake. I want the water to blur out, so I'm using a slow shutter speed, but instead of the water having that…that…"

"Feeling of motion?"

"Yes, exactly. Instead of that, the whole frame is blurry."

"You're using a tripod?"

"Of course," Gary said.

"How are you releasing the shutter?"

He blinked at her and held up a finger.

"There's your problem. You can't get away from the camera fast enough to avoid blurring the image. Do you have a shutter release cable?"

"I didn't bring one." He scratched the back of his head looking chastised.

"No problem. The way around that is to set up a timer on the camera. That way, by the time the shutter releases, you're not disturbing the frame."

Gary's eyes lit up. "Fantastic! I'm going to go try that out. I have time, I hope?"

"We've got wagons of time," Kristine answered, happy she'd been able to tackle her first question so easily.

"You're a good teacher."

Gloria's voice surprised Kristine. She scrambled to her feet, finding Gloria standing just off the trail. She'd been so absorbed talking to Gary that she hadn't even seen her approach, and she blended into the scene in her green and tan uniform. Her face was flushed from the exertion of the hike, and the pink on her cheeks under her ball cap instantly recalled for Kristine how beautiful she looked post-orgasm, splayed next to her in bed. Her own cheeks flushed red, so she tried to redirect her thoughts. "I wondered if you'd catch us during lunch."

"When you said you were stopping at Shadow, I took that as a challenge." She shrugged out of her pack and leaned it against a tree before hiking up to where Kristine had been lunching. They sat together in silence for a few minutes, Gloria with a sly smile perched on her lips.

"What are you smiling at?" Kristine finally asked, bumping her shoulder.

"I thought you were sexy in those short cowboy chaps you wear…"

"Chinks," Kristine said.

"Yeah, I thought you were sexy in your chinks, but that's nothing compared to hearing you give a photography lesson."

Kristine wrinkled her brow, puzzled.

"I think I need a private lesson on release."

The blush she'd been fighting to hide flushed crimson. "I don't think you need any help there, if I recall correctly," she whispered.

"Don't go hiding behind your hat," Gloria said.

"Yes, ma'am," Kristine answered, bringing her eyes back to Gloria's.

"For someone so tough, you sure blush easily."

"I'm not so tough." Kristine studied Gloria, loving how the lake and the sky made her eyes all the more blue. Too tempted to resist, she leaned over and kissed her quickly. She pulled away and slid back into professional mode, scanning the area for her students. "Want my apple or cookie?"

"Apple," Gloria said, accepting the food as well as the segue. "How's your trip shaping up?"

"It's going to be a long one. I don't know where Leo found this woman, Trish, to cook. Her jeans go so high-water when she's in the saddle that they show off all of her hiking boot. Hiking boots on a horse," she said, disgusted. "This morning I wanted to talk to the group about what equipment they'd want to pack in their saddlebags, so I thought she could get the horses ready for the trail. I said, 'You might want to check cinches before we get back.' She gave me this blank look and said, 'Sure. Just tell me which one is Cinches, and I'll check 'im.'"

"You're making that up."

"I wish I was. After our first rest, she asked me if I could make the thingies her feet were in shorter. Shouldn't an employee know what a stirrup is? I don't know what they'd have done if Nan was with them. She didn't know anything about stock." She wished that talking about her job would get her brain to stop thinking about how much she wanted to kiss Gloria again. Gloria wasn't helping at all. As she listened, her eyes kept drifting down to Kristine's lips, increasing Kristine's desire to lower Gloria back onto the soft bed of pine needles where…

"Daggummit!" Nard's annoyed voice rang through the trees. "Teeny! Where the hell are you?"

Kristine shot an apologetic look at Gloria as she stood.

"It's okay," Gloria said. "I'll catch up with you guys at the campsite. Thanks for the fruit."

Her expression suggested it was the kiss, not the apple she was thinking about, making it even harder for Kristine to answer Nard's page.

"Teeny!"

Reluctantly, Kristine waved goodbye and jogged down the trail to see what had him so worked up. "Up here," she shouted once she hit the trail.

"What the hell? Why are you all the way over here and not with the stock?"

"I've got my students," she said, exasperated. He never would have expected Nan to do more than ride her horse. Since she was already annoyed, Kristine took the opportunity to share her displeasure of the cook they had hired. "I left Trish with the stock. After I showed her how to tie them up since she was just tying a square knot at the base of a tree…"

"Well she's not with the stock, and that Lumpy horse you insisted on bringing is kicking the shit out of whatever it is you're riding." He looked pointedly from Kristine up the hill to Gloria. "Sorry to interrupt…"

"When my students are finished with this lesson we'll be along." She wanted to redirect his attention.

"There's no crazy bear up here at all, is there? That was just something the bear lady spun for my dad, so you two could have a backcountry lovefest?"

"You might want to give listening to what she's got to say a try. She's out here because she's worried we're putting people at risk. For starters, we could camp at Gladys instead of Rosalie. These riders could easily go the extra distance today."

"No go. It'll mess up our travel day and layover. We camp at Rosalie."

"You're the boss," she said, hoping her tone wouldn't goad him, not liking the look on his face when she said it.

As she figured, when she and her students returned to the horses, they were fine. Proud that she hadn't bent to Nard's goading, she did consider being more careful about the direction her thoughts so easily traveled. She didn't regret that things with Gloria had progressed, but she reminded herself that now more than ever she needed to concern herself with Nard who felt like the real backcountry threat.

CHAPTER TWENTY-EIGHT

Gloria spent the day hiking out from the campsite the Lodge always used by Rosalie Lake trying to determine what direction the bear had headed after trashing the camp. She radioed Rick and was glad that he said he'd stop to check in with her after he was finished up at Gladys. He'd spent the last few days talking to all of the hikers and campers in the area. None reported contact with the bear, which of course Nard took as an all clear. His condescending look said he doubted her competence, and the way he looked from her to Kristine told her that he suspected something between them. Even though she had wanted nothing more than to sit and hash out the day with Kristine, she didn't stay longer than she had to, reluctant to give Nard any ammunition.

As the sun set, she built a small fire to heat up her dinner, and sat jotting in her field notebook. She was spooked enough to have her gun at hand. Instead of making her feel confident about the safety of the campers in the area, the bear's aloofness disturbed her more, adding evidence to her argument that the bear's behavior had changed drastically. Had he returned, she would know that the animal was becoming food-conditioned. This they would treat with rubber bullet spankings or relocation. By not returning, the bear's afternoon camp trashing fell further outside of normal behavior. There was no easy way to tell what was happening with the animal, but of one thing she was certain: his behavior did not seem right. The sharp crack of a stick brought her to her feet, gun in hand.

"Don't shoot! It's me, Kristine."

Gloria let out the breath she'd been holding. "God, you scared me."

"Sorry. I wanted to chat with you earlier at the campsite, but Nard…"

"I know. He was watching me too." Gloria saw that Kristine's hands were full. "What do you have?"

"Not the world's worst coffee, but close." She handed Gloria the steaming mug. "And some cherry pie. That Jorge made, so you can trust it."

Gloria accepted the offering and sat back down on her sleeping bag, inviting Kristine to join her with the tilt of her chin. She dug in.

Kristine pointed to her notebook. "Anything new?"

"No. I really shouldn't let you keep feeding me like this. You're spoiling me."

"Only child, shouldn't you be used to it?"

"My parents didn't spoil me, just made me independent."

Kristine stared into the fire so long Gloria wondered if she'd said something wrong. "I wish I could say the same."

"You seem pretty independent to me."

"If that were true, I wouldn't have gone back to the ranch after my temp job ended."

"Have you ever considered teaching? I meant what I said earlier about you being a great teacher. You're clearly good at gaining your students' interest, and you sound like you know your stuff. You certainly have the skills. Your pictures take my breath away."

Kristine did her best to hide a smile. "They seem like a good group. I never have considered teaching. I've been so set on a professional career trying to prove that my degree wasn't a total waste."

"Well, I think you should teach. I'd sure like to be in your class."

"Yeah, you and your private lessons on release," Kristine joked.

"I'm not joking. And it opens up your job opportunities."

"Great idea. I promise to check it out when the trip is over." Her eyes drifted to Gloria's mouth, and Gloria thought of many things she'd like to check out when they were both back in Kristine's cabin. Kristine seemed to recall her surroundings and changed the subject. "You didn't seem convinced by Rick's read on the bear earlier."

"I wish I could agree that the bear's just stuffed after gorging on the ridiculous amount of food your boss allowed those fools to bring into the backcountry…"

Kristine held up her hands, surrendering to Gloria's rant about her boss.

"But for some reason, I just can't let go of the behavioral shifts. Usually, if a bear found food in a spot, he'd be back, right?"

Kristine nodded in agreement.

"But this bear hasn't been back to visit, and no one has seen it. What if that means the last time we saw it, it had just become sick, and now he's holed up and feeling more and more off? My worry is the next time we see it, it's going to be fully rabid, and I am at a loss for how to track it down on my own."

"What about Rick?"

"He stopped here earlier on his way out. He was finishing up his ten-day run. The bear's activity has started to convince him about relocation, but he doesn't feel we have enough to make it an urgent matter."

"And no bite on the rabies hunch?"

"He's not convinced."

"Let's say that it does have rabies. What chance does a camper have of fighting it?"

"Pretty good if you're carrying a rifle."

"So the rubber bullet setup Trish has is going to do no good?"

"That actually might aggravate attack instead of scare him off. Remember we're talking erratic behavior. You don't have a gun with you?"

"Nard probably has something. I've got my camera," Kristine answered.

Gloria mumbled not very well concealed insults about Leo while she stretched over to her pack and rummaged through it. She handed a flare gun to Kristine. "At least carry this with you, so if you get into trouble away from the group, you can signal for help."

Kristine tucked it into her coat pocket and stood. "I'd better get going."

Gloria rose reluctantly. "I wish you could stay."

"You don't know how much I want to."

Gloria leaned into a long hug. "I think I have a pretty good idea. Two more nights, and I think I could show you."

"I'd like that," Kristine said. "Tomorrow I'm doing a day ride with the group to the lake north of Shadow to do some mountain range work, and then we camp back here another night."

Gloria scowled.

"I know you don't approve. We probably won't see you or your bear friend."

"You realize that's still well within his territory…"

"Yes, I realize. And I'll make it up to you. I'll bring you dessert tomorrow evening," Kristine said.

"It's a date," Gloria said. She watched Kristine's smile travel to her eyes and loved the sparkle she saw there. As Kristine left the light of the campfire, she was quickly swallowed up by the dark night. It was happening far too often for Gloria. Until the issue at Fish Creek, she'd been taking her time writing up her final report for the grant because she wanted to spend more time with Kristine. Now the bear incidents demanded her full attention. She could feel the cold of the night that signaled the end of summer and knew that the Lodge would soon close, and there would be nothing to hold Kristine in Mammoth. Watching her walk away wasn't as easy as it typically would have been in the past when she found herself wrapping up a project.

CHAPTER TWENTY-NINE

"Let's see what we've got," Kristine said to her photography group.

Gary was already swapping cameras with his brother Rob, who had inherited all of the height but none of the hair. They took their lessons seriously and said very little, so she made sure to have a specific agenda to explore various shooting techniques each day. As usual, they huddled together analyzing the images, frequently agreeing to delete pictures that didn't meet their expectations even though Kristine kept encouraging them to share everything they shot.

The couple, Marilyn and her husband Bill, was the complete opposite, happy for instruction but happier to share and talk about what they captured. Where the brothers looked starched in the gear they'd obviously purchased for this trip, Marilyn and Bill looked like they lived in the mountains. Marilyn's lumpy sweaters and homemade scarves and her crazy, wavy, shoulder-length graying hair made her think of the hippies who attended the High Sierra Music Festival in her hometown.

They usually paired up with the only singleton on the trip, Ida, the closest in age to Kristine of all her guests. The three would huddle around one camera, ooohing and ahhing over the images. Photography was a new hobby for Marilyn since she'd retired from teaching, and while Bill supported her in this endeavor, he was along more for the scenery. His toned frame told of the hours he spent running in their hometown of Napa. Though he had a good eye for photography, he more often watched and encouraged his wife. The group viewed what Ida had shot before he, like a true gentleman, humbly presented his substantially smaller but talented offering.

He reluctantly accepted praise from Kristine, though she had much to give him. They had switched to their telephoto lenses for shots of the Minarets after the more tempting wide-angle shots captured the massive mountain range. Everyone had agreed that he'd been most successful in using the lens to flatten out the ranges, giving a very different texture to the landscape. One of the best images of the trip was his extreme close-up of the ridges of the peaks which, removed from the context of the whole mountain, took on the look of abstract art.

Bill waved her over. "Take a look at this one. It's magnificent!"

Kristine accepted Ida's camera and studied the image. "Were you lying on your stomach?"

The young woman nodded, her short light-brown curls bobbing. Though she was the most reserved of the guests, she often shared her radiant, toothy grin.

"I've never thought about framing before, and the horses seemed like such an obvious object to use."

Bill laughed. "I think horses and framing, and one side of my image has them. I don't think I can lie on my belly and make their legs and tummy three sides of the image."

"Really lovely," Kristine said, handing the camera back to Ida. She'd known what to anticipate from her students, having kept an eye on the stock during their lunch and shooting activity.

"I never would have thought to shoot from the ground until you said shoot from every angle available," Ida said.

"Thank goodness for the telephoto, though, or you'd have been putting yourself in a pretty unpleasant spot there!" Bill noted.

Everyone laughed at Bill's easy humor.

"What's next, Photomaster?" Marilyn asked.

"I thought we'd work with shutter speeds. When Nard sends the horses out, we'll do some pan shots. You're familiar with the technique?"

"Yes, but won't that be tricky at dusk?" Marilyn asked.

"Since this is a layover day, he'll turn the stock out once we're back, and we'll catch them back up and picket them for the evening. Otherwise, we risk them heading home for supper tonight."

"Why did he put a cowbell on one of the horses last night?" Ida asked.

"Two reasons. That's our bell mare. She's the only female horse on the trip, so all the other animals will stick to her. The riding horses are geldings, and they'll stay close because they think she's their girlfriend. The mules stay close because boy or girl, they think the mare is their mama. She wears the bell so Nard can find her easily in the morning after they've been grazing all night."

"What happens if the bell mare wanders off?"

"Then we're all in trouble. Some trips get held up a whole day because the stock follows her all the way home. There's nothing more valued than a loyal bell mare," Kristine said wishing that the women at the Lodge were treated as well by some of the cowboys.

"Have you worked with this outfit before?" Marilyn asked. "You seem to know a lot about how everything works."

"That's really my job," Kristine explained. "I'm a pinch hitter for them on photography."

"But you know so much about this, too," Ida said. "Is there anything you don't do?"

"Well, I've never cooked a trip." The group didn't say anything, and Kristine couldn't help thinking she'd do a better job than Trish even though she'd argued so vehemently that she wasn't a cook. Though she'd fought going on overnight trips all summer, she found herself grateful for the opportunity to teach photography and spend time capturing images she'd framed in her head when she didn't have time to stop. To break the silence, she continued. "For me, nature photography just goes with all this packing stuff."

"We sure can't ask for better scenery to shoot," Bill said.

"How's everyone feeling on horseback?" Kristine asked.

"Besides sore?" Ida asked.

Everyone laughed. "I mean are you confident that they aren't going to run away with you?" Kristine clarified. Seeing that everyone had acclimated to the riding on the trip, Kristine talked about what she wanted them to shoot as they rode. "Your horse is going to follow mine. Trust me. I've shot a lot of stuff from the front of the line knowing my horse is going to stay on the trail. You've got the added safety of being behind me. My horse isn't going anywhere, so feel free to explore what angles you can get from the saddle. You might also remember how Ida framed the picture Bill likes so much. One of my favorite images is the Devils Postpile seen between a pair of mule ears. Have some fun. Let's mount up."

After she helped everyone aboard, Kristine swung up and took the lead. In her saddlebags, she had her own camera, the remnants of her lunch and Gloria's flare gun. She'd been on alert all day, remembering Gloria's warning that their day ride hadn't taken them outside a normal bear's territory. Now heading back to Rosalie in the late afternoon, her tension rose. Whenever she stopped to afford her group a chance to shoot without the horses moving, she scanned the area, never allowing herself the distraction of her own photography.

They dropped back down to Shadow Lake, but before Kristine picked up the trail over to Rosalie, Gary called for her help. He'd seen Kristine pull off her sweatshirt and tie it to the back of her saddle and tried to do the same but dropped it. Kristine doubled back to retrieve the item.

Though he thanked her, Gary looked uncomfortable.

"Are your stirrups too high?" Kristine asked.

"No. It's my back. We're pretty close to camp, aren't we? Maybe I could just walk the rest of the way? I wanted more time practicing with the waterfall here."

"You may not make it back in time to snap the horses being turned out."

"That's okay. If it's no trouble to you, I'll hike back."

His brother seconded the request, and soon the whole group was in on the idea, opting to spend more time out of the saddle. Kristine hesitated, not wanting to leave the group on their own. Although they were close to camp, it still didn't feel right to leave them alone. She didn't want to worry them, but she didn't want to hold up Nard's plan to feed the animals before dinner. "I can give you fifteen minutes," she said. "But then, considering the bear activity, we'll all head back to camp together."

"Do you need any help with the horses?" Ida asked. She was the last to dismount.

"Oh, no thanks," Kristine said. She'd thrown a loose half hitch with each horse's lead rope on the next horse's saddle. "They'll be fine strung together like this until everyone gets back." When she'd helped Gary, she'd looped her own horse's lead through her belt, and now the horse tugged hard on the rope connecting them. Reflexively, she grabbed the rope, but she still had trouble controlling him. "Whoa, there, buddy," she said, trying to stay on her feet. One look at the whites of his rolled back eyes sent a wave of adrenaline through her body.

Time seemed to stand still. Every hair on her body stood up, and her ears strained to hear something, anything... She tried to pin the horse's fear on anything but what she feared, but failed. Her instinct screamed danger, too.

Bear.

Ice-like fear stabbed her. "BEAR," she yelled.

"Bear?" Ida repeated, her voice strained and quiet. "There are lots of bears out here, right? It doesn't have to be the one that Fish and Wildlife woman was talking about, does it?"

Kristine was still looking for it, but she also had a string of five animals that were keyed in, all of them dancing, swinging each other around. "Everyone stop moving wherever you are. We've got a visitor," she hollered.

"Do you want us back on the horses?"

Kristine considered but then rejected the idea. If they tried to outrun a bear on horseback, he'd have the advantage since he carried no extra weight, and she didn't want to risk someone coming off at a dead run. No, safer for them to stay put where they were and let her create a diversion. "Ida, grab my saddlebag, would you?" she barked, quickly working to untie the animals from each other. They continued to dance, trying to locate the danger they felt nearby. She pointed her own mount in the direction of Rosalie and swatted him on the rump. "Get out of here," she shouted, and the six horses galloped up the trail.

With the burst of motion on the trail, Kristine saw thundering movement up the hill. The massive bear crashed down the hillside targeting the animals. She had never heard of a black bear chasing after horses before. In all the summers she'd worked there, in all the stories she'd heard, bears had never bothered the stock. She'd ridden by mama bears and their cubs without being attacked or chased. Seeing it charge after the horses stopped Kristine in her tracks. This is what Gloria meant by abnormal behavior.

This was Gloria's rabid bear.

As the frightened horses scattered off the trail and into the surrounding woods, Kristine's guests ran to her. "What do we do now?" Bill asked nervously.

"Hope that the horses keep it distracted. If they take him all the way back to camp, Nard'll get 'im."

"And if they don't?" Marilyn asked, the edge of panic in her voice.

Kristine grabbed her saddlebags from Ida and shot off her flare gun. "Hopefully, Gloria is nearby and can help us out. Our best bet is to get out of sight, quickly, and stay still. Do not run. He can run faster. Normally, I'd say get as big as you can and scream like mad, but I don't think this guy is in his right mind."

"So we just hide and cross our fingers?" Marilyn said, her voice shaky.

"Head toward the outcrop of rocks. Get up there in a defensive position, and if you can find a large stick or something to help keep him away, even better."

Not that it's likely to do you any good, she thought to herself, remembering Gloria's comment about a gun being the only way to fend off the animal, but it seemed to calm them to have a plan, and for that she was grateful.

"I don't know how she's staying so calm," she heard Marilyn say as they crept off the trail.

Kristine was faint with fear and had absolutely no idea what she'd do if the bear came back. For the second time of the season, she cursed Leo for creating a problem she was not equipped to handle. In her first seasons, he had scared her by sending her off on unfamiliar trails. He'd draw a map in the dirt and tell her she couldn't get lost. Amazingly, she'd always made it to her destination, not always without consequence, but nothing that compared to where she found herself now, eye on the trail praying Gloria had seen her flare.

CHAPTER THIRTY

Searching the wilderness north of Shadow Lake, Gloria had finally found where her bear had holed up. She had intended to hike farther from Rosalie to see if the bear had headed toward Gladys Lake, but knowing that Kristine was heading in the opposite direction, she had changed her plans. If Leo insisted on putting Kristine in a dangerous area, she was at least going to stay as close to her as she could.

The bear had gone through quite a bit of food from the crazy guests at Rosalie that Kristine had sent her to observe. She'd finally stumbled upon scat that contained food wrappers and cursed that it was too old to give her any information about where the bear was now. He'd obviously eaten enough to satisfy his appetite, but she reminded herself that she was calculating with a "normal" bear in mind. She had no idea if the disease might make the bear hungrier.

A sharp hiss burst from the north side of the lake, and she saw her flare shoot up over the tree canopy.

Kristine.

Gloria slung her daypack over her shoulder and ran as fast as her feet could carry her in the direction of the flare that shot up right next to the lake. She skittered over rocks and leaves, her forward motion keeping her upright. She held onto her rifle with both hands, using it for balance. If the bear had been close to Kristine, and presumably it had for her to send up the flare, she knew she wouldn't have much time to get there to help. Kristine was unarmed and vulnerable. The image of a rabid bear crashing down on Kristine's line of horses flashed in her mind. She saw again the horse that had been mauled down at Fish Creek. Mauled by a sane bear. Imagine the damage a mad bear might do... She pushed faster.

Then stopped. Her heart pounded so loudly she couldn't figure out whether she'd been imagining the sound. Then she heard it again. Hoofbeats. She was nearing the trail and could definitely hear hoofbeats. Three riderless horses galloped up the trail. Kristine would have had more horses. Why were they running alone? Gloria knelt and brought her riflescope up to her eye hoping to see the bear following the stock. She swept over the area, searching but finding no sign of him. "Shit."

She jumped up and continued running just above the trail down toward Shadow Lake, trying to pinpoint where the flare had gone up. Ahead of her was a clearing. She heard hollering. Kristine's voice? She reached the trail. In front of her, a few of Kristine's guests huddled on a boulder.

"Where's the bear," Gloria demanded.

"It just came back down the trail. It was headed for Ida, and she jumped up in a tree. The bear started to climb it, too, so Kristine charged it."

"She what?" A wave of terror flooded through Gloria.

"She's trying to distract it. Can you shoot it from here?"

Gloria scrambled up the rock, locating Kristine on the opposite side of the clearing. As the couple had described, their fellow guest clung to the lower branches of a tree, and the bear seemed temporarily torn between her and Kristine. Gloria watched helplessly as the bear decided to go after Kristine who was now scrambling up her own set of rocks.

"Can't you take a shot?" the woman asked.

"Bad angle. We can't afford a wounded bear." Gloria scuttled down the rock and ran, faster now that she was on the trail. She needed to get in front of the animal, needed a heart shot…if she was faster…if Kristine got high enough fast enough…

The enormous brown bear lumbered up to the rock and began to get purchase. Gloria couldn't let him get up on that rock with Kristine. Kristine had nothing. The bear, about to gather his haunches beneath him, suddenly took a step back. Gloria passed the rock Kristine was on and dropped to her knee to set up her shot, hoping for a good angle at the front of the animal as it approached the rock again.

She glanced again at the whole scene before relying on the scope, making sure Kristine was well out of harm's way, and saw what had given the bear pause. Kristine had her finger on her shutter and was firing off shot after shot with her flash popping with each image. The light temporarily stumped the bear, long enough for Gloria to aim and fire.

The large brown form crumpled in front of the boulder, harmless. She fell back onto her butt rigid with fear. Kristine peeked over the boulder at the mass beneath her.

"Gloria?" She still hadn't seen her. Of course, she'd been too absorbed by the bear to see her hauling ass across the trail. Behind her, she heard the couple she'd been talking to.

"Over here!" she called.

Kristine scrambled down the rock and ran in their direction. As she reached Gloria, she threw her arms around her, shaking with fear. "Holy crap, I'm glad you made it."

The enormity of the situation, knowing what would have happened had she not made it, settled in Gloria's throat making it impossible to talk. Instead, she held on to Kristine, just closed her eyes and held on. Her mind whirred all the faster since her tongue was stuck. She couldn't do this anymore, couldn't be in the backcountry tracking bears and trying to intervene like she just did. She'd been right, she knew it without needing the forensics lab in Sacramento to confirm her diagnosis, though she'd see through with the necessary decapitation for analysis of the bear's brain. But no one had listened. She needed a job where people *did* listen.

Finally, she pulled away from Kristine. "Stupid risk," she managed.

"I don't think Ida would say the same," Kristine responded, ever stubborn.

"What would have happened if…"

"Shhh. It didn't. I'm okay."

For a moment, it was just her and Kristine. She was lost in Kristine's eyes, eyes that no longer held fear and only held her. She couldn't believe how fast it was all over, couldn't bring herself to think about the fact that she could have lost Kristine. They hadn't had enough time. She realized then how little of the summer they had left. How was she going to tell Kristine that she couldn't stand to lose her? Too soon, Ida and the brothers crossed the clearing, slowing as they neared, still wary of the bear. "I need to check him, make sure…"

"Oh, he's done. You got a real clean shot. And I got it all on film," Rob said, beaming, his bald head shining with perspiration.

"You took pictures?" Kristine gasped.

"Well, when I saw you get out your camera, I figured this was another lesson you set up special for us," he kidded, a wide grin on his face. "I gotta hand it to you. This was an awesome subject. Can't wait to see what you got on those frames you were firing off."

"I can't look," Kristine said, handing off her camera to him.

"The flash," Gloria said, finding Kristine's eyes. "Brilliant."

"So I'm stupid and brilliant." Kristine beamed. "All in the span of minutes. I've outdone myself. Well, folks. I'm sorry to say we're in for a hike. I'm sure Nard and Trish are worried about us. Come back to camp with us?" She reached for Gloria's hand.

Gloria took and squeezed her hand. "I've got to stay here with the carcass. I can't have anything getting to its head before I get it out of here."

"Tell you what," Kristine said. "I'll get my crew settled back at camp, pick up your gear and meet you back here."

Gloria nodded. "I'll take you up on it. After running all that way, my legs are jelly. I can't move."

"You don't have to." Kristine wrapped her arms around Gloria. She whispered for only her to hear. "Thank you for rescuing us. I owe you big-time."

CHAPTER THIRTY-ONE

"She was awesome," Bill exclaimed to a wide-eyed Trish back at the camp. "First she distracts him with the horses, and when he came back and went after Ida…" he and the rest of the group all looked to Kristine.

"I couldn't let him up that tree."

"Still, I couldn't believe it when you started running and screaming in the opposite direction," Marilyn said. "We thought you were toast."

"That's nice," Kristine laughed, trying to deflect their concern. Her body still hummed with the adrenaline, and the piercing look Nard kept trained on her didn't do anything to calm her nerves. All she wanted to do was get back to Gloria.

"She's a keeper, that's for sure," Bill said, putting an arm around Kristine's shoulders.

"You guys don't get to keep me tonight. I'm headed back over there to Ms. Fisher's camp." She felt funny calling Gloria by her last name, but she wanted to emphasize the professional relationship in front of Nard. She took her leave to gather her own things. She wasn't surprised to hear Nard's voice as she hauled her gear over to the stock.

"You have time to head back to camp after you take her gear over there," he said.

"I'll help her protect the carcass tonight. She's making arrangements to have the head picked up tomorrow, so she can get it tested."

"Guarding a dead bear isn't your job."

"I've done my job today, Nard. There's nothing more for me to do with the group tonight. I'll be back on duty tomorrow. You do your job. I'll do mine." And then we'll call it a summer, she thought.

"Still sneaking off to get laid."

A dozen comebacks buzzed around in her head, but she bit her tongue and kept on saddling the two animals she would take with her to the meadow. She would not let him bait her. She held her ground as he moved closer to her.

"Don't think you can run away from me again. Go have your fun tonight. But your girlfriend won't be at Thousand tomorrow night."

His voice echoed in Kristine's mind as she packed up her camp, as she rode back to Shadow and as she shared the exchange with a very serious and pissed off Gloria. Even after she'd convinced Gloria that she really didn't think it was a good idea for her to storm over to the camp and have a chat with Nard and instead pulled her into bed, Nard's threat kept her awake. She felt Gloria shift next to her.

"You don't owe this trip anything more, you know," she said. "Why don't you pack out with me tomorrow? You came back, you faced Nard. Let this place go. I love your loyalty, I really do. Even though it made me steaming mad when you weren't agreeing with me, I admire how you stand by them, but can you say that Leo has done the same for you?"

As tempted as Kristine was to simply leave the backcountry with Gloria, she couldn't run again. "I can't let him win again. I have to finish this trip. The whole pack station sees me as a quitter. If I come back in with you, I reinforce their idea that I can't see it through." Nard had been challenging and taunting her from the beginning of the season, and she realized that in avoiding his trips, she continued to let him lead. To take control of her own life, she had to see this trip through.

Gloria stroked her hair. "How did I know you were going to say that?"

"You're the one who said I'm stubborn."

"I'll be worried about you."

Kristine wrapped her arms around Gloria. "I'll be fine. I stared down a crazy bear today."

"If I'd been a minute later..." Gloria shuddered in her arms. "You really scared me."

"You think you were scared? Try staring down a bear. I was freaking terrified, but you know what? I faced it. I faced that huge thing with a front row seat to all those huge sharp teeth, but I knew I'd be okay. Whatever happens tomorrow, I can do it. I don't feel scared to face him, not after what I did today."

"I care about you, you know."

"Me too," Kristine whispered. "I'll be careful."

Gloria snuggled down and fell asleep. Kristine could feel her relax, her breathing deepen. Kristine lay awake thinking about what the next few days might bring, surprised that she felt no anxiety. She was ready to face Nard in the backcountry confident that she had followed the trail that she had set out on at the beginning of the season. Under the great expanse of the star-filled sky, she felt at peace. If she held her breath, she could hear the bell mare's bell carrying on the gentle breeze. Looking down at the woman next to her, fast asleep, the phrase Gloria had used to talk about short-term affairs, words she read every time she took the River Trail, slipped into her mind: Take Only Pictures; Leave Only Footprints. She knew that this summer, she would be taking so much more away from the backcountry.

CHAPTER THIRTY-TWO

The two days that Kristine remained in the backcountry flew by for Gloria with the responsibility she had for shipping the bear's head to the pathology lab in Sacramento and dealing with the aftermath. Scott required a briefing on the kill and had a mountain of paperwork for her to complete. When the Ontario office shared this second bear incident with the director of the state office, wheels were finally set in motion. They requested intricate details of her field notes from before the incident, as well as with whom she had discussed her concerns and how many people witnessed the attack in the meadow. Her calls were no longer met with sluggish promises to review the problems she encountered. She was now speaking directly with the State Director of Fish and Wildlife.

With nothing left to do but wait for the lab results in Mammoth, she used the opportunity of having clear cell reception to call her mother.

"This is a surprise," her mother said when she picked up. Gloria smiled hearing the delight in her voice.

"I had some business calls to make and thought I'd check in."

"Wrapping up?"

"Not quite. I've had quite an exciting week with two pretty major incidents. This last one might turn out to be a rabid bear. Sacramento didn't back me up on it, and now they're tripping over themselves to make things right. It might parlay into the promotion I've been wanting."

"Wait, back up. To test for rabies, don't you need the animal's brain?"

"Yes," Gloria answered simply.

"So in the last few days, my daughter has taken out a rabid bear. Any help with that?"

"Kristine was out there. She was protecting her guests, and I made it in time to neutralize the animal."

"I see. So that's why you're calling. You want to talk about love, not business. Let me get comfortable." Gloria had heard her mother puttering and knew the phone was tucked between her chin and shoulder as she completed some task as she talked. Now she heard water running, her mother pouring a glass of water, and the squeak of the back door which led to the swing she loved to sit on for long conversations. "Ready." Gloria had her full attention.

Gloria wanted to argue that it wasn't Kristine, but the promotion that she wanted to talk about. But she hadn't slept the night before, and while she'd tried to tell herself that it was the dreams filled with images of the bear running after Kristine, she knew it had more to do with how empty her bed felt without Kristine in it. They had shared a bed for a total of three nights, and each morning, it was Gloria who wanted to linger next to Kristine longer, Kristine who was up and out of bed jumping to work, leaving Gloria wanting to lure her back again.

"Since you're having your own personal conversation in your brain, let me see if I can help kick start you here," her mother said. "You're thrilled that you're finally in the position to take over the Eureka field office which you've had your eye on for years, but suddenly, there's Kristine, and what if living behind the Redwood Curtain isn't her dream of dreams."

"How do you do that?"

"Years of practice and a daughter who is gracious enough to share what's happening in her life with her boring old mother."

"But I haven't said anything about wanting to ask Kristine to come live in Eureka."

"You haven't said a thing about your work in any of your letters. It's all about Kristine. A mother knows what that means. Are you going to marry this girl?"

"Mom!" Gloria yelped. "I've only known her a few months."

"I know all about the U-Haul date, honey. Is that where you are?"

Her tone was serious, forcing Gloria to actually consider the question. She was used to being the one pulling away, not the one wanting more. "I have no idea where we are. This doesn't feel like anything I've done before."

"That's because you never met your forever before."

"She's got her own professional dreams. How can I ask her to follow me to Eureka?"

"What you mean is what if I didn't take the field office in Eureka where I can keep an eye on my sick mom. Well, factor me out. What does your heart say?"

"How can I just factor you out?"

"I'm dead. Now what does your heart say?"

A wave of nausea swept over Gloria. "Take that back. You're not allowed to say things like that to me."

"I'm not allowed to speak the truth? I'm not going to live forever. So you move back here, don't invite this lovely girl you've found to come with you. She's off pursuing her career and meets someone new while you're stuck wishing I would die…"

"Enough with the dying. I get it. How about the reverse? This is the time I can be there with you. I choose to go, you get worse, and I resent her for making me choose to be away from you." She knew she wouldn't be able to forgive herself if she left and her mother's health worsened. Just because her mother gave her permission to leave didn't mean she, herself, could, or even wanted, to do it.

"That's not very nice. Were you raised by wolves?" she said, humor in her voice.

"Mom, I called you because I'm stuck." She heard her mother sigh. "Are you okay?"

"I'm fine if you don't count being annoyed with you."

Gloria bit her lip, fairly chastised for how she automatically jumped to the conclusion that her mom wasn't being honest about her health at the slightest change in her tone. "Sorry."

"You want to be worried about me. You need to be worried about me because you've never taken a risk before, but the fact is, love is always a risk. And it's always worth it."

"Love?" Gloria said, surprised again.

Her mother laughed. "When you're with Meg, you're only thinking about what will make you happy. Now you're thinking about Kristine's dreams and what will make her happy. Time to ask her if you're part of what will make her happy."

Gloria looked at her watch, knowing Kristine was likely to be arriving at the Aspens soon. She wanted to be there when they rode in. "I miss you," Gloria said, her throat tightening. It always did when she had to say goodbye.

"Big kiss, sweet. I love you."

"Love you, too, Mom." Gloria clicked the phone shut and held it between her knees. Though she didn't want to admit it, she knew her mother was right. She had always thought of her career, her happiness first. That had always held her first priority, yet now anticipating the professional recognition she had worked so long and hard for didn't make her feel satisfied. Having Kristine did.

CHAPTER THIRTY-THREE

Kristine dismounted in the yard at the Aspens, a coating of dust on her skin and gritty between her teeth. Though exhausted, she now actually felt like the victor Gloria had insisted she was just for returning to The Lodge. The backcountry trip over, she could finally relax and think about the future. She hoped the immediate future included a lot more of Gloria. Just thinking about seeing her after two days away sent a thrill through her body. There was so much to fill her in on, but also so much to do. Her cheeks reddened at how many of the hours she'd had in the saddle that had been spent fantasizing about what she'd love to do with Gloria, most of which didn't include any clothes.

Work first, she lined up her guests for a group shot on horseback. Once they dismounted, Ida asked her to take a picture of her with her mount, and each guest issued the same request, adding a challenge for Kristine to demonstrate the techniques they'd been practicing. Perched high on the tie rail, she snapped Gary and his horse smiling up at the camera, the horse smiling because of the carrot in Kristine's hand that he reached for. While she worked, her gaze constantly drifted not up the mountain to where the pack mules would descend, but down to the road where she hoped to see Gloria. Nard soon arrived with the stock, so she had little opportunity to watch for Gloria in the chaos of unloading the animals and sorting out all of the gear.

For the first time in years, Kristine worked on the dock with Nard without distraction. During the last segment of the trip, she had not avoided him. She strode about camp with the knowledge that she had faced down a bear and the belief that she could now face Nard as well. With her attitude shift came the control she'd lost so many years before, and she kicked herself for taking so long to assert herself. She recalled the reprimand her father gave her when she refused to catch up a broodmare he wanted. Kristine had never liked the mare because she crowded Kristine and had stepped on her numerous times. Her admission had prompted half a day stuck in the round corral with her father showing her how to assert dominance over the horse. He explained how horses are constantly reestablishing the pecking order, and when she did not reprimand the horse for crowding her, she lost her dominance.

After hours of anticipating the animal's movements and blocking her, the mare gave Kristine her space and accepted that, though the smaller of beasts, Kristine deserved her respect. This trip in the backcountry had been another round corral, and she had been forced to assert herself around Nard just as she had done with the broodmare all those years ago. In her stepping forward instead of back, he, too, had finally granted her space.

Gear finally sorted and loaded into the appropriate vehicles, the guests said their goodbyes, thanking Nard and Trish for the trip and Kristine for the photography skills they had acquired. She shook hands with Bill and the brothers, Gary and Rob. The two women hugged her and shared the difficulty of parting forever, wanting to exchange contact information with everyone in the group. In past years, she'd seen strangers connect in the backcountry, but this group, after the experience in the meadow with the bear, had bonded at a deeper level. She watched them go with a little sadness, her first group of students.

Absently, Kristine picked up some grooming brushes that had been left in the feeders and returned them to the tack shed. The anticipation of Gloria's greeting distracted her. She was completely unprepared for the hand on her shoulder, spinning her around, the strong arms that pushed her up against the shed wall.

"My turn," Nard growled, pressing himself up against her.

She screamed deep from her gut, the scream she should have let loose to call for help years before. "Get off me!"

Nard stroked her cheek. "Not this time."

"Get it through your thick skull. This is not happening."

"You've kept me waiting long enough."

She pushed against him, and he retaliated, slamming her back up against the wall and putting his elbow to her throat. "I like the fight, too. It makes the ride all the more exciting." She felt his rough hands on her throat, loosening the bandana she wore there. "No more talking," he said, sliding it up into her mouth.

Fear washed over her, gripping her belly. It felt like a crushing weight against her chest. Nard smiled. She was helpless again, staring at the smile that had haunted her for six years. He had to release her to work her belt. She felt paralyzed. How many times had she found herself in the same position in her dreams, unable to scream, rigid with fear. She willed herself to move, even just a tiny bit. He was too strong to overpower, she knew that. But she couldn't give up, not again. She opened her hand and placed it on the wall, inching it to where she and Gabe stored the hay hooks.

His eyes dropped to her hips, and she made her move, grabbing one of the hooks and digging it between his legs. He howled in surprise, and Kristine pushed harder, forcing him to take a step back. With her other hand, she pulled her bandana out of her mouth.

"You asshole," she gasped. "Get the fuck off me."

"What do you plan to do?" he challenged.

She tugged the hook, piercing his jeans and silencing him. "Oh, there's a lot I can do."

He laughed nervously. "You'd like to think you have the balls."

"The way I see it, I'm about to get yours." She pulled upward, slicing through the fabric. His gasp told her she'd nicked him.

"You'll fucking pay for this, Teeny."

She responded by ramming the point of the hook into his flesh. When he hollered with rage, a figure blocked out the light in the doorway, startling Kristine. "You need any help in here, Kristine?" Sol asked.

"I'm the one who needs help here," Nard snapped. "She's fucking crazy."

"Shut up, Nard," Sol said. "Pretty clear who the crazy fucker is."

Kristine looked up to see Gabe, a look of pure shock on his face.

"Kristine?" He looked from her to Nard, understanding dawning in his eyes. "You never said…"

Nard screamed, "She's fucking gelding me! Do something!"

Sol held up both palms and took a step back. "You put yourself there, boy. You ready to tell your daddy why she felt the need?"

Kristine dropped the hay hook, her muscles relaxing. He'd need some doctoring. That was enough. She could walk away knowing he'd have to explain his injury. She kept a piercing eye on Nard. "Get your stock loaded up and get the hell out of here. Don't come near me again. Don't even think about me," she stated with finality.

Sol grabbed him by the collar and roughly pulled him out the door. "Let's get the stock loaded and deliver you to Leo. You're done here."

Gabe stood there for a moment, an awkward silence growing. Kristine placed a trembling hand on his shoulder. She didn't know what to say either.

He wrapped his arms around her, holding tight. "All those years ago…" He spoke into her crown, his breath warm but his voice cool.

Kristine closed her eyes, wishing she could go back six years and at least have the maturity to explain why she'd left. She took a step back, realizing he was probably thinking the worst. "It's not as bad as you think," she said. Though the dark of the saddle shed offered a place to hide, she had to get away. Standing there, she could still feel Nard's hands on her. She stepped out into the light and walked to the pack dock and sat perched on the edge. She took a deep breath and told Gabe what she'd told Gloria. He stood in front of her, arms crossed, face growing angrier as she explained how Nard had caught her after she'd snuck off in the woods with someone.

Gabe dipped his chin to his chest, his breath labored as she explained the good timing of the bear that had saved her from a different fate. When she'd finished, he looked back up at her, processing what she'd said. Without a word, he stepped back into the saddle shed, emerging a minute later with a flask in his hand. He sat next to Kristine, his long legs extended in front of him, and took a deep swallow from it.

"What the hell's that?"

"Sol's emergency medicine for when his 'old bones are fucking with him.'" He took another draw before handing it to Kristine. "I don't understand. Why didn't you tell me when you took off? Why invent that stupid story about Coppertop nailing you in the head? You made me cover up for that asshole." He stood again and paced away from her. "Why would you do that to me?"

Kristine took a small swig from Sol's flask, enjoying the burn at the back of her throat, struggling not to cry. "It would have been obvious who I'd been screwing around with," she said quietly.

He stopped pacing but didn't turn until he'd figured it out. The hurt in his eyes was exactly as she'd imagined it would be. The years she had avoided it by lying to him did nothing to dampen his wounded expression. "You slept with Nicole? My Nicole?" His voice cracked.

Kristine bowed her head. "Yeah, I didn't know about that until after...when she said..." She did not want to share or even remember the post-sex revelation she experienced when Nicole compared her kissing to her brother's.

Gabe strode back to the pack dock and snatched the flask from Kristine and took a deep swallow before he sat down next to her, shoulders hunched. "You slept with my first love and then the two of you talked about me? That's even worse." His voice rose.

"If I'd known, I never would have let it go so far. I..."

"How could you not know? I told you I was in love. I talked about her all the time."

"You never said who. You flirted with everyone. I thought you were into one of the day-ride girls, someone your age." She took a deep breath, realizing her defensive answer came from trying to hide the truth. She had to own up to everything. "I was too busy screwing around to notice. Dad told me to watch out for you, and I didn't. I did what I always did when I got away from Quincy, and I felt like such a shit when she told me." Kristine flushed. "My head was spinning on what I could do to make it right, and then Nard was there shoving it in my face, saying I couldn't keep going around hurting people leading them on. I knew how angry and hurt you'd be and thought you'd feel like I deserved it."

"You think I'm that low?" he demanded angrily.

"If I'd told you about Nard, you'd have found out about Nicole. Everyone would have found out, and I couldn't live with that. You know the grief you would have gotten if they found out that your sister had slept with..." She couldn't make herself say it even now. "I had to get away from you as much as anything. I didn't want to see the look you're giving me right now."

Gabe turned away from her, rubbing the back of his close-cropped hair. "You let them think you were a flake instead."

She shrugged. "I didn't have to work with them anymore. You did."

"So you were watching out for me." He sounded doubtful.

"Trying to find a way to make it up to you. Why do you think I came back this summer? I still feel bad about it."

"You should. I really liked her."

"I know. We all knew. When I saw you at Christmas, you were still licking your wounds."

"She said she'd write. I thought she liked me…I never knew why she cut me off like that." His head hung low as he passed the flask from hand to hand.

"You can't ever know what's going to come from a summer fling," Kristine said gently, remembering how hard she fought her feelings for Gloria because she fretted about the sting that would come at the end of the summer.

"So that's what it was for you?"

Kristine put her hand on Gabe's shoulder. "I knew that for you it was serious. That's why I had to go."

"But you knew for her it was a fling," he said pointedly.

"You didn't need to hear that from your sister."

"Now all I can think about is whether she was thinking about you when she was kissing me. Thanks," he grumbled.

Kristine bit her lip. "She wasn't the best kisser."

"Enough!" Gabe tipped the flask back again, then offered it to his sister.

She declined, and they sat staring at the mules waiting to be put away for the night. Kristine shivered as the cool evening air settled around them. Her thoughts spun on the regret of lying to Gabe tangled with the fear and anger from Nard's attack. It felt the same as it had the night she'd left six years ago. She wished she could change the course of events and make things right. She wanted to know what Gabe was thinking but at the same time wished there was a way they could just forget about it. A new reality hit her. "I have to tell Dad now, too."

Gabe nodded beside her. "Better call him before Leo does."

"On the ride back home that night, I had convinced myself that it would jeopardize Dad's business with Leo."

"You're more important than that," Gabe said frankly.

She rested her head against his shoulder. "I'll call him tomorrow. I don't feel up to it tonight."

"You should have told us back then. Even though I would have hated you."

"I never said I made the right choice," Kristine said. "Do you hate me now?"

"Yes."

Kristine's head shot up.

"Because you still get the girl." His eyes were on the road, on Gloria approaching with her knapsack slung over one shoulder. "I get dumped, and you get the girl. Go on," he said with a resigned sigh. "It'll take some time to sink in, but I don't hate you."

"Is everything okay?" Gloria's voice was heavy with concern as she approached them.

"It is now," Kristine said, standing to wrap her arms around Gloria. She felt something different in Gloria's hug and stepped back to look in her eyes.

"What's going on?" Gloria asked, looking from one sibling to the other.

"I gotta put the stock away," Gabe said. He tipped his hat and left them.

"Kristine?"

Kristine let out a long breath, feeling tears threatening again. "Gabe knows."

"Did something happen?" Gloria asked, alarmed. She took Kristine's hand.

"I'm okay. I'll fill you in." She stroked Gloria's cheek, tickling the stray hairs of her ponytail at the base of her neck. She wanted Gloria to hear the details of her afternoon, but she was puzzled by the way Gloria held herself. Something was different. She seemed distant. Guarded? "What about you?" she asked.

"I'm fine," Gloria said, smiling. "I talked to my mom earlier."

Kristine's face went pale. She was so caught up in what had happened with Nard that she didn't even consider that something may have changed with Gloria's mother's health. "She's okay, isn't she?"

"I was just checking in with her. I didn't mean to scare you," she said.

Distracted. Kristine finally placed it. Gloria was distracted by something.

"Hello, by the way," Gloria said, leaning forward to kiss Kristine. Kristine loved that they had a hello kiss. Fairly quick, but warm, supple, the sigh of a soft place to rest after a long day. She returned the kiss, moving beyond the hello kiss into the kiss of want, the one that said she had missed Gloria and had every intention of removing all her clothes as soon as possible. Gloria hummed in response, and when they broke apart, her eyes were all fire and desire and it felt like she was fully present again. "Really?"

"Like you're surprised," Kristine answered, swatting Gloria on the ass. "I know you're going to make me talk it all out, but don't think you're going to be able to keep me from having my way with you."

"I wouldn't dream of trying to stop you," she answered, slipping her hand into Kristine's.

CHAPTER THIRTY-FOUR

"Sorry I'm so late," Kristine said, dropping her boots by the door and a kiss on Gloria's cheek. "Lemme just get the top layer of grit off, and then I'm yours."

"I like the sound of that," Gloria said, turning to snatch a quick kiss before Kristine cleaned up. In the week since Kristine's return from the backcountry, they'd fallen into a routine. After Kristine told Leo the truth about why she had left all those years ago, he sent Nard back to Bishop, put Gabe on Nard's last few overnight trips and sent other people up from the Lodge to help for the day if more than one spot trip was leaving out of the outpost. Thus, after Kristine had loaded stock that was headed back to the Lodge into the truck or put them up in the corral, they had the place to themselves.

Gloria listened to the water running in the bathroom and knew that Kristine was up to her elbows in soap. Once she'd removed the day's dust from her face, they'd eat dinner together, catching up on their respective days. While Gloria did dishes,

Kristine finished her chores before it got dark. They then had the rest of the evening to lounge and read. She smiled thinking about how many nights they got distracted by each other. What started as an innocent backrub or foot rub quickly evolved into another exploration of each other's body.

Being with Kristine was so different to anyone she'd ever been with before. She didn't feel crowded by her like she did by Meg. Intuitively, Kristine gave Gloria the space she needed. When she had to work, Kristine might pause to run her fingers through Gloria's hair or kiss her neck just behind her ear, but then she'd move to her own project, not threatened by the demands of Gloria's work.

At the same time, she felt more deeply connected to Kristine than she had with any of the women she'd hooked up with during her other temporary assignments. She and Kristine shared more than sex, and she found that she didn't want to give up that compatibility.

Kristine emerged with a clean tee and freshly scrubbed face and neck. She'd run her wet fingers through her short hair, accentuating the natural wave. She looked beat.

"How many hours were you in the saddle today?"

"Too many," Kristine said, sinking into her chair.

"When I came back from Mammoth, your stock was here, but I couldn't find you anywhere."

"Typical Leo. He overbooks at the end of the season, forgetting who is going off to college early. Takeisha helped Dozer out of the yard, but she brought my stock home since she wanted to get on the road and still had her cabin to pack up. I got to finish up the drop with Dozer."

"Did he give you any grief?" Gloria knew that Kristine hadn't wanted a big deal made out of what had happened with Nard. Leo's sending him off to Bishop had thrown a wrench in her hoping for a quiet resolution. As Kristine had suspected, Nard was quick to reveal her indiscretion with Gabe's girlfriend. She wondered if the fallout was as bad now as Kristine had always feared it would be.

"None. I expect Gabe's getting the worst of it, but he won't say anything when I ask."

Gloria waited for her to continue. Typically, Kristine chatted about her guests and events on the trail, but tonight they ate in silence. Their normal easy dinner conversation had stalled. Kristine looked to be chewing on something more than her food. Gloria certainly was, having finally received confirmation from the lab that she'd been right about the bear she'd shot and wanted to share the news with Kristine. "What are you thinking about over there?"

Kristine smiled at Gloria's question. "You can tell, huh? Guess I'm pretty easy to read. It's just this conversation with Dozer I had. Like I said, he didn't mention Nard, but he was surprised that I wasn't on Leo's case for keeping me in the saddle all day or using stock that should be done for the summer. I explained to him that I spent all these years feeling guilty for walking away, but today, I got to see that Leo makes do. He always manages to get someone in the saddle to keep things going. It's not my responsibility. It never was. It isn't my place anymore."

"You said all that to Dozer?" She found it difficult to picture the conversation happening between Kristine and the man she'd shot in the ass at the beginning of the summer.

Kristine laughed. "That's the thing! He just kept working, totally uncomfortable. I said we don't usually talk about this sort of stuff, and he said, 'Yeah, don't you have a girlfriend?'"

Gloria's eyes widened and Kristine shrugged shyly. She didn't know what to say. She'd very much like to be Kristine's girlfriend, but they weren't going to be here in the cozy cabin for very much longer. She had to leave, and she was still scared to ask Kristine to come with her. She hadn't let anyone stand in the way of her career and certainly didn't want to hold Kristine back in hers. She saw Kristine start to worry over the silence. She pushed her food around on her plate, her eyes hidden. Gloria realized she had to level with her, she had to let her know why it wasn't that easy. "I got the promotion."

Kristine's eyes shot up. "What?"

"Leo came by to say he got a call from Scott. He seemed grateful I'd saved his ass. Mauled guests might have had a negative impact on business and all."

"Not that he'd ever come out and thank you."

"No. But he came by. It was a nice acknowledgment. I went up to talk to Scott about it all. He seemed pretty impressed to get a call from the Director of Fish and Wildlife. He relayed that it's actually me they want to talk to. Long story short, they want me in Sacramento to formalize my recommendations for how to decrease the contact between humans and bears in this area, and then I have my pick of field offices to run."

Kristine set down her fork. "Wow. That's super." Her voice sounded strained. "When do they want you in Sacramento?"

Gloria reached for Kristine's hand, hating the trepidation she saw in her eyes. "Tomorrow."

"So that's it." Kristine pushed away from the table, clearing her plate. She stood at the sink with her back to Gloria.

"I don't want it to be," Gloria said. She rose and crossed the kitchen, putting her hand on Kristine's shoulder. "I can tell them I need time to think about which field office would work best for me. We could get lucky. You could get a job in a city that has a field office. Then we'd be set."

Kristine turned. "That's ridiculous. You've wanted the Eureka field office forever. You have to take it." Gloria's heart sang with the knowledge that Kristine knew her so well but sank when she saw the defeated look on Kristine's face. "We've talked about the schools out there, about the possibility of teaching there, but if that doesn't come through…"

"I know you have to follow your dream," Gloria said. "I would never ask you to give that up."

"But the same is true for you. I couldn't ask you to pass up the chance to be near your folks."

"Where does that leave us?" Gloria whispered.

"Making the most of tonight?" Kristine asked hopefully.

Gloria wanted more than one night and was disappointed in Kristine's flippant response. It wasn't that she didn't want

Kristine. It was that she wanted Kristine in the long term. She wanted *all* of Kristine's nights, but she knew she couldn't ask for that. Kristine's hands pulled at the fabric of Gloria's shirt. She raised her hands allowing Kristine to remove her tee. She shuddered as her lover unclasped her bra, freeing her breasts, her nipples already tight buds, begging for Kristine's mouth. Gloria smiled as Kristine pulled off her own shirt and bra. Kristine's comfort with her body was one of the sexiest things about her. But Kristine shirtless, all feminine and soft on top, remained rugged below, still clad in her cowboy boots, jeans and belt buckle. The contrast of her bare breasts and belt buckle illustrated Kristine's complexity perfectly. She raised an eyebrow and led Gloria to the bedroom, pressing her back to the mattress, stripping off her jeans and panties.

Hungry for more, Gloria unfastened Kristine's belt buckle, pulling her belt slowly through the loops. Kristine held her gaze as the belt slipped away from her waist. "This is mine."

"Fair enough," Kristine whispered. She wrapped her mouth around Gloria's nipple, pulling hard. "This is mine."

Gloria writhed beneath her, trying to pull Kristine to her, wanting to press her whole body to Kristine's.

Hovering above her, Kristine whispered, "And this," she said, nipping her ear lobe. She continued down Gloria's frame, skimming her belly, her hips, ankles, the back of each knee, claiming Gloria with her words and mouth, and Gloria let her, knowing Kristine's words were true. She was Kristine's.

Gloria panted as Kristine traced the inside of her thigh with her tongue, and she sank into Kristine when her mouth finally touched down at her center, on fire from the moment Kristine's lips and tongue began to dance across her throbbing clit. Her hips matched the rhythm Kristine set, wanting more contact, more pressure, more of Kristine.

"I want you inside," she whispered.

The pressure built as she felt Kristine trace the path her tongue had taken with her finger. Instead of honoring Gloria's request immediately, she teased, circling her clit with her finger, slipping down to Gloria's sex but leaving just as Gloria was ready for Kristine to fill her.

"I need you inside," she growled.

Kristine's thumb replaced her mouth. Gloria groaned her disappointment and frustration but gasped as Kristine's tongue batted her nipple. She arched into the contact just as Kristine finally slid her fingers inside her, releasing Gloria's orgasm. Gloria continued to buck against Kristine, her arms tight around her lover as she rode the aftershocks.

When she stilled, Kristine raised her head, finding Gloria's eyes. "This isn't goodbye," she whispered. "We'll figure it out."

Gloria tilted her head away from Kristine's look of determination, tears falling onto the pillow. She ducked her head and wiggled free of Kristine's grasp, kissing a swift path down Kristine's tummy, her tears mixing with the salty tang on Kristine's skin, her long hair tickling its own path. She was as quick to her destination as Kristine had been slow, smiling at the surprised gasp that escaped Kristine as Gloria's tongue found Kristine's slick folds. Using lips, tongue, pressure and feather touch, she lost herself in her lover.

She tasted like rain, Gloria realized, which made her think of tears and goodbyes. It suddenly made her feel more homesick for the Northcoast than she had in years, cementing the truth that she did, in fact, have to take her hometown field office. But Kristine felt like home, too, and Gloria longed to share foggy, cold days cuddled up with Kristine in her arms. Kristine didn't last long under Gloria's tongue, hissing her pleasure as Gloria entered her, calling her name as she finished. Gloria pressed her face to Kristine's damp thigh as she caught her breath, loving the smell of their combined sex in Kristine's bed.

Kristine pulled her up into her arms, and Gloria rested her head against Kristine's chest, hearing her heart beat wildly beneath her ear. "I love you," Kristine whispered.

Gloria absorbed Kristine's declaration, her breath catching, tears threatening again. She'd heard the words before but her heart had never echoed them like it did now. "I love you, Kristine."

"We don't need to be on the same trail to be headed in the same direction," Kristine said.

"I'm going to miss your cowboy logic." She traced lazy circles on Kristine's belly. "And your belt buckles. Your sexy chaps."

"Chinks."

"Whatever. I'm going to miss you."

CHAPTER THIRTY-FIVE

Kristine let the screen door slam behind her as she entered through the kitchen of her parents' home. After Gloria had left for Sacramento, Kristine's need to finish with the Lodge had intensified. Without any spots out of the Aspens, she and Gabe had moved their stock down to the Lodge and dined with the remaining skeleton crew. Afterward, she had stood with Leo and Sol outside the café, reviewing what a good season it had been, Leo saying she shouldn't have stayed away so long. She had never dreamed that he would back her up after he found out what happened in the backcountry. Typical of Leo, he'd dealt with the situation and moved on. She'd followed suit and told him she might be convinced to help on the photography trip next year. But she was very clear in her plan to have a full-time job by then.

She had heard Sol's voice telling her not to be a stranger, and felt the strong clap on her shoulder before he shuffled off. She'd miss them, but they would no longer hold any power over her.

"Kristine? That you?"

"Yep. Hope you're ready for Gabe's appetite. He's right behind me."

Her mother joined her in the kitchen and gave her a tight hug. She wore a long dress with a sweater buttoned over it. Her shoulder-length hair, a shade lighter than Kristine's, was pulled back at the nape of her neck with a leather stick barrette. "Well? Was it worth it?"

"It was." Kristine reached in the cupboard for a glass and filled it with water before turning back to her mother. "I hate that it had to involve Gabe."

"Of course you do, but he'll get over it. The bigger question is whether you will, too."

Kristine smiled. "I think so. I feel good. Different."

"You look different, lighter somehow."

"Yeah, I think I know what a mule feels like carrying empty bags."

Her mother laughed. "You sound just like your father. He's working with the two-year-olds in the round corral."

Kristine did not move to join him. "Now that I'm back in civilization, I want to go through my mail, check and see if there are any new job listings."

"Of course," her mother said hugging her again. "The stack is in your room."

Kristine nodded. During the summer, she checked her email weekly up in Mammoth but had her mother open any mail sent to the house. Since she'd agreed to call if any letter of interest came in and hadn't ever called, Kristine knew the stack on her desk was all rejections. Another bonus of working away from the ranch all summer: she didn't have to face the mailbox every day and could simply tally all of them in one sitting.

She spent several hours cataloging the rejections and adding the jobs she had applied for while she was in Mammoth, most of which were teaching positions she'd sought after the success of the photography trip.

During dinner, they recounted the highlights of the summer, with Gabe doing much of the talking. Kristine said little, reflecting on how many of the highlights included Gloria. She was similarly quiet while they fed the stock after dinner, her father catching them up on what he'd done with the new foals, the yearlings, the two-year-olds, noting the state of the fields. Normally, Kristine would have asked questions, made mental notes on where to get started. Instead, she felt the same detachment that she did leaving the Lodge. She felt no guilt about these animals being her father's project, and not hers.

After stomping their boots at the door, her father headed for his den. "Kristine, let's go over the books. We need to start thinking about what to do with the broodmares in the spring."

He cast his words like a rope meant to pull her in. She looked down, expecting to find the loop that would yank her off her feet. She'd felt her whole life shift in the last few weeks, yet he continued as if she hadn't been gone at all. She retrieved her computer from her room and met him in the den.

"Still bugging me about going digital, huh?" he grumbled.

"No. I have some incredible shots from Mono I want you to see."

"Still carrying that camera around," he said, his voice tired. "What in God's name were you doing out there?"

"I had a day off and Gloria invited me to go with her."

"Ah." She thought she saw the edge of his lip curl toward a smile. "Still chasing girls, too."

She thought about his statement, thought about the whole summer spent with Gloria. "No," she answered honestly. "Not chasing anymore."

"What does that mean? She means something to you?"

"Yes. She's taking over the Fish and Wildlife field office in Eureka, so I put in an application for a teaching job over there. It's part-time, but it's in photography. I'm still waiting to hear from them."

"No sense in taking a job across the state that you could have here at the community college. We need to start working with the yearlings. You know Gabe doesn't have the knack for it you have."

"You could get students from the equine training program to help you. It would be good experience for them."

"You're out of your mind. No one knows these animals like you do. You know their mamas and have trained their siblings. The college can't teach that."

"The important thing is that these kids are a hundred percent set on training as a career. They've got their whole heart into it, and I don't."

"How long do you expect this to last? You go to this town for this girl and work a job with no guarantees? It's just another seasonal job that could be gone anytime. A job like that'll make you start to doubt yourself. Job like that is like a burr under the saddle. It'll get you squirrely enough to get to bucking."

Kristine tried to keep her expression neutral and not show her frustration. She had grown up on these metaphors and no longer fought being compared to the animals that their family raised and loved. The best way to deal with her father was to join him in the metaphor.

"You're assuming that she's putting this saddle on me, and you're forgetting that a saddle isn't permanent. But at least I'm in it, riding through instead of sitting out."

Her father considered her words. She knew that he was studying her, shaping her up. The more she talked, the more information he gathered, and he'd use it all to push her where he wanted her to go. Guide the energy and make the horse think it's his idea had been one of his mainstays. He rubbed at his bottom lip with his thumb, something he always did when thinking hard, and Kristine sat across from him. For the first time in her life, she was conversing with him as an equal.

"You think that I'm trying to talk you out of going. I'm not," her father said. Kristine blinked in surprise, never expecting her father to say that. "You think I'm keeping you here on the ranch, but you've always kept yourself here. I wanted you to be sure about your decision to pursue photography, and I thought you were when you paid for graduate school in Santa Cruz. But then you came back here. I thought maybe you'd find your own direction when you went back to the Lodge this summer. You say this college job is part-time, but folks get comfortable. You do that. Look at how hard it is for you to leave Quincy. I don't want you to find yourself in the same place in a few years, looking for a way out of another job that isn't right for you and resent this Gloria. It's natural for you to resent me. That'll help you establish who you are. But if you resent your partner...well, then you're pretty screwed."

She mulled over his words seriously, realizing how she had misinterpreted his parenting for so many years, always assuming that he was trying to push her in the direction he wanted her to go. Now she saw that he had been showing her the open gates. In the round corral, there's a moment when the barriers between horse and human drop, when a horse lets down its guard and understands intuitively what the human has been trying to communicate. She finally understood.

With this new understanding, Kristine watched as her father studied the slideshow she'd put together from her best Mono Lake shots. With him intent on her photographs, she looked around his office, seeing it anew. She always felt like he was humoring her when he hung her images on the walls: Suzy-Q as a newborn, the foal framed by the mare, the image softened by morning mist; her father working a pair of Belgian mares in front of their red barn; a string of loaded mules crossing the Silver Divide on the John Muir Trail. It never occurred to her that he had hung them with pride. He pushed back from the computer, the love in his eyes confirming her realization before he issued a challenge. "These are as good as anything you've ever shot. So what are you going to do? Waste your talent or do something with it?"

CHAPTER THIRTY-SIX

"C'mon, boss," Adam said. He was as trim as he had been when she'd interned at the field office during high school, but in the last few years, the hair on his head had migrated to the bushy beard on his face.

Gloria looked up from her desk piled high with papers she had yet to sort or make sense of. She smiled at the sass in his voice, relieved that taking over the office had not upset her former mentor.

"It's going to take more than a week to find any order in the mess Carl made of this place. Give yourself a break."

"Easy for you to say. You don't have Sacramento expecting a report on Monday."

His eyes twinkled. "One of the many reasons I never wanted your job." His expression grew more serious as he sat in the chair across from the cluttered desk. "Are you using the job to avoid something?"

"You know me better than that. I don't hide at work." Gloria frowned. She didn't convince herself, and the look on Adam's face said he didn't buy her words, either.

"Come to the brewery with us. We'll get a pitcher and catch up."

Gloria glanced at the clock.

"Pack it in. Call it a week."

"Give me ten minutes. I'll meet you there."

She ran by her camper on the way to change into dark slacks and the blue blouse she'd worn on her "supper" date with Kristine. A half hour later, she climbed the stairs at the Lost Coast Brewery, looking for her employees. Adam waved her over to a small table. "Jim's trying his luck at the bar."

Gloria looked over and found the younger man chatting with a woman. She already felt out of place, wishing that Kristine was there next to her. Instead of helping her take her mind off Kristine, being out trying to socialize made her more acutely aware of how much she missed her. An hour. She promised herself she'd give it an hour.

"You still seeing Meg?"

"Oh, no. We were never serious."

"Your mom thought you were."

"Yeah. That made it a lot harder for Meg to hear that I'm with someone else."

"New love, and you're at the office late every day. Are you sure you're with this one?"

"She's not local."

Adam tilted forward, encouraging her to share more.

"We met in the backcountry. She might get a job teaching over here, though."

"So until then, you're distracting yourself with work."

"Something like that."

Adam poured a glass of beer for her out of his pitcher. "Well, Jim's bad luck with dating is a great distraction. Ah, here he comes. Any luck?"

"Waiting for her boyfriend," Jim explained. He looked surprised to see Gloria. "Hey, boss."

"Gloria. Hope you don't mind my joining you guys."

"No. Not at all. As long as you move your chair toward Adam there. Don't want anyone thinking you're my girlfriend."

He ran his fingers through his thick sandy hair, arranging it just so.

Gloria looked at Adam to gauge whether Jim was genuinely concerned.

Adam nodded. "He takes this seriously."

"The way I see it, how am I going to get a date if I don't ask? You've got to put yourself out there, you know?"

Gloria nodded and sipped her beer. Fifty minutes. She could last fifty more minutes, especially if the band started soon. "Who's playing tonight?"

"A local Cajun Zydeco band. You'll like them. Very upbeat," Adam answered.

"Easy to dance to if you know the two-step or have done any swing," Jim added.

"I don't dance, but I love to listen," she said, wishing that she was curled up in Kristine and Gabe's cabin listening to them sing their cowboy songs. She'd never danced with Kristine, Gloria realized. She glanced at her watch. Forty-five minutes. Jim and Adam chatted about work, and she peppered in a few questions and tried to avoid looking at her watch. Then the music started.

Fiddle, accordion, guitars and a swinging beat did distract Gloria. Though she resisted at first, she finally gave in to Jim's requests to dance. He was convinced that if other women saw how well he could lead, he'd get more to agree to dance with him. Gloria found that he really could dance, and she lost herself in the energy and movement. After a few songs, she retreated to the table for more beer, giving Jim a chance to ask someone else to dance.

"There's the smile I've missed," Adam said when she returned.

Gloria touched her face, not realizing that she had been beaming the whole time she'd been out on the dance floor. "Sorry."

Adam smiled. "No need to apologize. Looks like it does you good to get out, though. I hope you continue to join us."

"I think it does too," Gloria said, taking a long draw on her beer. She would like to dance again and wondered if Kristine would mind. A little wickedly, she wondered if a little jealousy might help remind Kristine of her promise to visit. She scanned the crowd and watched a group of women. One of the women had Kristine's athletic build and coloring. Her hair was longer and styled, and she wore makeup to accentuate her eyes. She was wondering if the woman's eyes were solid brown or whether they had the golden flecks she loved studying in Kristine's. She blinked back to Adam, suddenly self-conscious. Part of her hoped the woman would approach, though she didn't know if she could accept a dance. She wouldn't want to mislead anyone. It was one thing to dance with a colleague and a whole different story to dance with a stranger. As if reading her distress, Adam held out his hand.

"I'm not as good as Jim," he warned.

She shrugged off his self-deprecation and joined him on the dance floor below. Hours flew by, and she was stunned to be watching the band pack up their instruments. She followed Jim and Adam out of the bar into the cool of the night, thanking them genuinely for the fun evening. Fog had rolled in from the bay, muting the world around her. Joining Adam and Jim had been the right decision. Like the fog, it softened the corners of her missing Kristine and might give her something to look forward to each week. As she waited for her sedan to warm up, she closed her eyes, knowing Kristine would be in bed already, wishing she was on her way home to climb into her warmth.

CHAPTER THIRTY-SEVEN

The ranch looked different when Kristine stepped away from her truck, having finished tying off the tarp covering her stuff in the bed of her pickup.

"Think it'll hold?" Gabe joked, butting her shoulder. "I could check your tie-off."

"Shut up." Kristine butted him back. "I taught you all your hitches." She looked over her shoulder at the house where their folks were. They'd already said their goodbyes. Gabe leaned against the frame of the truck, looking out over the yearling pasture. Something in his posture, in the way he wasn't looking her in the eye kept her from climbing into the cab.

"You driving the canyon down to the interstate?" he asked.

"Yep," Kristine said. "Quickest way to the interstate."

"You're not going by Indian Falls?"

It was a favorite spot of hers. When they were young, the large rock formation below the falls had always looked like a giant St. Bernard, its head resting on its paws. For years her father had tried to show them how it also looked like a woman bent over, washing her hair in the creek. Once she'd been able to see both images, it had become a ritual to stop by. Coming back home for holidays, she'd often stop there first, and if it was warm, she'd swim before completing the last leg of the trip.

"It's not a huge detour to stop there and still take the canyon to the interstate," she said, ignoring what he was really asking her. He knew she had promised to visit Gloria on the Northcoast. If she took Highway 36, which passed Indian Falls, she'd be heading west to the coast which had been her plan before she'd received the job offer, before she'd heard the words that were supposed to fulfill her dreams. "We'd like to offer you a job."

In a week, she'd be receiving her first assignment from the nature magazine she'd thought was a long shot when she applied. She still couldn't believe they had hired her. Gloria had been thrilled and countered Kristine every time she said she couldn't believe it, reminding her over and over how great her portfolio was and how much she deserved the position. Maybe she had hoped for Gloria to be disappointed, for her to say that she had hoped Kristine would ditch the offer and come to Eureka as planned.

"Dad's proud of you."

Kristine smiled. "Yeah. Hearing him say that is almost as good as it was seeing him eat dirt back when we were training Crackers. I loved that horse for throwing him off. I think I know what she felt like now."

Gabe laughed at that. Kristine waited, knowing he had something on his mind that he was trying to phrase. He looked down the road she'd be taking in a moment and said, "Don't you think San Diego is a long way in the wrong direction?"

Kristine laughed. "No, I don't think San Diego..." She dropped her voice to match the timbre of his "...is a long way in the wrong direction." She studied her brother, thankful for his concern but firm when she said, "It's my dream job. It's what I always wanted."

"What you want now, or what you always wanted?" Her brother waited until she met his eyes. "It's good to be sure of that." He pushed away from the truck and knocked his knuckles on the hood as he walked back to the barn, calling out, "Safe trip," over his shoulder.

Kristine climbed into the cab and said goodbye to the ranch, knowing she would only ever be back to visit. She rolled down the window and rested her elbow on the doorframe to enjoy the familiar turns of the mountain road and the fall foliage decorating the riverside. She took the Highway 36 turnoff. *It's only a five minute detour*, she thought, turning the wheel to the right. Just a few minutes past the turnoff, she recognized the rock face she was looking for, catching a glimpse of the woman washing her hair before the road curved, and trees blocked her view. She slowed even more, looking for the tiny worn "falls" just off the road. No cars were parked at the trailhead, always her preference.

Letting the steep trail pull her, she jogged quick switchbacks down the mountain, recalling how many times she and Gabe had raced ahead of their parents as they called warnings to be careful to deaf ears. She was out of breath by the time she reached the water, collected in a wide, clear pool at the small slip of beach. Climbing the rocks to her left, she scampered closer to the wide waterfall and sat on an outcrop of rocks, enjoying the roar of the water drowning out everything else in the world. The mist from the falls kissed her skin, awakening her senses. Determined to sort through her thoughts, she hiked downstream until she could see the rock face that still mesmerized her as it shifted from one image to the other.

The job offer was everything she'd wished for and worked toward, and as she'd told Gabe, she relished the pride she saw in her father's face when she shared the news. But Gabe had said something that stuck with her. Was that her current dream or what she had once dreamed? She hadn't shared with Gabe how hard it had been to tell Gloria about the job. She left out how she thought Gloria would tell her not to go and how she would not have argued if Gloria had asked her not to take it.

She thought again about the photography trip at the Lodge. She enjoyed her guests, getting to know them as well as teaching them. Watching them master new techniques was hugely satisfying. Hadn't she felt happy coming in from that trip, like she'd really accomplished something? She'd been completely fixated on using her MFA artistically, teaching held no appeal. She'd regularly rejected her father's suggestion to teach photography at the local community college if she "had such an investment in playing with her camera." She considered the parts of backcountry trips that she liked so much, the parts that fit nicely with her gregarious personality. She enjoyed explaining the things she knew and loved about the backcountry and packing to guests. Wouldn't that be similar in a classroom setting? New students and new classes each semester would mirror the series of trips she led in the backcountry. She'd always known she was good at drawing people out, but she hadn't realized how satisfying that was when linked with watching someone learn. Thinking about it that way made teaching seem not like a dead end but rather a promising trail.

But she'd heard nothing from the art department at Humboldt State, and the position they'd flown was for the spring semester, anyhow. If she turned down this job in San Diego, she'd be in the same position she'd always been in at the ranch, dependent on someone else.

She stared at the rock face until she could see the St. Bernard's face and saw herself, off on assignments with her camera around her neck like the dog portrayed with the cask of brandy around its neck. She'd be a wanderer. And alone, still trying to prove herself to her father. Then there was the woman, the other choice, a tantalizing woman completing the domestic chore of washing her hair. She visualized herself making a home with Gloria. Two choices. Professional or domestic. She heard her father's argument again and wondered if he was right, that if she sacrificed the magazine job and found no full-time work in Eureka, she might eventually grow to resent Gloria just as she had her father for so many years.

For the first time in her life, she actually wished she didn't have the job offer in front of her, pulling her in a direction she was no longer sure she wanted to go. She looked at her watch.

If she left now, she'd make it to San Diego by suppertime. Or Eureka by lunch. She decided to ask the universe. She shut her eyes and concentrated. She would open her eyes and let the first image the rock face offered determine her decision. She cleared her mind, took a deep breath, and opened her eyes. She let out a long, slow breath cementing the image before she hiked out of the valley.

Her whole body tingled with anticipation by the time she reached the truck. She slid behind the wheel and pulled up to the road. To the right, the Northcoast and Gloria; to the left, the more direct route to the interstate and San Diego. Calling up the image she'd seen when she opened her eyes, she eased out the clutch and pulled onto the road.

CHAPTER THIRTY-EIGHT

"It sure is nice having you home," Gloria's dad said, balancing the level on the shadowbox she held in place. A pencil sat behind his ear in scraggly blondish hair.

"I'll look for a place of my own soon, I promise," Gloria said.

"Funny. I thought I just heard myself say that we enjoy having you home."

"If I don't get an apartment of my own, Mom will start to think I'm worried she's sick."

Her father set down the level, lines crossing his high forehead exposed by his receding hairline. "So it's a covert mission."

"Exactly." Gloria shifted under the weight of the shadowbox.

His light blue eyes twinkled as he marked where he wanted to insert the hanging screws.

"Mail call," Gloria's mother called from the kitchen. "Looks like you got a card from your backcountry babe."

Gloria glanced down the hallway but didn't move.

"Set it down," her father said, removing his glasses and rubbing them on his shirt. "I'll get the screws in, and we'll hang the box later."

"About time," her mom said when Gloria joined her. "What if she's sent a picture. I want to see," her mother said, waggling the card.

"You can open it," Gloria said, not wanting to hear what Kristine had to say after their conversation. She felt foolish for finding comfort in Kristine's idea that though they weren't on the same trail, they had a shared destination. She poured a glass of water as her mother opened the envelope.

"Oh, this is lovely." What she always said. "Is that you?"

Reluctantly, Gloria held out her hand. On the front was a black-and-white shot at the trailhead to Shadow Lake. In the foreground of the lower left-hand corner was the "Welcome to the Backcountry" sign. Blurred in the upper right-hand corner was a backpacker. Kristine must have been on her belly on the trail, emphasizing the last lines of the sign, Take only Pictures; Leave only Footprints.

Her stomach dropped reading the words she'd spoken back when she was trying to convince Kristine to have a summer fling. Had she decided that was all their time together was after all?

She flicked open the card and read Kristine's words. *Lovely Gloria, Thank you for understanding why I need to pursue this job offer. Bear with me, please. Love, Kristine*

"What happened to her coming out here to capture our wonders?"

Gloria sat down at the table. "She got a job."

"That's fabulous news!" She paused, studying her daughter and then sat next to her at the table. "That's not fabulous news."

"It's in San Diego."

"San Diego is perfect. Isn't that just a few hours from the Ontario office? Surely they'd have you back."

"Yes. But she's being stubborn about wanting to go down there on her own. She has this thing about how I'm already successful, and how she needs her chance to establish herself."

"Stubborn as the mules she raises?" her mother laughed. She pointed at the card. "May I?"

Gloria nodded and watched her mother read Kristine's words a few times. "What do you think?"

"She's witty. I like that. Maybe this will be like an old-fashioned courtship. And you're in the same state for heaven's sake. There are people who live on opposite coasts who make it work. You're the one who was always saying people crowd you and how much you like your independence."

Gloria picked up the card, considering it from the angle her mother proposed. Kristine got her need for space and quiet. Even if they were in the same room, Kristine had a way of not crowding Gloria. Even though the cabin and her camper were tiny, she never felt her typical need to escape.

"I want everything. I want her and you. I want my job and the redwoods. I sound like Meg. When she says that, I want to run. I don't want to sound like that and push Kristine away. I want to trust her when she says long distance can work."

"But?"

"I don't know if I'm cut out for long distance. I want to know that it all works out."

"You always were a read-the-end-of-the-book-first kind of girl."

"How else do you know if it's worth reading?"

"Faith. My sweet. You're supposed to have faith that the storyteller wouldn't be telling you the story if it wasn't worth it. And Kristine seems worth it."

Gloria hmphed and leaned into her mother's hug. She knew that her mother was right, but that didn't make it any easier to accept.

CHAPTER THIRTY-NINE

The familiarity of the college town instantly put a smile on Kristine's face. She parked across the highway from campus and found a coffee shop. She bought a local paper to read while she had her lunch, though she barely turned any pages, thinking instead of what she was going to say when she walked over to campus and whether their answer mattered much in this crazy decision she'd made to follow her heart.

Once fortified, she strode purposefully toward campus, her portfolio under her arm. She marveled at the redwoods that stood as a backdrop. Gloria had been right about how much she'd want to capture her beloved Northcoast on film. She dawdled at the footbridge, admiring the artful graffiti before tackling a steep set of stairs.

She stood nervously outside of the art department door even after she'd caught her breath and figured out what to say. Finally, she reached forward, turned the knob and pulled open the door.

"I'll be right with you," a harried man maybe five years older than Kristine said before returning to his phone call. She nodded and studied the office, the flyers announcing opportunities for scholarships and graduate programs, a few students filling out paperwork at the counter. She wasn't trying to eavesdrop, but she realized she'd been listening to lists of schedule conflicts. Sounding more frustrated by the minute, the man wrapped up the phone call. He closed his eyes, stretched his neck and brought his attention to Kristine.

"How can I help you?" he asked, still seated.

Kristine gulped. "I hope I haven't caught you at a bad time and that this doesn't come off as inappropriate," she began. "I filed an application for adjunct work, but my contact information has changed. I'd like to update it."

"Please tell me you're Kristine Owens," he said, sounding hopeful.

"Yes," she said, surprised he had her name at the tip of his tongue.

"I'm Aaron, the office administrator." His face brightened immediately. "I've left message after message for you at the number you provided."

"I'm so sorry," Kristine said. "I just wrapped up a job in the High Sierras where the cell reception is poor, so it's the business number you have. They've all cleared out for the season now."

His hands flew through piles of papers, finally landing on what she gathered was her application. He scanned through it, his expression changing in front of her from harried to surprised to excited. "Not a problem now as long as you're still interested in working for us."

"Of course."

"Can you meet with some people today?" he asked.

"Yes," she said, stunned and a little confused about the rush.

"And you could start right now."

It was a statement, not a question, which confused her. "I, uh…yes I could," she said, taken aback.

"Let me grab our department chair."

Even more confused, Kristine simply nodded.

"Don't move. I'll be right back." He looked at her again as if committing what she looked like to memory. After he left, she self-consciously checked what she was wearing. Her outfit was more appropriate for a barn than an art department, but at least her jeans were on the newer side and her shirt and boots both clean. She sat, wondering what was happening with the department chair. She hadn't had time to create an answer when he was back with an older woman on his heels.

"Miss Owens?" the woman said.

Kristine nodded. The woman's suit jacket was the only part of her that implied management. Her jeans and loose blouse suggested she felt more at home in a studio. She'd swept her long gray hair back in a messy bun held by what might have been a red chopstick.

"I'm Natalie Stettner, Department Chair. We've been trying to track you down for days." The radiant smile and extra squeeze of Kristine's hands when they shook conveyed just how excited she was.

"Yes. I'm so sorry about the defunct number I had on file. I promise you can reach me easily now."

"Let's talk in my office. Aaron, you'll put together a packet for me?"

"Already working on it," he said.

Though confused by their exchange, Kristine followed the chair down the hall to her office, which confirmed her guess that Natalie was herself an artist. Oil paintings, sketches and watercolors covered the walls. Her desk was piled high with papers, and the floor had various stacks of books. "I really should use the chair's office back in the department, but it still doesn't feel right to me. I'm a little new at this—my first semester as chair," Natalie explained. "An associate professor became ill and is facing complications we knew would keep her from returning next semester. But her health has declined rapidly, so we're having to cover her classes for the rest of this semester as well. We need a substitute immediately. Aaron's been striking out all week, and then he calls with this news that the perfect replacement is standing in the office."

Kristine blinked. "Perfect replacement?"

"You do have your MFA?" Natalie said, flipping through Kristine's application.

Kristine nodded. Her afternoon was going nothing like she'd planned. She had hoped to get a feel for the department. When she'd opened her eyes at the falls and recognized the image of the woman washing her hair first, she felt the pull of the coast, of Gloria, and responded. She'd hoped, at best, for some positive feedback about her application for any part-time classes for spring semester, but had never dreamed of something being available right now.

"And you've taught before?"

"I taught a few undergrad classes while I finished my graduate degree. But since my internship photographing museum pieces ended, I've been working on my portfolio, thinking that I wanted to pursue a professional career."

Natalie's gaze shifted to the portfolio at Kristine's side. "May I?"

Kristine nodded, handing over her work. She watched the woman's facial expressions as she studied the pages, feeling hopeful as she inspected each photo closely rather than scanning them quickly. When she finished the portfolio, Natalie sat back in her chair. "It's an impressive portfolio. I'm surprised you haven't found anything in the professional realm."

"Actually, I just did. I have an offer from a magazine down in San Diego, but this summer changed my priorities in a lot of ways. I had the opportunity to teach on a photography trip for a pack station in Mammoth." She described her students, the terrain and the techniques they had covered during the five-day trip. "Until that trip, I hadn't even considered teaching as an option, but I'm a social person, and when I really started to think about accepting the magazine's offer, I realized it wouldn't be as good a fit for me."

"And Humboldt is a good fit?"

Kristine thought of the primary reason she was here, and when she thought of Gloria, she blushed, but she remembered Gloria saying she'd love to see the Northcoast through Kristine's lens and quickly tapped back into her professional brain. "Look at this environment! Who wouldn't want to be teaching photography here?"

"Indeed," Natalie said, smiling. "I've seen enough to know that you can handle this job. The nature photography class will be a lot like what you described doing this summer. I see in your portfolio that you have the skills to teach our studio photography classes. The only question left is whether you want to take over as instructor of record on Monday. We're three weeks into the semester, and I do want to warn you that these classes are off to a rocky start. They've missed multiple sessions while we've been struggling to find someone."

Kristine could see the chair waiting for a response, but every cell in her body was busy going haywire, making speech impossible. What would Gloria say? She hadn't even asked, but it was Friday. Clearly, this woman needed an answer before the weekend. The universe had opened a door, so she bravely took a step forward. "Yes, absolutely."

"You seemed to hesitate. Are you committed to your professional offer in San Diego?"

Kristine rushed to assure her. "Oh, I'm thrilled. I'm just shocked is all. Your offer feels like an answer to a prayer."

Natalie Stettner sank back in her chair, a look of relief relaxing her considerably. "Thank you for saving us," she said. "Aaron was just starting to think I would have to take over the classes. What a disaster that would be, a sculptor trying to teach photography!"

"I'm sure you'd have been fine," Kristine said, laughing. "I can't tell you how excited I am to have this opportunity. I'm used to picking up all sorts of assignments on the fly, so I am confident that I can step in here to help the students through the rest of the semester."

"Another quality I think makes you well suited for our department," Stettner said, smiling. She glanced at the clock.

"We have a lot to do to get you legal, but I'm worried folks are going to start to disappear. Let's take a quick tour and get you acclimated to the facilities and see if Mark Briggs, the full-time professor is still hanging about."

Even the quick tour impressed Kristine. She couldn't wait to return to spend more time checking out the studio, traditional darkroom and computer lab where they did their digital work. For a smaller department, she was pleasantly surprised by the setup. Natalie introduced her to many faculty who taught art history, ceramics and drawing but was disappointed not to find Mark on campus.

With promises to introduce her on Monday, Natalie returned Kristine to the office. When he saw them, Aaron immediately jumped up from his desk with a stack of papers in his hands. Before he whisked her away, Natalie shook her hand. "I have to remind you that this is a temporary full-time assignment. I can't guarantee what next semester looks like. We can rush the paperwork for this emergency hire, but for spring, I'll have to go through the formal steps."

"I understand completely," Kristine said.

"Aaron will get you started on the paperwork and make sure you know where you need to be on Monday."

"Thank you, again. I can't tell you how excited I am."

"Trust me," she winked at Aaron who was waiting for her, "you're not the only one!"

So began the whirlwind of tasks to complete. Aaron dragged her up and down campus, through human resources and security, the library for a temporary faculty card and finally back to her office where he weighed her down with the books, syllabi and a flash drive containing course materials and assignments for the classes she was taking over. Hours later, they returned to the department office. Natalie emerged from her official office.

"How did it go?" she asked.

Kristine took a deep breath. "I have a long weekend in front of me to prepare for Monday."

"But you don't look like you're scared, that's good." She smiled at Aaron.

"Feel free to email either of us with questions over the weekend. It's going to be a tough week, but I'm certain you'll settle in quickly." With a quick squeeze to Kristine's shoulder, she slipped back into her office.

Kristine walked into the fog creeping in from the bay as she descended the hill and collapsed behind the wheel, closing her eyes to try to soak in the enormity of the day. A wave of anxiety passed through her when she thought about seeing Gloria. She glanced at her watch, gauging whether she'd be likely to find her at the brewery with her friends yet. Hoping she'd made the right decisions over the course of the day, she cranked her key, turning over the old engine. As it roared to life, so did her confidence. Her heart beating home, home, home, as she pulled onto the highway, closing the distance between herself and Gloria.

CHAPTER FORTY

Gloria sat on the edge of her bed, her head in her hands, trying to find the strength to change and make it to the brewery. She checked her cell again even though she knew it was working and didn't really figure she'd missed a call while she sat there feeling sorry for herself. She hadn't been able to reach Kristine all day, which probably meant that she was still driving. She pictured Kristine excited about her new job, giddy with anticipation, and couldn't help wonder about the other opportunities she might find. Should she have asked Kristine to give up the job? Adam and Jim had given her a hard time all day, telling her that she should have lobbied for her to choose love over her job, but Gloria understood her need to prove herself in her field. She couldn't ask her to turn down a job when she, herself, wouldn't have been able to.

She flopped back on the mattress, wishing she could just stay home, but she couldn't stand up the guys. Not after she'd spent all of the lunch break defending Kristine's decision, convincing them as she tried to convince herself that the long-distance relationship could work and was worth keeping. Doubt crept into her thoughts, though, when she wondered what would ever change. If it was true that she loved the Northcoast and Kristine loved her job, shouldn't they just break up instead of drawing out the inevitable?

Maybe she shouldn't go. Surely, they wouldn't miss her one night. No. If she missed, they would know she was lying. She had to put her happy face on and get over there before they suspected.

She shucked off her uniform and grabbed an old pair of jeans and a tee from the closet, not caring what she looked like. For a moment, she hesitated, considered really dressing up and tempting the crowd, just to feel picked by someone. She discarded the idea immediately, knowing that she really wanted for Kristine to pick her and that it wasn't productive or mature—satisfying, maybe—but definitely not fair to play that kind of game just because she was feeling melancholy. Instead, she pulled Kristine's belt on, pressing her hand against the buckle, wishing that she was back in the cabin at the Aspens using it to pull Kristine toward her.

The band was already in full swing by the time she made it to the brewery, and she found the guys at their favorite spot on the second floor by the rail where they could watch the band and the crowd but not be pulled easily onto the small dance floor below.

"Told you she wasn't bullshitting us earlier," Jim said loud enough for Gloria to hear as she joined them.

"We wondered if you'd changed your mind. I thought you'd at least be to Fort Bragg by now."

"No, I'm not chasing after her. She's worth trusting."

"Well, since you did make it, I'll get the pitcher," Adam said, heading off to the bar.

"There are really good opportunities down in San Diego," Jim said. "I don't see why you're holding onto the headache of management when you could be doing something with wildlife. Working with people all day..." he shivered. "That alone would make me want to relocate. You could find something on the sly, surprise her. You don't really think she'd say no if you showed up on her doorstep, do you?"

"You forget again, my friend, that I like my job, the power, the responsibility…"

"Still think you're the biggest liar ever." He smiled.

"Think what you want," Gloria said, accepting Adam's pitcher of Downtown Brown Adam. After pouring a round, she turned to watch the band. She hoped that Jim would get the message and let the topic of her extended long-distance relationship go. He didn't.

"I can't believe you changed out of your uniform into that," he said. "Lots of women are into the uniform."

She rolled her eyes but kept her chin inclined toward the music, really not in the mood to engage in his working the crowd.

"Unbelievable," he said.

"What?" Gloria asked.

"Even looking like she does tonight, she still caught the eye of the hottest woman in the place."

"Where?" Adam asked.

"There at the bar. She's been staring at Gloria since she got here. Every time I look over…"

Adam interrupted, "…hoping she'll be looking at you."

Jim nodded. "Hoping to get her to look at the person who is actually available at this table, she's got her eyes glued on Gloria. I think she's your type, too. She's got cowboy boots on."

"Will you please shut your trap?" Gloria said, finally exasperated. "No more talk about long distance, about hooking up, about cute girls. I'm not in the mood, okay? I just want to have a good beer and listen to the music."

The men eyed each other. Adam shrugged.

"Your loss," Jim said. "I'm not telling you to cheat on Kristine. I just thought that a dance with a pretty lady might make you feel better."

"Good company might make me feel better, too," Gloria muttered. She finally turned her head, meaning to suggest that good company might be found somewhere other than their table, and her eyes locked with Kristine's. Her Kristine. Sitting there at the bar in cowboy boots, her trademark tight blue jeans, sexy tank top tucked in and yet another belt buckle. Her breath caught.

"Told you," Jim said in a congratulatory tone. "It doesn't matter who you are, what's going on in your crazy mixed-up love life. A woman like that should not be ignored. You should so go talk to her."

His jaw dropped when Gloria responded by pushing back from the table. Adam hooted encouragement as she walked away from them. She could barely feel her legs as she walked to the bar. She kept waiting for her eyes to reveal the trick they'd played on her, that there was someone there who looked like Kristine. But then she stood right next to her, and unmistakably, the woman who should have been in San Diego rose to her feet.

"I'm such an ass," Kristine said.

Gloria stared at her, unsure of what to make of the woman standing in front of her. Maybe she'd just decided to take the scenic route on her way to San Diego. She'd be gone in the morning, making Gloria even more heartsick. Though she wanted to throw herself into Kristine's arms, the unanswered questions kept her an arm's length away. "Knowing how the family business relies on asses, I'm not sure how to take that."

Kristine belly laughed and pulled Gloria into an embrace. As they parted, her eyes wandered down Gloria's frame, filling Gloria with desire. When she reached Gloria's waist, Kristine smiled and reached out to touch the belt buckle. "I wondered if you'd been wearing this." Her eyes found Gloria again, and Gloria saw hesitation in her gaze. "Sit with me?"

Gloria nodded. She glanced back at her friends who looked utterly awed by what they were watching. She pointed, mouthed "Kristine," and watched both of their eyes widen. She sat, her heartbeat competing with the band.

"Everything I said on the phone, I meant. I know you belong here, and I know that a professional job is what I've always wanted," Kristine said. She reached for Gloria's hand, and Gloria closed her eyes at the touch, her heart breaking.

Kristine traced the back of Gloria's hand with her thumb. It felt to Gloria that her whole body was being touched in a way no one ever had before. She knew that Kristine had realized what she did too, that they were only drawing out the inevitable split-up and she had come to do the honorable thing by breaking up in person. She took a tight hold on Kristine's hand and felt tears threatening. She didn't want to let go, ever.

"Gloria, look at me. I came to say that I was a fool to tell you that we could be long distance."

Gloria swiped at a tear that escaped, still trying to avoid Kristine's eyes, not wanting to hear what she feared Kristine would say out loud.

"Would you please open your eyes and look at me? I want for you to have a say in our future." She grabbed a newspaper off the bar and waved it in front of Gloria's face. "I want you to help me find an apartment. For us."

Gloria blinked. "What?"

"I want the next place we live to be our place. I don't want to live alone. I want something like the cabin at the outpost, a place that I know when I come home, you'll be there."

Gloria stared at the paper in front of her blindly. "You're not breaking up with me?"

Kristine sat back, surprised. "Of course not. What makes you think I drove here to break up with you?"

"Your card. I thought you were reminding me not to get attached. I thought you were saying you were happy to have a memory."

"Didn't you see that you were in the frame? I needed you to know I want to be where you are. You were right. You've always been right. This," she waved her hand in between the two of them, "is the most important thing."

"So you're saying you want me to go with you?" Gloria asked, unsure how that made her feel.

Kristine gently shook the newspaper in her hand. "I'm saying help me pick an apartment. Here. Please."

Gloria finally registered the words on the newspaper in her hand. The local paper. Why was she holding a local paper?

Kristine, she realized looked equal parts radiant and scared. "I don't understand."

"I signed a temporary contract with Humboldt State. I start Monday."

"You start in San Diego in ten days."

Slowly, Kristine shook her head. "I couldn't accept it. A wise horseman told me it was a long way in the wrong direction, and I finally listened."

Gloria felt like she was floating, like the number of emotions she was experiencing finally took over and suspended her above herself. It sounded like she got to have everything she wanted, the girl, her family, her job, her friends. Did she deserve all of that? She felt like if she moved or breathed, the fragile bubble that was keeping everything together would pop.

Kristine squeezed Gloria's hand. "Could you please tell me I didn't do the wrong thing?"

"What about regret?" Gloria whispered.

"What about faith?" Kristine answered.

"What about your dreams?"

"She's sitting right here in front of me refusing to kiss me. Punish me for being stupid, but please tell me you want me here."

Gloria did better. She showed Kristine. She wove her fingers through Kristine's hair and pulled her into a deep, deep kiss, a new kiss, one full of promise.

"Really?" Kristine said, coming up for air.

"Forever. I want you here forever."

"You better be sure about that. I'll be stuck on you like a mule stuck on a bell mare."

Gloria swatted Kristine. "You are my everything. You're supposed to be stuck to me."

Kristine smiled. "Just making sure." Her eyes left Gloria's and drifted across the room. "I think you'd better introduce me to your friends."

Gloria flushed red. She'd forgotten all about them. "Only to tell them that they're on their own for the rest of the night. I have other plans."

"I think I like the sound of your plans," Kristine answered.

Gloria kept hold of Kristine's hand as they wove back through the crowd, finally on the same trail, one that they would travel together.

Bella Books, Inc.

Women. Books. Even Better Together.

P.O. Box 10543
Tallahassee, FL 32302

Phone: 800-729-4992
www.bellabooks.com